Fresh MEET

ALSO BY JASMIN MILLER

Brooksville Series

Baking With A Rockstar - A Single Parent Romance

Tempted By My Roommate - A Friends to Lovers Romance

The Best Kind Series

The Best Kind Of Mistake - A Workplace Romantic Comedy

The Best Kind Of Surprise - A Surprise Pregnancy Romantic Comedy

---

Standalone

The Husband Checklist - A Brother's Best Friend Romance

Kings Of The Water Series

Secret Plunge - A Surprise Pregnancy Sports Romance

Fresh Meet - A Single Dad Sports Romance

KINGS OF THE WATER SERIES

JASMIN MILLER

Fresh Meet
Copyright © 2020 by Jasmin Miller

All rights reserved. No part of this book may be reproduced, distributed, or transmitted in any form without the prior written consent of the author, except in the case of brief quotation embodied in critical articles or reviews.

This book is a piece of fiction. Names, characters, places, and incidents are the product of the author's imagination or are used fictitiously. Any resemblance to actual persons, living or dead, things, locales or events is entirely coincidental.

Published: Jasmin Miller 2020
jasmin@jasminmiller.com
www.jasminmiller.com
Editing: Marion Archer, Making Manuscripts
Proofreading: Judy Zweifel, Judy's Proofreading
Cover Art: Najla Qamber, Qamber Designs & Media

To my children,
For providing me with endless book material.

PROLOGUE
JACE

WOMEN ARE CRAZY.

I will probably deny ever having had this thought, but they are absolute nut jobs.

Especially the one standing in front of me.

Or maybe it's just my shitty talent of picking them.

With one hand poised on her hip, and her other one clutched tightly around the now empty wine glass, Sandra has a bigger resemblance to a snake-loving Medusa than the beautiful and exotic bikini model I enjoyed spending some of my down time with.

Used to enjoy spending down time with.

As of three minutes ago, right after I told her we should stop seeing each other—and she unceremoniously dumped her red wine on me. I'd say the breakup was successful.

Which is exactly what I wanted.

But I could have gone without the drama.

If her pursed lips are anything to go by, we're not done for tonight.

"Jace Atwood, I can't believe you're treating me like this. I thought we had something special. You're . . . you're . . . such an egomaniac asshole." Her voice is so high and screechy, I'm afraid every glass in this restaurant is going to burst any moment.

I'm not sure anyone would notice since everyone's attention is on this very public display of my newest failure of "How to dump a fuck-buddy-slash-casual-date in public."

I don't often indulge in women because spoiler alert, I'm still clueless on how to pick a woman who actually means it when she says she wants casual.

My bad judgment is apparent by the drenched light blue dress shirt that's clinging to my upper body like a second skin.

My bad.

I should have known better.

At least I was smart enough to ask for the corner table in the back of the restaurant.

With the help of the host, we get a very upset Sandra into a cab in less than ten minutes.

It's a quiet evening otherwise, and George, the host and long-time fan of my career, waits with me for the valet to get my car. "How's training going?"

Pushing my hands in the pockets of my black slacks, I kick a pebble onto the wet streets and chuckle. "It's going. I definitely feel my age."

The grin on his face comes fast, bringing out every last laugh line. I'm sure he's earned every single one in his life fair and square.

His hand comes down on my shoulder. Hard. "You're twenty-eight, Atwood. I'm almost three times your age. That's when you're allowed to complain about your aches and pains. Gosh, when I was your age . . . I would have given everything to be a professional swimmer, but you know that."

I do. I come here regularly, either by myself or with company. Partially because of George, not that I'd admit that to him. I'd never hear the end of it.

The valet stops at the curb with my SUV, and I wave at my friend as I make my way to the driver's side. "I'll make sure to remember that. Tell that lovely wife of yours I said hi."

He salutes and sees me off as I leave downtown Berkeley.

I'm not surprised to see a black Mercedes in my driveway when I get home, my best friend Hunter leaning against the sleek passenger side.

After stepping out of my car, I walk past him, knowing he's going to fall in step with me. "I swear, George is the biggest gossip I know. And fast."

Hunter chuckles. "You know he's sharp as a nail. He just enjoys pretending otherwise sometimes." He elbows me, pointing at my shirt. "But I was going to come over anyway. I had to see the damage for myself."

"Great." My teeth clench as I unlock the front door.

As if he knows I've had enough for today, he holds up his hands before clapping one on my shoulder. "Sorry, bro." He reaches behind his back and pulls out a DVD. "I brought entertainment, that Aquaman movie you've wanted to watch, so get cleaned up."

I grunt and walk to my bedroom to take off my sticky, wet clothes.

After a quick shower, I feel marginally better and head back to the living room, my naked feet cold on the hardwood floor.

Hunter is stretched out on one of the sofas. It's a familiar scene, something we do as often as our demanding training schedules allow. We met during summer swim camp when we were teenagers—alongside our friends Noah and Ryan—and despite competing against each other throughout our careers, our friendship has remained tight.

"Finally, dude. I'm not getting any younger here." He throws a piece of popcorn at me as I walk to the kitchen to get some water.

I shake my head. "Doesn't look like you had any interesting plans tonight anyway."

He's a bit of a loner, like me. Like all of us are. Except Ryan. He's got Harper now.

It's not always easy to fit in a healthy social life with the little time we have outside the pool and gym, which is exactly why I haven't attempted a serious relationship.

Hunter's about to say something—most likely another smart-ass retort—when the doorbell rings. We both frown, knowing I didn't expect anyone. And as much as Hunter likes to drop by uninvitedly, he wouldn't invite others without asking.

When I open the front door, there's an old lady on my front porch. With short, dark gray hair, and a sad look in her eyes, she wordlessly holds out an envelope to me. I take it, too perplexed to say anything.

She watches me, her eyes slowly roaming over me from head to toe. Inspecting me. Appraising me. For what, I have no clue.

"Who are you?"

"I'm Bette. My contact information is in the envelope. I'm sure you'll have questions, and I'll try to answer them as best as I can, but I have to go home for now. Have a lovely evening." Her voice is gentle. She sounds tired.

I barely register her departure as I rip open the envelope with a sense of foreboding.

I'm not sure how long I stand there, but at some point, Hunter leads me into the house, practically shoving me onto the couch.

"You're as white as a ghost. What's going on?" The unsure tone in my otherwise steady friend is what makes me look up at him.

My mouth opens, but words still evade me.

Hunter rubs over his short hair, a frantic look on his face. "You're starting to really freak me out. Who was at the door and what does the letter say?"

"It's from . . . it's from a woman. A fling. Hookup." The words sound stale coming out of my mouth. Like by saying them out loud, I'm inadvertently calling her bad names. "She . . . she . . . um, she died."

Hunter drops on the couch like a sack of potatoes. "Fuck, man. I . . . I'm sorry."

I look away. Disbelief tears through my body.

"Hunt, she had a son. Apparently, my son."

ONE

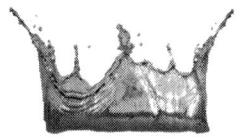

EMILIA

"What about a chicken sexer? That can't be that hard, right?" I grind my teeth together to keep from laughing as I peek over my laptop screen at Nicole.

We sit at opposite ends of my bed, and she cocks her head to the side as if she didn't hear me correctly. "Did you just say chicken sexer?"

"Mm-hmm." Gosh, it's hard not to laugh.

"What the hell is a chicken sexer?"

And I lose it and laugh loudly.

Nicole shakes her head and smirks. "Does that even exist?"

When I've calmed down, I nod and squint back at my screen, silently willing the letters to stop from jumping around. "Apparently, they sort chicks by gender."

Nicole raises her eyebrows.

"I swear, I'm not making this up. They actually make some good money too." I turn the laptop around so she can see.

"Well, you learn something new every day." Her phone vibrates next to her, and after typing on the screen, she looks back at me. "Have we moved on to looking for crazy jobs now?"

I shrug. "Sorry, I've been looking at normal job listings all day and can't find anything that would work for me. I needed a break."

She gives me a sympathetic smile, knowing how stressful it's been trying to find something new.

Nodding, she leans back against the headboard. "Okay, let's take a break then. Have you found anything else fun? Let's hear it."

I'm not ashamed to admit that I'm excited at her question, eager to share my newfound knowledge with someone, no matter how irrelevant it is. It's the little things in life. "I'm so glad you asked. One moment please."

She adjusts her position a few times before pulling my soft teal blanket over her legs, patiently waiting for me to pull up my info. "So, there are hippotherapists, crime scene cleaners, live mannequins, and fortune cookie writers. Those were my favorites. I might be down for a live mannequin job. Apparently, they pay one hundred bucks per hour."

Nicole shoots up. "No way."

"Yup. Crazy, right?"

"Seriously." She points to my laptop. "What's a hippotherapist? I can read it if you want."

Shaking my head, I search through the million tabs I have open in my web browser. "I still have the app open. Let me pull it up."

Nicole doesn't blink an eye. She's used to this on an

almost daily basis. Thank goodness for technology. It makes my life so much easier, and so much less embarrassing.

After finally finding the right window, I push the play button to start the robotic voice.

"Hippotherapy is an occupational, speech, and physical therapy that uses the natural movement of horses to provide sensory and motor input. It is used for patients with mental and physical disorders—mostly children—to help improve sensory processes and neurological functions."

The narration stops and my wide gaze finds Nicole's. "Awesome, right? But it needs a ton of education—understandably—or I'd be all over this. It's amazing they're able to do that. Being able to help those little ones is so special."

Nicole leans forward until she can reach my arm, giving it a gentle squeeze. I've missed her. Ever since she got together with Justin, we've seen less of each other. I don't blame her though, because they were made for each other, but I do miss our daily contact.

Roommates since graduating, best friends, it's hard to put a label on our friendship, but I'd be lost without her. I still can't believe it's been three years since we graduated college.

She smiles at me softly, her brown eyes studying me. "You know you do a lot for kids too, right?"

I huff out a frustrated breath of air. "Not anymore, no."

She crosses her legs to get comfortable, grabbing one of the throw pillows for her lap. "But you will again, I have no doubt about it. I still want to go after your sleazeball ex-boss and rip off his balls for firing you at that kids' show."

That's why she'll always be my best friend. She gets so worked up and offended in my honor.

Her hand flies in the air as she shakes it. "Downsizing, my ass. He made a move on you that you didn't reciprocate, it's as easy as that. But of course, his ego couldn't take that. Asshole. But Millie, you're special. So very special. I don't think you see how talented you are with kids. They absolutely adore you."

"Yeah?" Familiar unease whenever my "job" is brought up washes through me, and even though I know Nicole is nothing like my family, I'm still waiting for the criticism, for the words that voice disapproval for my occupation—or as other people like to call it, my childish attempt at embarrassing my family.

Because apparently, I live for that. At least, according to the people who are supposed to be my biggest supporters.

As if Nicole can sense the path my thoughts have taken me, she continues, "I haven't seen a kid whose smile couldn't light up the whole damn planet if it was possible. Your old boss will figure out soon enough that you were the biggest part of that show. He's going to lose his mind when he hears that your dream show came knocking on your door."

I snort. "Please tell me how you really feel."

She pokes my side. "I mean it. I just know they'll invite you to audition, and you'll nail it. Even if I have to listen to you sing your nursery rhymes all day long."

This time I chuckle, knowing exactly how much she likes to pretend to hate those. But I've overheard her humming them when she thinks she's alone. "Thanks, Nic."

Her phone beeps again, and after giving my knee a pat, she picks it up. "Alrighty, sister from another mister, let's get back to real jobs."

"If I have to."

She fixes me with a glare and points her finger at me. "Listen, I know you don't really want to do any more nanny jobs after the drama with the last family, but I told my grandma you were looking for a job and she knows someone who's looking for a nanny tout de suite."

"Ugh." I close my laptop and grab my gummy bears from the nightstand. "Does she have any more info?"

"It's the son of one of her aqua aerobics friends, so it's a legit job offer."

"Legit, huh?"

The corners of her mouth twitch. "Her words, not mine."

We both crack up. Nicole's grandma is hilarious and tries to stay trendy, and hip, as she likes to call it. "Do we have any more info? A possible jealous wife I need to know about?"

"I hope not, but I can ask her." She taps on her phone a few times before looking at me. "You sure?"

I let out an exaggerated breath that portrays how I feel about the possibility of taking on a nanny job. "Yeah."

The mom of the last family I nannied for slapped me after accusing me of sleeping with her husband. Apparently, the jerk conveniently failed to mention that his affair was with his assistant, not me. The mom apologized, but at that point, it didn't really matter anymore. The damage was done.

"If everything goes according to plan, you can quit in a few months when the people over at *Kinder Street* realize you're the most perfect addition to their successful kids' TV show." Her smile is radiant and filled with promise.

It also makes me giggle. "You sound like one of their spokespeople."

"What can I say? You've talked me into watching it

enough times that I can see the appeal. To kids of course. Even though I'll miss you like crazy."

"I know. I hate the thought of moving away too, but at least it's in California." I bite the head off a green gummy bear, my thoughts still stuck on her little speech. "They actually need to invite me to the audition first though."

"They will." She winks at me before lifting her phone up to her ear. "Hi, Nana."

The volume of her voice has risen a few levels like every time she talks to her grandma. She listens and nods. "Yes, yes, thank you. And, yes to Millie too. She has officially succumbed."

They both laugh—her grandma easy to hear—and I shake my head. Her family might be on the crazy side at times, but they've welcomed me with open arms to family dinners and celebrations like I'm one of their own, so I'm not complaining.

In fact, I'm so thankful. I never fear criticism when I'm with them. So different to my own family. I'd take that a hundred times over the thick tension that surrounds me like a suffocating cloud every time I step foot into my family home.

"Okay, Nana. Sounds fab. Thanks. Love you too. Bye." Nicole wiggles her phone with a satisfied smile.

"Sooooooo? Are you going to tell me what she said?" I poke her arm for good measure, making her flinch.

"Not if you poke me again." Beautiful black curls fall across her face as she laughs.

With her olive-toned skin and dark features, she's the opposite of me and my light complexion. In addition to my copper-colored hair, I live with an explosion of freckles across my nose and cheeks.

"Nana will text me the number of her friend in a

minute. I swear, this woman is even more technology-fixated than some of the teenagers these days. Sometimes I think she ignores phone calls on purpose, just so she can text."

"She's a strange one but awesome."

"That she is." Just then, her phone vibrates with a message on the screen. Nicole holds out her hand. "Go get your phone or something to write."

I grab my phone and open a new contact. "Ready."

"Okay. Her name is Patricia, and she's Hottie McTottie's mom."

I pause and glance up at her. "Hottie who?"

"Hottie McTottie. That's Nana's nickname for him. She's caught a glimpse of him once, and it looks like he left an impression." She lifts a shoulder.

I blink at her, not sure if this new info is good or bad. "Uh ... okay."

"You know Nana." After slowly rattling off the number, she drops a kiss to my cheek and gets up. "I hate to run, but I'm meeting up with Justin. You've got this, you hear me? It's better than eating ramen noodles for the next few months. Let me know how it goes, okay?"

Groaning at her remark, I nod. "You just had to bring up the ramen noodles, didn't you?"

She winks at me, knowing how much I hate them. "Better than becoming homeless."

"Yeah, yeah. Go have fun with your boyfriend." I shoo her away. "And thank you."

"Always." She blows me a kiss and leaves.

I stare at the spot she just disappeared for a moment before lifting my phone to stare at the screen.

Looks like I might interview for a job with Hottie McTottie.

Let's hope Nana had her prescription glasses filled correctly.

Or maybe it's better if she didn't.

The jury's still out on that one.

TWO

JACE

It's official: I'm a *crazy*-chick magnet.

If I'm honest, after a long day of disappointing job interviews, I had high hopes for my last one. The candidate came highly recommended by my mom's friend, for fuck's sake. That should count for something.

Now that I'm face to face with Emilia, I feel like everyone's lost their damn minds.

Or maybe I have the worst luck. Maybe I'm cursed. There must be a reason for everything to go downhill in my life lately.

My mom did a preliminary check on all applicants via phone interview. According to her, the five women were the best of the best. At least the ones that were available on short notice.

It's depressing, and I want to go home.

All I can think about when I look at Emilia is Pippi Longstocking mixed with Mary Poppins. Her red hair is pulled back in two ponytails on the sides, a big bow adorning the top of her head. Freckles decorate the bridge of her nose and cheeks, and she's wearing the biggest tutu I've ever seen in my life.

I'm not even sure how she manages to sit on her chair.

Like I said, crazy-chick magnet. Right here.

Branded for life by some invisible force.

I'm about to cut this short and thank her for meeting me when the door of the coffee shop bursts open and my mom walks in with Tanner. A quick glance at the clock tells me they're early.

With all candidates, we agreed on her coming in after about fifteen minutes of the interview. If the applicant was still around, it would allow us to gauge Tanner's reaction to the possible nanny prospect. I don't want to hire anyone my son doesn't like. Seems counterproductive to me.

My son. I'm still grappling with that concept. In the few weeks since I've known about him, my whole life has turned upside down. But then again, so has his.

And here we are, trying to find someone who can uproot their life and be a good fit for Tanner.

So far, two people were gone by the time my mom and Tanner arrived. Tanner started crying with one and running away the other time.

I'm not sure who's more frustrated at this point. Him or me.

But I'm quickly learning that kids moods change quicker than some people can change their underwear.

Tanner has only been with me for a few days—after a thankfully short paternity-establishment in court—and I still feel like I got on a roller coaster but haven't gotten off it yet.

My brain constantly feels like it's rattling in my head, all while my heart doesn't quite know what to make of this whole situation.

It's not often that you gain custody of a two-year-old you didn't even know existed until a few weeks ago.

My mom doesn't waste any time and goes right for Emilia, holding out her hand. "Hi, Millie, I'm Patricia, Jace's mom. After our conversation, I wanted to make sure I got to meet you in person."

Interesting. She didn't stop by to ensure she'd meet any of the other candidates. Conveniently, she's avoiding my gaze, making me wonder if there's something she didn't tell me.

Emilia, or apparently Millie to my mom, gets out of her chair, beaming at my mom. "It's so lovely to meet you."

Her tutu puffs out on all sides, barely avoiding her coffee cup on the table.

I'm about to get up too—feeling awkward being the only one sitting—when a high-pitched shriek rings through the room.

Holy crap. What the heck is that?

When I look down, I realize it's Tanner. Oh crap, he's terrified of Emilia too. What the hell do I do now?

But then I look at him . . . really look at him. He's sporting a huge . . . *grin?*

Well, huge for him. The only thing I've seen of him so far has been a tight-lipped attempt at a smile. If you can even call it that. I'm sure I've seen the corners of his lips twitch though.

Right now, there's no doubt. He's definitely smiling.

And . . . *hopping?*

What is happening?

His hands are flying through the air in front of his small body.

Wait a second, is he . . . humming?

Emilia's responding smile is so wide, I can barely see her eyes.

Then she crouches down in front of Tanner and starts singing, the melody of her words matching his quiet humming. Her hands move in a similar fashion as his, but so much more distinguishable in their execution that I see for the first time what he's doing.

What he's *been* doing all along.

And we had no clue.

My gaze finds my mom's, who is now covering her mouth with shaky hands, her eyes shiny and wide.

Shit.

He's been trying to talk to us. With his *hands*.

Why the fuck didn't the old lady Bette tell us about that? After all, she was the one who took care of him after his mom Lila died. Since Lila and I didn't do much talking when we met, I don't know much about her, or what happened the last three-plus years. Obviously.

In her letter, she said that she was admitted to the hospital for a terrible case of pneumonia and that they diagnosed her with bacteremia. When I looked it up, it mentioned that it can lead to septic shock, which is often fatal in as little as twelve hours, even to a healthy individual.

Since Lila's medical history is protected under law, and Bette confirmed complications with pneumonia, that's my best guess as to what happened because Lila was gone the next day.

She wrote the letter when she wasn't sure if she was going to make it. Explaining that I had a son, telling me she only figured out recently who I was when she saw me on TV.

Confessing that she's wanted to contact me but couldn't. Telling me about Tanner. Begging me to take good care of him, and to tell him how much she loved him.

My chest tightens just thinking about her words, about the things she went through and what it ultimately led to. The things she lost.

What Tanner lost.

I swallow the lump in my throat and focus on Emilia instead.

She's still at eye level with Tanner. "Hey there. You must be Tanner. You did such a good job with that song. Do you like to sing?"

Tanner nods, his small head of brown waves bobbing up and down. Then he shakes both hands in the air, almost like jazz hands, before putting his right index finger on his left wrist as if he's pointing at a watch.

Emilia's smile widens, her focus solely on the boy in front of her. "Do you like to watch *Wiggle Time*?"

Wiggle Time? I faintly remember my mom telling me about Emilia having worked for a kids show with that name.

Tanner nods again, right before he launches himself at her, his arms going tightly around her neck.

Emilia closes her eyes as she enfolds him in her arms. Then she looks at me before settling her gaze on my mom. "I didn't know he signs. You mentioned on the phone that he doesn't talk, even though it seems like his hearing is okay."

My mom swallows several times before clearing her throat. "We . . . we had no idea." Her gaze flicks to me. "Things haven't exactly been . . . conventional with Tanner."

"How so?" Emilia's clearly confused, her gaze ping-ponging back and forth between me and my mom, all the while Tanner clings to her like he's a koala and she's his favorite eucalyptus tree. And she doesn't look concerned at all. In fact, it looks so natural for her. Wow.

Under other circumstances, I'd find her question direct, but I understand her need to know what's going on.

My mom lifts her chin in my direction, and I take that as my cue.

After letting out a pent-up breath, I point toward the abandoned chairs around the round metal table. "Let's sit down."

Once everyone's settled, I look into Emilia's green eyes. "I didn't know about Tanner until roughly two weeks ago. I received a letter from a woman I used to know. She . . . she got sick, and there were complications, and she—"

I can't finish the sentence, not with Tanner right there. I'm not sure how much he understands, but talking about his mom's death with him right there feels wrong.

Emilia nods in understanding, her lips pressed into a thin line. "I'm so sorry. And now he's with you?"

My throat feels dry, and I take a sip of my coffee. "He is. The court was willing to speed things up as much as they could since we had all the necessary paperwork and paternity tests done right away."

She turns her head and looks at the little bit of Tanner's profile she can see, which isn't a lot with the way he's pressed his face into her neck.

Her smile is weak and she blinks slowly before gently cupping the back of his head. "That's good. I'm glad he's got you now. And it helps so much that he signs. A lot of parents teach their babies and toddlers simple signs. It helps tremendously with communication, especially when they don't talk yet."

My mom leans forward in her chair. "So it's normal? Even for his age?"

"You said he's two and a half?"

"He's turning three in three months."

Emilia nods. "I'm clearly no doctor or speech therapist, but I've met and worked with a lot of kids. Most children can talk at his age. Some can talk your ear off while others don't at all. One of the girls at the show had full-on conversations at eighteen months while another boy excelled at signing but didn't start verbalizing until three. And then he started reading at the same time. Their little minds are something else, and we can't put them all in the same box."

"Is there a specific program that you recommend? The faster we can start learning some signs, the better." My mom picks up her phone, probably getting ready to order the program right now.

"Of course. I love *Baby Signing Time* and *Signing Time* by Two Little Hand Productions. They have several other amazing programs for older kids as well. And they use real ASL —real American Sign Language—which makes it even better."

"Perfect. Thank you." My mom types away.

"Of course."

I shift around in my seat to get more comfortable. "Did you learn how to sign at the show you were on?"

"I did sign on *Wiggle Time*, yes. But I learned how to sign when I was younger. One of my friends from elementary school was hard of hearing and she taught me how to sign. At least, the basics." Her hand moves up and down Tanner's back. "Young kids respond so well to it, even as babies, way before they can ever talk."

"Is it hard to learn?" My voice sounds rough, the words hard to get out of my throat.

Emilia shakes her head. "No, it's pretty straightforward, and the signs are easy to learn. Since you're using it with a toddler, you won't communicate in full sentences. The way you sign is similar to the way they talk."

"What do you mean?"

Just then, Tanner turns his head and coughs over her shoulder before pulling his head back to look at Emilia. He lifts his hand to his face, palm facing to the side, and holds up his fingers to tap them on his chin.

Emilia mimics his motion, even though she only holds up three fingers, her thumb and pinky held down in her palm. "You want some water?"

Tanner nods, giving her a small smile.

My mom immediately jumps into action, grabbing his water bottle from her backpack, and holding it out to Tanner. "There you go, sweetie."

"Did you see that?" Emilia smiles at Tanner before looking at me. "He signs water like if he'd say 'water' at this age, or maybe 'want water.' The most important thing is that you continue to talk normally with him, in full sentences and sign along the few words you know."

I nod. "That makes sense."

"I also like to repeat back what they sign in a question like I just did. Instead of just giving him the water, I asked him if he wanted some water and signed water as well. The more words they hear, the better."

We all watch as Tanner finishes up most of his water, sighing loudly when he's done.

My chest squeezes, thinking about the times he's tried to tell us something and we didn't understand him. Where both Mom and I tried to guess what Tanner wanted, only able to go by his nods and headshakes—if at all—not knowing he's been trying to communicate with us via sign language this whole time.

Just like that, my opinion of Emilia changes, this whole situation bathing her in a new light that has highly swayed my first impression of her.

She's the youngest of all applicants at twenty-four, and I went into this looking for someone with more experience. Maybe someone with a less quirky attire. From the looks of it, we might have to go with Tanner's reaction and hope for the best.

Mom will be there to help if I need her, but she still works, so I will have to learn how to trust someone else with my son. The clenching in my stomach has loosened slightly at the knowledge that Tanner won't be miserable while I'm training. At least not because of his nanny.

Other than that, who could blame him? His whole world changed in a way that's not only irreversible but also irreplaceable. For a short time, at least by law, he was an orphan, right before he was thrust into someone's arms he'd never seen before in his life.

Me.

His *dad.*

Something we both have to get used to, and I know it will take a while.

Lila mentioned that he went to daycare, so I hope that

will make it easier for him to get used to us and my rigid routine.

Without a doubt, I need all the help I can get because I haven't been around kids much. None of my friends have kids yet.

Hunter has a bunch of nieces and nephews that I've seen at family gatherings before, but that doesn't make you ready for twenty-four/seven care of a little boy. I think I'm still in shock, if I'm being honest.

I study Emilia. The way her lips quirk up at the corners when she murmurs soft words to Tanner, and the way her eyes shine when she giggles with him.

I clear my throat to get her attention. When her eyes are on me, I do the only plausible thing. "The job is yours. When can you start?"

I will take good care of him, just like I vowed after reading Lila's letter. She never had the chance to finish it, but I'll be damned if I didn't at least try my best to honor her last wish.

Dear Jace,

I've dreamed of contacting you so many times, and now that I'm sick, I finally learn your name, from the hospital TV broadcasting one of your races of all things. There are so many things I want to say. So many things I want to ask, but this is about Tanner, your son. I'm sorry to spring something this enormous on you in a letter, but I want to be prepared, just in case.

Our one-night stand three years ago resulted in pregnancy, but since I didn't know your full name, I couldn't contact you. I was scared to do it all by myself, but the moment I saw Tanner's sweet face, I knew I could and would. He's turned my life upside down but in the best possible way. He's my whole world, and the only family I've got. I love him so much, and if things get worse, I hope you tell him that daily.

I'm begging you right now with my whole being to take him in and to take good care of him if I don't make it. He's my best buddy and has the biggest heart. I had hoped we could co-parent him, and the thought of not being able to watch my gorgeous baby grow up breaks my heart. I know that you'll love him too and if I'm not there, help him grow into the amazing man I know he can be.

Even though he doesn't talk yet, his communication is wonderful as you'll quickly learn. He's the smartest and happiest boy and very well-loved by his daycare friends.

I'm getting tired, so I'll try and write more later. The doctor is hoping I'll be out of hospital next week.

THREE

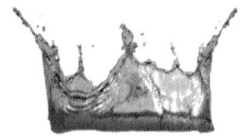

EMILIA

Tanner might just be the cutest kid on earth. I owe Nicole and her grandma big time because this new nanny job might be the easiest job I've ever had. One I also enjoy. Not to mention, I make more than I did at my previous online show gig. Talk about win-win.

Tanner and I are cuddled up on the couch reading books when the alarm system beeps, indicating that one of the doors was opened. Less than two seconds later, the front door shuts and footsteps echo across the wooden floor, coming closer to the living room.

Footsteps I know belong to Jace.

It's been a week since I started working for him, but we haven't interacted much.

I'm practically sleep-walking into his house at an insane hour in the morning, just for him to grab his duffel bag and slip out of the house for his morning training session. In the evening, we do the same the other way around. He comes home exhausted from his afternoon training, and most nights, I hand off a sleepy Tanner to him who's ready for bed.

Now it's a bit after ten in the morning, and Jace is here. With us. For the first time. It's strange and oddly intrusive.

Even though it's his house.

His son.

More than once this last week, I thought about Jace when I was lying awake in bed at night. Trying to put myself in his shoes. His situation and what happened to Tanner's mom is sad, but also strangely fascinating. Probably not unique, but unique enough I'd say. I'd hope.

Something that's hard to fathom. To not know you have a child, just to have it practically shoved into your life—a very busy one at that—after learning the woman you were involved with died.

A shiver runs down my back at the thought alone.

Kind of creepy, probably making the whole situation even harder to get used to. Especially since Jace seems a bit awkward around Tanner, but hopefully he just needs to warm up to the situation. From the little I've seen them interact, it has improved already.

Some people aren't kids-people by nature, I've seen my fair share of those over the years. But he doesn't seem like the kind of guy either who'd say "No, please take my son somewhere else, I don't want him." I wonder how much experience he's had with kids prior to Tanner. If I had to guess, the answer would be not a lot. But he's trying. At least, he smiles at Tanner and is nice to him, which is worth a ton.

Now he's there, right in front of the couch. His long legs clad in gray sweatpants, hanging low on his hips, a black T-shirt tucked messily into the front of it. "Hey."

His voice is deep and rich, his gaze barely skimming over me before landing on Tanner.

Then he walks around the couch table and sits down on the edge of the cushion, leaving a good distance between us, like he's unsure of how to approach Tanner.

Tanner lifts his hand sideways with his fingers spread wide and touches his forehead with his thumb several times. Then his gaze drifts over to me as if he's looking for reassurance.

I nod, giving him a big smile. "Yes. That's Daddy." I lift my hand to copy his motion, confirming he did the correct sign. "Say, Hi, Daddy."

Tanner repeats the sign once more before waving at Jace. Then he launches into a string of incoherent babbling.

I realized on day one that Tanner does talk, a lot actually, but it's mostly random babbling that no one but he understands. In a word, he's incredible. When Jace told me what had happened to Tanner, I truly thought I'd have to deal with a distraught, confused, and very quiet young boy that I'd need to coax and calm and coddle.

But Tanner has been so happy, so . . . adaptable. Patricia mentioned he was in daycare, and it makes me think he started at a young age. Not surprising if his mom was a single mom with no other relatives around to help. He's simply accepted that I'm his nanny, and that Jace is his daddy. Amazing.

He turns to me, his fingers rushing through a set of movements not a lot of people would recognize because they're so sloppy. But I do. The letters of my name, the same ones I signed in every episode we filmed during my introduction. Tanner's trying though, and the first letter m looks actually pretty recognizable.

I point at myself, before fingerspelling my name too, extra slow this time. "Yes, I'm Millie."

Movement to my left makes me lift my head to stare straight into Jace's blue eyes.

"Does everyone call you Millie?"

I shrug. "Mostly. That's what my friends call me, and what I went with for the show. I think kids like it better, and I do too."

"Your family doesn't call you Millie?" His eyebrows draw together, the only motion on his face.

Well, crap on a pretzel stick. He's a straight shooter. Of course, I walked right into that one.

The last thing I want to do is talk about my family.

He doesn't look away, just keeps studying my face as I have a heated debate inside my head. Thank goodness no one can see what's going on behind my mop of hair.

"No." I return the penetrating gaze, silently challenging him to say anything else.

"Okay." He turns to Tanner, who's been happily looking at his books, before gazing back at me. "He hasn't eaten yet, right?"

Shaking my head, I check the time on the Blu-ray player on the media center. "No. I was going to turn on a show for him after we're done reading so I can get his lunch ready."

"I can read with him." He looks hopeful, and . . . nervous I think.

I sit up straight, my stomach churning once. "Oh, of course."

Turning to Tanner, I brush a hand over his hair. "Daddy is going to read to you, okay?"

He puts his hands together, palm to palm, before opening them like a book.

"Yes, book. Good job."

His eyes flicker to Jace for a moment, a hint of uncertainty in them as he watches his dad repeat the book sign as well.

Jace's eyes are trained on Tanner, the corners of his mouth lifted in a friendly grin. "Should we read a book together, buddy?"

Tanner gives me a smile that melts my heart. I return it and get up, going to the kitchen. Trying hard to push down my other emotions. The pity. And compassion. Sympathy. I think it's just sinking in how hard this is for Jace. For both of them.

They are, in every possible way, absolute strangers, and might not know how not to be.

The urge to help, to push this along is strong, but I'm not sure that's the best thing for them.

Before sadness takes over, I busy myself with Tanner's meal. Some scrambled eggs and cheese toast. Something quick and easy he loves and has devoured each time I've made it so far.

I last about two minutes before I glance up. Tanner has moved on from the books, a car and a truck now in each of his hands as he drives them along the edge of the cushions. Jace sits on one end of the couch, holding the big parking garage wide open for Tanner to drive into.

My eyes close as relief washes through me. This is good. Really good, and exactly what both of them need.

Belatedly, I realize I didn't ask Jace if he wants something to eat too. Dang it. I'm pretty much done with Tanner's and mine, about to put it on our plates. I could offer him mine.

I clear my throat. "Jace, do you want some too?"

He turns to look at me over his shoulder. "Nah. I've got my prepped meals. But thanks."

"Okay." My stomach rumbles, and I barely contain my chuckle. Close call.

I grab the plates and walk over to the table. The second Tanner sees me, he drops everything and runs over. After I pull out his chair at the head of the dining table, he climbs into it, his butt firmly planted in the highchair. I buckle him in and push him to the table before handing him his green spoon—his favorite color.

"Here you go, buddy. Bon appétit." I put his plate in front of him and ruffle his hair before sitting down in the chair to his right.

"You speak French?" Jace's questioning eyes are on me.

I shrug. "Not really. But enjoy your meal doesn't sound as good. Much prettier in French."

"I guess."

Tanner and I eat while Jace takes out several food containers from the fridge to heat up in the microwave. The fridge is filled with meals prepared by a local chef, but we've never eaten together.

My jaw falls open when he brings his food to the table, or rather when he *starts* to bring it over because it doesn't seem to end. Back and forth he goes, loading up the table with what looks like enough food for Tanner and me for a whole day, if not two.

When he sits down opposite me, the corners of his mouth

twitch. It might have something to do with me staring at him like he's grown a third eye.

My eyes bounce from the food to his face when I finally snap out of my stupor. "Are you seriously going to eat all of this?"

"Yup."

I bite my tongue before a curse word slips past my lips, but boy, does it want to get out. "Holy guacamole."

Jace takes a bite of what looks like pasta with chicken, right as his stomach lets out an angry growl. After chewing another mouthful, he puts down his fork and wipes his mouth with a paper towel. "Believe me, I need it. If I didn't eat this much, I'd easily lose five pounds or more a week."

"No way." My answers keep getting more brilliant by the minute.

"I burn a lot of calories every day."

I nod, unable to wrap my head around eating so much food, or burning so many calories.

When I don't say anything else, he picks his fork back up, and works his way through bowl after bowl. Besides the pasta, there's also a large sandwich, some fresh fruit, and a sports drinks.

When I pick up my toast, I stay quiet, my eyes mostly trained on my plate or Tanner. He's too engrossed in eating to notice much around him, happily shoving small pieces of scrambled eggs in his mouth with his chubby fingers, his spoon long forgotten.

His eyes have grown tired in the last half hour, his body knowing that his nap is coming up when he's done eating, which is the reason why we usually have an early lunch. Looks like Jace is on the same schedule.

"I'm sorry I wasn't around much this last week." Jace's voice is gentle. Hesitant.

He picks up his drink and unscrews the cap, the bottle opening with a swooshing *pop*. "I missed a lot of training the last few weeks with everything going on, so I had to catch up and get back in the groove."

"It's okay. You told me your schedule is crazy." My plan was to ask him about it once we're more familiar. It's not like I need him here or that my working hours would change. But I'm definitely curious.

Jace shakes his head. "It is, but it's not always this bad. I train twice a day either at the aquatic club or at the pool at Hawkins University. Usually, I come home between my sessions for lunch though. And, if possible, a nap."

"A nap?" The words are out before I'm done processing what he said.

"Uh-huh."

Honestly, I have no clue about swimming, or swimmers for that matter. For some reason, I didn't expect them to nap though. I'm not like some people who think it's ridiculous for adults to take naps, that it's for kids, but it still throws me for a loop. It sounds silly coming from a guy like him. "That's . . . fun."

He blows air out of his nose at my answer, and I look down, hoping he won't see my cheeks because they feel like they might burn holes in my face.

"Consider it my secret weapon, one of my special training techniques." He takes a bite of his sandwich, chews, and swallows, his Adam's apple pulling my gaze to the smooth skin of his neck. Everything about him is smooth. "Or maybe I just like to sleep."

No argument from me there so I nod. "You've been to the Olympics before, right?"

Wow, Millie. Way to expose you've been looking up your boss online.

"I have. Next year will be my fourth one."

I stare at him for a moment, trying to wrap my head around that. "Wow. That sounds like a lot of work."

Jace chuckles. "It is. It's pretty much been my life since I was a kid."

"That's a long time."

"It is." His expression has turned serious.

What must that feel like? To dedicate everything to a sport like that. Is it really worth the sacrifices?

I focus back on my lunch, but not before noticing how oddly quiet it's been. When I look over at Tanner, he's sound asleep in his chair, his head tilted back and to the side, his mouth wide open. Only kids can pass out like that.

I'm about to push back my chair, when Jace beats me to it.

"I've got it."

For some reason, his statement takes me aback, but I nod anyway. "Okay."

I guess I feel that if I'm on the clock, I should do all the responsibilities of the nanny. But, this is new to both of us, so I'll go with whatever Jace thinks is best. It's also nice to see Jace so keen to do things with his boy. It's undeniably cute.

Jace hesitates for a moment with his hands midair before gently grabbing Tanner under his armpits, pulling him out of the highchair, and up to his chest, where Tanner's head flounders to the side on his dad's shoulder.

It's a sight to behold.

This tall, lean mountain of a man gently cradling his little boy he didn't even know about until recently. He's lost almost three years with him he can never get back, and Tanner deserves every bit of affection, especially after losing his mother at such a young age.

From the outside, it seems like Jace has it in him to give Tanner exactly that. Because how can someone who's so passionate about his life and what he does with it, even devoting most of it to his job, his sport, his dream, not have any devotion left for his child? How sad that would be for a little—

How sad that would be for any child...

The hairs on my back suddenly stand up when the realization hits me hard.

Because that is familiar territory. Because I know just how sad that is... how damaging.

FOUR

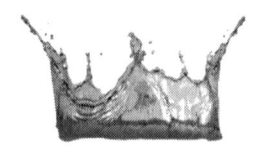

JACE

My fingers grace the wall of the pool, and I lift my head in relief. Maybe I pushed too hard during my cool down, but I felt so tense that I needed to let out some extra steam toward the end.

Hunter crouches down next to the starting block, right in my face as I push up my goggles. "I'm so happy you kicked that punk's ass. Your times were awesome."

I also had to push a lot harder than normal to get those times. But I don't tell Hunter that.

He squeezes the cap in his hand and casts a glance in the direction of the group that has gathered on the side of the pool. A bunch of cocky college freshmen.

Maybe I should have trained by myself at the aquatic club today after all. Instead, I went to the university pool to see my coach, who alternates between both training locations depending on availability. But then, I wouldn't have seen Hunter either, who's here with his coach.

"I didn't do anything." I roll my shoulders, willing this damn tension to go away.

His gaze finds mine, and he shakes his head. "Of course you didn't. It's not like he has a chance against you. They don't call you king of the water for no reason."

"They're kids, Hunt."

He moves to the side so I can get out of the pool, even though my arms feel like Jell-O.

"Doesn't mean they have to think they're better than others and act like jerks. It serves him right to learn some respect. Hopefully, that'll put them all in place."

I walk over to the bench to grab my towel. "We were just as bad back then. Thinking we were better and faster than everyone else."

"Maybe you were, but I wasn't."

I pause with my towel right above my chest and look at him. His shit-eating grin confirms he's full of it. "If I was bad, you were worse. You pretty much challenged everyone back then, thinking you were the hottest thing professional swimming had ever seen."

His casual shrug portrays Hunter's personality more than words ever could. "I *was* the hottest thing, still am."

A chuckle escapes my mouth even though it's the last thing Hunter needs. He doesn't need to be encouraged. Not one bit. Two years younger than me at twenty-six, he's often still a young punk at heart, exactly like the ones he just mocked.

The only difference is, he has enough gold medals to back up his confidence. Even though his ego is big enough without the medals.

"Speaking of hot things . . . how's that nanny of yours doing?" He wiggles his eyebrows.

The pointed stare I give him does nothing to deter him.

Instead, I pretend I didn't hear him, gather my things, and wave to my coach before heading in the direction of the showers.

I only have a few hours before I'm back after my lunch break and a nap if I can manage it. I could really use one.

Hunter doesn't miss a beat, grabbing his stuff and falling into step beside me. "Oh, come on, dude, give me something. She's smoking hot."

His comment makes my step falter, and I turn to look at him. "How would you even know? You haven't met her."

Now that I think about it, it actually surprises me he hasn't shown up on my doorstep unannounced.

"You're kidding me, right?" Hunter stops me with a hand on my bicep. "Please tell me you've googled her and checked out the YouTube channel of her old show. I mean, *come on*. What kind of employer are you?"

Why do I feel like he's interrogating me? I didn't have time for this stuff when I was trying to find someone for Tanner, nor did I feel like it. Hunter has nieces and nephews. He's probably familiar with a lot of the kid's stuff. Me on the other hand? Not one bit.

"My mom checked out her social media." He knows how much my mom loves everything online. "And, of course, I ran some background checks."

"That's something, at least." It's such a quiet mumble I almost miss it.

"Do I have to be concerned that you think she's hot after watching her on a kids' show?" I know he doesn't discriminate when it comes to women. He likes them all.

Shaking his head like I'm the weird one in this scenario, he judges me. He so does. "I think we have to get you to a doctor. It's been like fifty-seven years since you've been with someone, and I'm afraid they've retracted your man card."

I blink. My best friend, the exaggerator.

As usual, he ignores me. "Jace. She's hot, like, seriously hot. And you're acting like *I've* lost my mind. Her tits in the tight yellow shirt she always wears, her long legs under that tutu. Makes me wonder what's underneath and how it would feel to get in close and shove up that skirt—"

"What the hell, dude?" I'm relieved there's an actual reason for her strange yellow outfit, but the feeling only lasts for a moment. "That outfit seriously does it for you? I don't get it."

His eyes go wide at my words. "She comes to your place dressed like that?"

My shoulders rise and fall. "Something like that, yeah."

He looks at me like he's never seen me before. Or maybe he's wondering why he's my friend. He rubs his hand over his face like I just did something inexcusable, and I have no clue why.

He rubs his chin. "Are you sure you're not gay? You know that would be okay, right?"

Since I can't decide if I should roll my eyes or punch him in the face, I walk away.

Naturally, he's next to me two seconds later as we walk into the locker room. "Sorry, I'll shut up about her."

"Thanks." I inhale deeply, my chest suddenly feeling tight. "She's my nanny, you know? She's at home with my . . . with my son."

Absolutely no need to talk about her beauty.

A quick glance around confirms that we're alone. I don't want someone hearing about my private life.

Hunter doesn't crack a smile this time. His big hand lands on my shoulder. "I know, dude. How are you both holding up?"

I unzip my bag, giving the contents my full attention as I think about his question.

How the hell do I explain that my whole life has been altered? That if I want to go to the store to grab something last-minute . . . that if I want to take a shower . . . nap. Forget hookups. Gone. I can't do that anymore.

I. Have. A. Son. A tiny human that will be my responsibility for at least the next fifteen years. *How are we holding up?*

"I have no fucking idea what I'm doing, Hunt. None. Everything I thought was my path, my future . . . Everything's changed. I used to hit my pillow and sleep. Now . . . now I wait for him to wake up and cry, because he's lost his world too. During the day, he's fine. Because he has Emilia. He really likes her."

"Don't blame the guy. He's got good taste."

Not wanting to talk about this anymore, I grab my things for the shower and get cleaned up quickly, so I can go home for lunch.

With my kinda cute son and my totally-not-hot nanny.

Everything goes downhill afterward.

Damn Hunter.

It's like he's planted a seed in my brain, and I'm desperately trying to figure out if there's any truth to his statements.

Which there isn't, right?

I'm Emilia's boss and definitely not attracted to her.

She wears a giant bow in her hair, for fuck's sake.

When I step out of the car at home, the music from inside the house is loud enough to hear outside. Looks like someone's having a party. Naturally, neither Emilia, nor Tanner, hear me walking into the living room. They both have their backs to me, giggling, as "Head, Shoulders, Knees, and Toes" plays from the speakers.

Tanner's eyes are glued on Emilia and her movements, touching all the correct body parts along with the music. Head, shoulders, knees, and toes.

Since it seems to be my *un*lucky day, Emilia bends all the way down to touch her toes, her ass high in the air and on full display.

Thank fuck she's wearing leggings underneath her skirt, even though at this point, she might as well be naked since the black fabric clings to her like a second skin, doing nothing to hide her shaped ass cheeks. They are round and perfect, and shit . . . they're sexy. So damn sexy.

This is all Hunter's fault.

The song ends and Emilia squeals when she turns around and sees me standing there like a total idiot.

After holding her hand over her chest, she looks at Tanner with a big smile. "Look, sweetie, there's Daddy." She spreads her fingers and touches her forehead gently with her thumb to sign daddy.

"Hi." Tanner waves in my direction with a shy smile and I return the gesture.

Most of the time, I'm still not sure how to act around him. Am I expected to go hug him? Does he want me to hug him?

Do I *want* to hug him? So many questions I don't know the answers to.

None of this seems to come natural to me, and I'm beyond grateful to have Emilia and my mom. I'd be utterly screwed without them.

Emilia walks in my direction, her skirt swaying around her hips like it's trying to pique my interest. "Hey, are you okay?"

Shit.

This is the absolute last thing I need in my life right now. My plate's already full to the max.

"Do you own anything else besides this hideous outfit?" The words leave my mouth while my brain's still trying to reboot after my Hunter-might-actually-be-right-and-Emilia's-sexy realization. Because, man, I'm so not okay with that.

I probably should have worded it nicer, sound less like an asshole, but it's too late now.

Emilia impresses me by flinching for only a moment before she goes straight to cover up her emotions. But I can still see it. In her green eyes. The spark is gone, an emptiness lingering in its place. *I* did this, and she's put up her guard.

Tanner comes up next to her and roars before lifting his right arm in the air.

He actually roars at me. What the hell?

"Does Daddy seem mad?" Her face contorts, the friendly expression from a few minutes ago long gone, furrowed eyebrows and an upturned mouth in its place. But when she bends down to get on Tanner's eye level, the look on her face has softened.

Emilia starts singing quietly—a song about feeling so mad that you want to roar, from a Daniel Tiger episode I vaguely remember—while they do a dance with their hands. The song helps Daniel to calm down in the show.

I'm too stunned to react, watching the scene unfold in front of me.

Does that make them crazy or me?

When they're done, Emilia takes Tanner's hand and ignores me. They walk to the dining table where she helps him in his highchair. After giving him a coloring book and some crayons, she's off to the kitchen.

Her damn skirt taunting me some more.

Short of cussing, or worse, slamming my head into something, I go to my bedroom, planning on meditating for a few minutes before I get my lunch.

Fucking Hunter.

FIVE

EMILIA

It's my first real evening off all week, and I spend it worrying about my boss.

Something is off with Jace. He's been acting strange all week, ever since that day he barked at me because of my outfit. I'm actually pretty sure he's been avoiding me as much as possible.

Suddenly, there are longer training sessions again, he packs up his lunch in the morning and has it someplace else, and whatever other excuse he can come up with to avoid coming home.

If he won't bring it up soon and tell me what's going on, I will. I hate any sort of conflict or confrontation, like *really* hate it, but constantly wondering if I did something wrong is a lot worse for me and will drive me to the edge of insanity.

Something must have happened to get that reaction from him, and I've been wracking my brain to figure out if I did anything but keep coming up empty.

Now this worry is taking over my free time too, and I hate it.

My phone beeps on my dresser, and my heart does an extra flip when Jace's picture pops up on the screen.

Speak of the devil.

He doesn't know I took a photo of him one afternoon, but I wasn't going to ask him if I could. I just wanted it for his phone contact.

Talk about an awkward conversation.

It makes my life easier when I don't have to try and decipher names when I get a call, so I use photos as often as I can.

I sit up in bed and straighten my tank top as if he could actually see me. Then I mentally berate myself. I don't need that added stress in my life.

After clearing my voice about five times, and taking two sips of water, I swipe the button on my screen to answer the call. "Hello?"

"Emilia."

I still can't decide if it irks or amuses me that he still calls me by my normal name when barely anyone else does. Except my family, of course. With them, it definitely gets a rise out of me.

"Hey, Jace." Very casual and aloof. Good.

Maybe he called to talk about what stick has been up his butt. I'd definitely be up for that conversation.

"I need your help, please. It's Tanner." He's out of breath, and if I'm not mistaken, his voice is shaky.

That definitely gets my attention, and I'm immediately on alert, my body tight with tension. "What's going on?"

A breath rushes out of him, making me hold my own for a moment. "I think his cough has gotten worse. He woke up and started crying. I gave him some water, but it doesn't seem to help. And now he sounds weird, kind of like a seal. I know that sounds stupid, but I don't know how else to describe it."

"Did you say seal?" Just then, Tanner coughs in the background, and I grab the edge of my comforter to pull it off my body. He got a cold this week and started coughing this morning, but it didn't sound anything like this. "Take him to the ER, Jace. I'll meet you there."

"ER?"

I'm so focused on finding some clothes in my messy bedroom that I almost miss the panic in his voice. When his next gasp registers, my chest tightens, making my own breath expel.

"Yes, emergency room. Sorry, I didn't mean to freak you out. I'm sure he's fine, but the pediatrician's office is closed by now, but it could be croup, which means his airways could swell closed. My motto is better safe than sorry, especially when it comes to kids." I put on whatever is within reach, not paying much attention to what it is, before grabbing a few things to throw it in my purse.

When he still hasn't said a word a moment later, I stop what I'm doing, trying to give him my undivided attention, even though it feels wrong to stop moving right now. "Do you want me to come to the house and get you guys?"

His next exhale squeezes my chest again. It's shaky, and it might sound odd, but it sounded sad. "No, it's fine. Just meet us there."

There's a hint of strength returning to his voice, so I nod to myself and adapt to his behavior. No need to freak out now. "All right. You know where it is, right? The children's hospital?"

Their devotion and ability to deal with sick children day

in and day out is miraculous. I don't think I could do it, but I'm beyond grateful there are people who can. Both children and parents need them.

"It's the one over on fifty-second, right?"

"Yes, that one." I nod like he's standing right in front of me. "You'll probably beat me to it, so I'm just going to call you when I get there."

Tanner's hushed cough in the background snaps me out of my frozen state, and I throw my purse over my head to secure it across my body. Nicole's spending the night at her boyfriend's place—like most nights—and the house is dark when I make my way through it. After grabbing a few things from the kitchen, I shove my feet into my shoes, snatch my helmet, and lock the front door.

Having any sort of emergency with kids makes me nervous, my cool facade slipping the tiniest bit when I climb on my moped.

I know Tanner's going to be okay, but I need to see him with my own eyes.

When I get to the hospital, I'm covered in goosebumps. I should have worn something warmer but didn't want to waste the time to drive back home to change clothes.

I storm into the hospital like my butt's on fire, just to come up short at the check-in window. I'm not even sure how I'm supposed to get back there. The doors to the emergency room wing are locked. Dang it.

"Hi. May I help you?" The lady behind the glass gives me a tired smile as I step closer.

"Yes. I'm here to see Tanner Atwood." It's taking every last ounce of self-control to keep my voice steady.

Her gaze goes up and down my body, her dark eyes friendly but stern. "Are you related to him?"

"I'm . . . no, I'm not. Not directly." Why didn't I think of this before? "I'm his . . . Jace Atwood is my . . ."

The corners of her mouth lift the slightest. "Oh, that's right. You're Jace's new girlfriend, aren't you? Or was that his other swimmer friend who has someone new?" She shakes her head and chuckles softly. "I'm sorry, my daughter is a huge swim fan and keeps up with all of this stuff, telling me about it if I want to hear it or not."

Heat floods my face, and she must take my stunned silence as an admission.

"Well, for what it's worth, you two make a lovely couple. Can I see your ID, please?"

I'm too chicken to correct her, focusing on my purse instead. Which naturally has everything I could possibly ever need to survive any kind of apocalypse, except for my wallet. Just great.

I'm about to inform her about my misfortune when my phone begins to vibrate in my hand, Jace's photo covering the whole screen. The lady behind the security glass sees it and winks at me, and I want to disappear into thin air.

Hurrying up to escape this discomfort as soon as humanly possible, I answer the phone. "Hey." I hope he doesn't notice my voice sounding all breathy.

"Where are you?"

"Just outside the ER doors, trying to get in. It's not—"

"I'm coming." And then my ear fills with the beeping sound of the dead line after Jace hangs up on me.

I send another awkward smile at the employee and feel so relieved when Jace opens the ER doors that I want to kiss him. Which is a very random, and very odd, thought because I don't *really* want to kiss him.

Tanner is in his arms, clinging to him like he's afraid to fall off the mountain of a man, a.k.a. his dad. The second he sees me, his lips start to quiver and he lets go of Jace's neck to stretch his arms toward me. My heart twists, and my stomach quivers, as I inhale a reassured breath at seeing that he's okay.

"Aww come here, monkey. It's okay." He wraps his small limbs around my neck and waist in a grip that could rival a python's, pressing his warm face into my shoulder. I start rubbing his back with one hand while casting a glance over his shoulder at Jace.

He must have talked to the lady while I took Tanner from him, ushering me forward to the door he's still holding open with one long arm. "Come on, the doctor should be there any second."

I don't dare glance over at the lady, but I'm pretty sure she has her eyes on me. *Us.* When Jace puts a hand on my lower back to guide me through the door, I'm certain I hear a sigh coming from her direction.

Oh, brother.

Jace guides me down a short hallway until he steps around me to pull back the curtain of one of the rooms. "In here."

Not wanting to disturb Tanner, I walk over to the bed to lean against it. Jace stops a foot in front of me, his gaze focused on his son. Lifting a hand, he brushes back Tanner's hair from his forehead, touching his knuckles along my neck in the process. I involuntarily shiver at the contact, but either Jace doesn't notice or he ignores it.

Thank goodness.

Before either one of us can say a word, a woman steps into the room, closing the curtain and glass sliding door behind her, sheltering us from the bustle of the emergency room. "Hey, guys. I'm Dr. Shelton." She looks down at her chart. "And you're here because of Tanner? Tell me what's going on."

Jace opens his mouth as a nasty coughing fit trembles through Tanner's small body. It sounds painful, and his eyes get watery as he looks at me as if I alone can make this nasty sickness go away. My throat tightens. There's nothing I'd like to do more than make him feel better. The need to do something fills me to the point of frustration.

"Ah yes, poor guy." Doctor Shelton makes a note on her chart before placing it on the counter and washing her hands. "Tell me about his symptoms. When did it start? Have you given him any medicine yet?"

Jace sends me a look I can't decipher. Is he freaking out about this? Could I really blame him though? This is his first real sickness with his child, and it's definitely a learning curve.

I turn my head away from Tanner as much as I can and clear my throat. "It started as a regular cold. Stuffy nose, normal cough. He had a bit of a temperature, around one oh one, and I gave him some Motrin before bedtime around six."

The doctor dries her hands on a paper towel and nods. "Okay. Let's take a look at him."

She pats the examination bed, and I slowly lower Tanner on it.

The exam is quick, and she constantly reassures Tanner, who never once lets go of my hand, leaning into my side as if he's trying to establish as much contact with me as possible.

"Good job, buddy." She nods to us, signaling she's done as she puts her stethoscope back around her neck. "His lungs sound good, but I can't tell for sure if it's croup. His breathing is a bit noisy but kids also like to suppress their cough when it hurts, so it might clear up the next time he really coughs. Since his cough sounds a little like barking though, I'd like to give him some steroids just in case. And keep giving him pain medicine to keep the temperature down. You can switch back and forth between Tylenol and Motrin."

Jace nods next to me, even though I can't tell if he actually knows what she's talking about. One of the kids I used to nanny for had it once, and that's the only reason I know about this.

Dr. Shelton walks to the sink to wash her hands once more before picking up her clipboard to scribble her notes on. "If you have a humidifier, I'd put it in his room. If the cough continues like this, you can take him outside when it's cool or even have him take a few deep breaths in front of an open freezer. I'll send you home with an extra dose in case things aren't better by tomorrow. The most important thing is that he gets a lot of rest. And lots of fluids."

Jace and I have both turned into mimes, constantly nodding our understanding. Dr. Shelton laughs.

"I know, it's a bit overwhelming, but Tanner will be fine. Just check with the pediatrician in a few days." She holds out a piece of paper and Jace takes it while I'm back to rubbing Tanner's back in rhythmic movements.

After we say our goodbyes to her, a nurse comes to give

Tanner his medicine and some juice. I hum quietly to him and watch Jace take the discharge papers, happy we can finally get this boy back home in his bed.

We walk out of the hospital in silence, Tanner's head heavy on my shoulder as his breaths slowly even out and his grip loosens around my neck.

Jace unlocks the car and opens the back door so I can put Tanner in his car seat. Somehow I manage to get him buckled in without waking him up. Poor thing is probably exhausted.

After one long look at his son, Jace lets out a stifled breath, rubbing his hands over his face. He gazes into the distance, and I give him this moment to decompress, before he sets his gaze on me. "Where are you parked?"

When I point to my Vespa in the parking spot right next to us, he just shakes his head before opening the passenger door. "Of course you have a moped. It's way too cold to drive that at night, especially the way you're dressed. Come on, I'll take you. We'll pick it up tomorrow."

Too bad he's right. I was freezing my booty off on the way here and wasn't looking forward to the drive home.

I cast a nervous glance at the hospital. "Do you think it's okay to leave her for the night?"

"I'm sure it is."

He's probably right. I mean, some people actually have to stay the night here, right? They can't know which vehicle belongs to which patient or relative. "All right."

Jace has his arm perched on the open car door, so when I step past him, I'm close enough to smell his clean, musky scent. It's a smell I've gotten used to over the last two weeks working for him. Even when he's not at the house, it still lingers in the air or on the furniture.

My body decides that this is the right moment to pull up a memory of that tiny moment an hour ago when he brushed his hand along my throat.

Well, it wasn't *really* a moment, and he wasn't actually trying to touch me, but my brain seems to think I liked it anyway.

My skin tingles just thinking about it as I get in the car and buckle in. I'm so distracted by my thoughts that I miss him shutting the door behind me and getting into the car himself.

He lets out an impatient huff and I look at him. With his head on the head rest, and his hands loosely in his lap, he inhales deeply several times.

When he rolls his head to the side, and his gaze lands on me, it's so intense, I feel it deep in my bones. He was closed off this whole time, looking cool and controlled from the second he opened that door to the emergency room.

Now, his whole posture is slumped, like he's sunken into himself. His eyes are wide, unblinking, as they stare at me with an almost tormented look that makes my stomach tighten in response.

"You okay?" Before I know it, my hand moves across the middle console to touch his arm. He doesn't seem affected by the cooler night temperatures, his muscles taut under his warm skin as he remains unmoving.

I'm not sure if I'm crossing some sort of boss-employee line, so I only squeeze once before I retreat back to my side, clasping my hands together in my lap.

"Yeah." He swallows and nods, his gaze never leaving mine.

Then we stare at each other like we just survived a zombie apocalypse and can't believe we're still alive.

"Emilia?" My name is barely a whisper on his lips.

"Mmm?" Muscle tension has me frozen to my seat, apprehension rushing through me, a certainty settling inside me that this won't be an everyday question.

"Will you come back home with us and stay the night?" The words are barely out of his mouth when he breaks eye contact, dropping his gaze to his lap. "Just in case?"

My heart breaks at his question. He made himself vulnerable to ensure his boy is safe and sound. He didn't have the chance to give Tanner the unconditional love every child should get from their parents from the moment they're born, or even before that.

But he's here now, and he's trying. And that's all anyone can ask of him. To do whatever is in his power.

"Yes. Of course."

Jace nods at my words but still avoids my gaze as he starts the car and drives out of the hospital parking lot with a quietly snoring Tanner in the back seat.

SIX

JACE

If I didn't have high blood pressure before, I'm sure I have it after tonight. Of course I've worried about other people before—my friends and family—but I've never experienced anything like the last few hours.

The feeling of being choked or smothered has lessened only minimally. There was a moment—when Tanner first woke up with his bad cough and started crying uncontrollably—where I felt like I wasn't able to get enough oxygen.

And that's coming from an athlete who was taught to hold his breath for long periods of time. Thankfully, that technique was retired long ago, but not once have I ever felt this kind of chest tightness before.

The chance of something bad happening to him when I just got him was unbearable to imagine.

Thank goodness for Emilia.

She might be a bit odd at times and dress crazy, but tonight, she saved me from going overboard, from losing my shit when I had to keep it together for my son.

My son.

The concept still seems surreal most days. Sometimes I catch myself staring at him, unable to fathom that he's actually part me.

Every moment I've wrestled with this intrusion in my life, every ounce of anger and frustration I've felt over my career being in danger, was put on the backburner.

"Is the baby monitor not good enough?" Emilia's voice is a soft whisper in the quiet house.

She peeks around my body in Tanner's room, his night light bright enough to see his curled-up body in his crib, his rhythmic snores oddly reassuring.

We both take a step back, and I close the door quietly before heading to the kitchen.

"The monitor's fuzzy." I hold up the offending device, and the corners of Emilia's mouth twitch.

"That's what I thought." She nods, but I can see the gleam in her eyes.

I look at her, *really* look at her for the first time tonight.

I sweep over her body from top to bottom, taking in her jean shorts and long-sleeved striped shirt. "So, you do own normal clothes."

How on earth did I not notice this outfit before?

I saw at the hospital that her outfit wasn't fit for a nightly moped ride, but my brain didn't register what she was actually wearing.

She lifts her arms to cross them over her chest but not before I notice her hard nipples through the thin material.

Just what I need tonight on top of everything else.

Her chuckle sounds strangled, a flush creeping up her

neck and face. "Um . . . of course I own normal clothes. You didn't think I do?"

My shoulders lift and fall. "There was a possibility your closet's filled to the brim with yellows shirts, yellow-black tutus, and gigantic bows."

A loud snort escapes her a second before she shoves my shoulder. Hard. Then she chuckles quietly. "You're funny, Jace Atwood. I wasn't sure you had *that* in you."

I continue to stare at her as she brushes a strand of her long red hair out of her face. Her *hair*. No pigtails or bows. I might as well have walked around with blinders tonight for all I've noticed.

"Your hair." This moment might go down in the book of oddest conversations.

She breaks eye contact and pushes her locks behind her ear. "I . . . I left the house in a rush, so I didn't have time to tame it."

"I like it."

"Thank you." Emilia smiles before yawning, and I'm unable to keep from copying her.

The exhaustion crashes down on me like a sledgehammer, and a quick look at the oven clock confirms it's late. Almost midnight. I can't remember the last time I stayed up this long.

Emilia points a thumb over her shoulder in the direction of the bedrooms. "We should probably head to bed. Who knows when Tanner will get up."

"True. But you're off the clock, so there's no reason for you to get up early. It's already bad enough you lost most of your free time to help me." I scratch my neck, trying to get rid of the prickling sensation under my skin.

There's absolutely nothing wrong with asking for help, but I don't do it very often, usually having no reason for it.

My life is incredibly structured. Everything from my training sessions, to my meals, and the times I go to sleep and wake up. It's all scheduled, and I love it.

Normally I'm in bed at nine the latest, much later and I'll probably regret it the next day during training. At least that's my normal bedtime when I get in my one-hour nap, which hasn't happened a lot lately. More than once I've passed out at eight, my body's way of telling me that this new schedule isn't really working too well.

I thrive on routine and quickly get frustrated when things veer off route. It's hard for me to adjust to change, and my mom always says I've been like this since I was little. She loves to tell me about all the meltdowns I had over simple things no one should get upset about.

Having Tanner in my life quickly showed me that acting like the world is about to end over a broken cracker is pretty much included in the job description of a toddler.

Another round of yawns fills the space between us, these ones bigger than before.

I wipe my eyes. "Definitely bedtime. Let me know if you need anything, all right?"

She nods, waving a hand before she turns around.

"Emilia."

"Yeah?" She looks over her shoulder, her red hair framing her pale face like a burning halo.

Seeing her like this stuns me for a moment, like I'm seeing her for the first time.

Her beauty is intangible.

Clearing my throat, I shove my hands in the pockets of my sweats. "Thanks for tonight. I really appreciate it."

"Of course. I'm glad you called and that Tanner's okay."

I nod. "Me too."

She gives me a hesitant smile like this is the first goodbye we share. "Night, Jace."

"Night, Emilia."

As I watch her walk away, I realize that this was the first conversation we've had without anyone else acting like a buffer.

Somehow, I hope things will get easier, more natural, between us because I'm starting to get used to having her around.

Maybe even liking it.

After a restless night, the morning is there way too quickly. I was tossing all night long, checking the baby monitor every time I woke up.

On a positive note, the medicine seemed to have helped, or it wasn't croup to begin with. Even though Tanner's still coughing, it sounds normal again.

He takes a big sip from his water bottle before taking another big bite of his pancake.

"Are those yummy pancakes, buddy? Maybe we should make them a Sunday morning tradition, huh? Would you like that?"

He smiles at me, as much as he can while chewing.

I take that as a yes, quickly understanding what Lila meant about him being great at communicating. The signs and reading his body language isn't a foolproof system of course, but then, what is?

He picks up his water bottle again and drinks until it hits air instead of liquid, the straw making a loud slurping noise. Tanner's fingers go up to his chin at the same time he holds out his water bottle to me.

"You want some more water? Is your water bottle empty?" I repeat the sign for water with my fingers on my chin, my thoughts jumping back to the first interaction with Emilia at the café. How things have changed.

After I get a refill for Tanner, we continue to enjoy our meal in comfortable silence when Emilia walks into the room.

She's rubbing her eyes, her hair still a wild mess, and I can't help but notice how she adds color to the room. I've never thought about my house lacking color, but the vibrancy she's added to my life—not only with her colorful appearance and looks, but also with her personality—can't be ignored anymore.

My life was good, pretty perfect really. Filled with purpose, going after my dreams day in and day out, my natural sense for competition and wanting to be the best giving me the drive I need to chase my goals like my life depended on it. Give me a competitor's new best time, and the need to crush that is born.

Sure, it might seem a bit too focused and simplistic to some people. All the training and strict rules I live by, barely having a social life except the occasional evening or Sunday I spend with the guys, my mom, or the rare date.

It does sound a bit sad and isolated, but I liked it.

I *chose* it.

But seeing Emilia and Tanner smile at each other as if this is the best day of their lives, does something to me.

Thoughts invade my mind of how life would be if it was more normal.

A normal job. Possibly a wife and children. A family to come home to. Actually having the time to hang out with them.

I never even thought much about having kids. Always thought I'd get to that point when the time was right and *after* I achieved my goal of being the most decorated Olympic swimmer.

Getting better and setting new world records is always my goal, but once the goal was within reach to have more medals than any other Olympian to date, my need to surpass the current record holder kicked in. All I need is two more medals.

Maybe I was cocky, but this whole time I thought it would pretty much be a walk in the park.

Now, there's Tanner.

Even though he only reaches to mid-thigh, he turned out to be the biggest distraction I've ever had in my life.

But then there are moments like these. Watching Tanner's face light up. Hearing him giggle when Emilia tickles him, unable to keep a smile off *my* face in response.

Tanner's squeal snaps me fully out of my thoughts. Emilia's bent over his chair, pretending to eat him, and he absolutely loves it, pulling her closer every time she moves away from him.

After a moment, she straightens up and shakes her hands left and right a few times. "All done, buddy. Millie's hungry." She rubs her stomach for emphasis, my eyes snapping to her hand immediately. When I lift my gaze, I meet hers. "If that's okay with your Dad, of course."

My brows immediately furrow at her question. "You don't ever have to ask. Not on a normal day, and especially not after you just did me a huge favor, *and* I asked you to stay."

Her hand tugs at the hem of her shirt as she nods. "Thank you."

It's then that I realize she's wearing something different from last night. A pair of tight black workout pants paired with a pink T-shirt. "Your clothes."

I've truly turned into a caveman overnight with limited vocabulary. Apparently, I do that a lot when I'm around her.

Brushing over her shirt, she shifts her weight from one foot to the other. "I always keep some extra clothes in the bedroom closet, just in case. It's good to be prepared with kids. I can put them somewhere else if you want."

"Yes. I mean, no, of course not. That's totally okay. I told you to use the room however you see fit in your free time."

I'm unable to stop my perusal as I stare at her curves. They are on display more than they've ever been before. And damn, if those aren't some sexy curves.

Hunter's words jump back into my mind at lightning speed.

Makes me wonder what's underneath and how it would feel to get in close and shove up that—

It suddenly does feel like it's been fifty-seven years since I've been with someone.

Maybe there will be a knock on the door at any moment with someone wanting to retrieve my man-card. The man-card I most definitely want to keep, now even more than before.

Because, damn, if those curves don't do something to me.

Which is bad, like *really* bad.

I give myself a mental slap, hoping my face doesn't show my very inappropriate thoughts, and clear my throat. "I made some extra pancakes for you."

Her head tips to the side like this surprises her, like me making her food is about the last thing she'd expected me to do. "No chef-cooked meals today?"

I shake my head. "No. The prepared meals are usually for days when I have training and don't have the time to cook."

I don't tell her that it took me twice as long to make them with Tanner around. Another thing I'll have to figure out and get used to.

"Ah, that makes sense. Well, thank you. That was . . . very nice of you."

"I'm keeping you away from your day off, so it's the least I could do."

She nods, tucking her unruly hair behind her ear. "Don't worry about it. I didn't have much planned anyway. I'm free until my meeting tonight." Her eyes go wide as the words come out of her mouth, as if she said something she shouldn't have said.

What on earth is this about? What kind of meeting?

Emilia blows out a shallow breath and breaks eye contact. "Anyway. I'll get some food. Thanks again for making it."

"Sure." My eyes stay fixated on her as she walks to the kitchen, taking a pancake from the large stack, and putting it on a plate and into the microwave.

When she comes back, she sits down next to Tanner, brushing her hand softly over his forehead. "Hey, monkey. You feeling better?"

He nods, *mmh-ing* around his mouthful of food. That boy might just have his appetite from me.

After eating a bite of pancake, Emilia lets out the smallest, sexiest moan I've ever heard. I doubt she even realizes what she did, but my body most definitely did.

Looks like I've officially—and very unintentionally, and sort of unwillingly—joined the Emilia Davies-is-incredibly-sexy club.

Just what I need in my already complicated life.

She leans in close to Tanner. "You still need to relax a lot today. No crazy running around, okay?"

He gives her a grin and nods, right before he sneezes.

Snot flies everywhere. On the table, and everyone's plates.

"Uh-oh." Emilia grabs the wet wipes from the table and pulls out a few. After taking care of his nose and face, she starts on the table.

Good thing Tanner and I were mostly done anyway. Poor Emilia didn't get so lucky, but there are more pancakes in the kitchen. "Why don't you get another one. I'm going to clean up the rest."

She studies me for a moment before getting up with her plate. "Okay."

I make quick work of wiping down the mess, making Tanner giggle when I pretend to wipe his neck and ears.

The sound is music to my ears, my heart hammering happily behind my ribcage. "Should we get you out, buddy?"

He turns his hands several times, his palms moving back and forth. *All done.*

"Yes, good job. All done."

I use the washcloth I prepared earlier and wipe him down once more before getting him out of his chair.

He immediately runs to the kitchen and throws his arms around Emilia's leg, swaying left and right, like he's ready to dance. I had no idea kids could bounce back so quickly. Not twelve hours ago, he was pale and listless. Yet, despite the coughing, he looks undoubtedly better. Is this normal? I have no idea. Although, Emelia doesn't look that surprised.

She laughs before bending down to pick him up. "Looks like a movie might be our best option to keep you from jumping all over the place, huh? We don't want to make your cough worse."

He nods and raises his fist up and down. *Yes.*

"Yes? That's what I thought. Why don't you pick something with Daddy while I eat my pancake?" She rubs her hand up and down his back when he snuggles closer, a small smile on her lips.

The two of them look so serene together, so natural and content, like they've been a unit their whole lives.

For a moment, I feel like an intruder.

A prickling sensation runs down the back of my neck, and I run my hand over it, willing the tension to subside.

I grab everything from the table and put it away in the kitchen.

Tanner turns and reaches for me. My limbs feel heavy as I close the distance between us and mimic his position, grabbing him under his arms as he halfway jumps into mine.

Even though he's so small, he feels solid against my chest.

He fits perfectly as he wraps his arms around my neck and squeezes. I squeeze right back, gently, as he pulls back to press his forehead against mine.

The room is completely quiet, except for Tanner's heavy breathing, as he leans back to stare at me. His gaze is intense, and I don't dare blink as he lifts his hand to his forehead to sign *dad*.

I swallow hard as I nod. "Yes, buddy. I'm your dad. Can you say that? Daddy?"

Tanner nods and grins, but doesn't say anything. Instead, he gives me a puckered kiss. The contact barely registers, but shit, the meaning of it is strong enough to almost knock me off my feet.

Emilia seems to feel the same, a quiet gasp coming from the kitchen, while Tanner has apparently already moved on, pointing at the TV in the living room.

Toddler attention span. Figures.

Emilia joins us a moment later, Tanner directing her to sit right beside me, so he can sit on both of our laps at the same time.

My fingers brush Emilia's as we both try to settle with a wiggling kid on us.

When I look at her, she gives me a warm smile. I'm sure it mirrors mine, impossible to hold back the joy after the bonding moment with my son.

Strangely enough, the moment was even more special because Emilia witnessed it, but I'm not ready to analyze that fact or the shitstorm that could come from exploring anything Emilia.

SEVEN

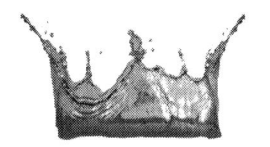

EMILIA

My hand is sweaty, curled under Tanner's tiny body, and pressed against Jace's thigh.

Why did Tanner insist on having us sit together like this to watch a movie? The same movie he's missed most of because he passed out about ten minutes in, lying across our laps, consequently rendering both of us immobile for the rest of the movie.

So Jace and I watched *Moana* by ourselves, pressed together from shoulder to toes on the wide chaise part of the couch. Awareness has been spreading along my skin like a layer of lotion, slowly sinking in but leaving me with the knowledge that it's there. And once that bottle has been opened, it was impossible to seal up again, just like those pesky pump bottles.

Why on earth am I suddenly thinking about lotions?

Maybe because you want to rub yourself all over him?

Bad, bad, bad.

I've also acquired a thigh fetish while watching a kids' movie. Feeling his hard muscles on the backside of my hand has made me all antsy, ready to crawl out of my skin this very second.

My thoughts are interrupted when Tanner coughs. My whole body goes on alert, but thankfully, it's still a normal cough. From the sound of it, it's also one that triggered a fit and doesn't want to stop.

He's curled into his side, his whole body shaking with each new ripple.

Tanner's eyelids flutter as he wakes up but continues to cough.

My gaze lands on his empty water bottle on the table.

Oh no.

I press my hand into Jace's leg. Hard and urgent. "Jace, can you fill up his water bottle please?"

"Of course." He helps Tanner sit up before jumping off the couch and speed-walking to the kitchen, sippy-cup in hand.

The cough grows louder and worse as Tanner's face turns red, his poor body unable to give him a break to recover.

"Jace, hurry." My gaze flickers to the kitchen nervously, but it's too late.

Tanner's gag reflex kicks in and he throws up. Heave after heave rocks through his body until there's nothing left. All I could do was snatch a blanket so it wouldn't all land on the couch. Or me.

Somehow it still went everywhere, even though most of it seems to be on the blanket. The smell is so bad, I have to focus on breathing through my mouth, barely keeping my own gagging at bay.

"Dang it." Jace rushes back over to us, cursing under his breath. "Oh, buddy."

Tanner shoots a surprised look at Jace and then me before he closes his eyes and starts crying. Loud wails echo through the room while sobs ricochet through his body. He's unable to keep his snot under control, wiping it everywhere his tiny hands can reach.

When I think I can safely breathe without joining the vomit club, I take a deep breath and look up at Jace. He's frozen in place, only a few feet away from us, looking like he just witnessed a crime.

It kind of looks like a murder scene, in a very abstract way I suppose. No one ever needs to see this many body fluids and stomach contents at the same time, that's for sure. Or ever, really.

I rub Tanner's back with my clean hand, probably one of the only clean exposed body parts I've got left. "It's all good, sweetie. We'll get you all cleaned up in the bath, okay?" Jace still hasn't moved. "Jace?"

"Huh?" His eyes are wide as saucers when his gaze snaps to me.

"Bath? For Tanner. Now." I'm still trying to talk without breathing through my nose again by accident. My stomach's already churning enough from the whiff I caught before.

Jace finally jumps into action, dropping Tanner's sippy cup on the coffee table before taking off to the bedroom in a sprint. When he comes back a minute later, he's holding out a large bath towel in front of him.

Stopping in front of us, he holds out his covered arms. "Can we get him on here?"

"Tanner, can you climb into Daddy's arms? Just right there on the towel?"

Jace wrinkles his nose, his head pulled back as much as

the position allows him. His nostrils flare as he's forced to step closer so Tanner won't faceplant or set foot on the floor in his messy state. "Come here."

When he finally gets a hold of him, he wraps him in the towel, holding him away from his body like he's a bomb about to explode. He speed-walks across the living room and they disappear down the hallway to the bathroom.

I close my eyes for a moment, not looking forward to cleaning up this mess. Vomit is at the very top of my things I like to avoid at every possible cost.

I wish Jace would have taken the revolting smell with him, but sadly he didn't. My stomach churns as I slowly fold together the ends of the blanket, careful not to touch any more throw up, even though it's impossible to avoid.

So gross.

I take the liberty and get a trash bag from the kitchen to throw the blanket in. I've tried cleaning up a similar mess before, and the blanket ended in the trash after four rounds in the washer, so I'll save myself that dilemma. I'll buy Jace a new one if he's upset about it. It'll be worth it.

After dumping the stinky bag outside in the trash can, I make my way back to the kitchen to wash my hands and scrub my arms as far as I can reach. My shirt stinks, but I want to take care of the mess before getting cleaned up too. I take a moment to at least brush the pieces off my shirt though and into the sink.

Then I grab a pair of gloves, along with some cleaner and a sponge—sadly no face mask—and make my way over to the couch.

It takes about fifteen minutes, but I manage to clean up

every last bit of the mess. A few rounds of Febreze and we should be good. Or at the very least, a lot better.

I'm putting away the supplies when Jace walks in with Tanner in his arms. "Why are you still out here?" He looks around and takes a whiff. "You didn't need to clean this mess, Emilia. I thought you'd jump in the shower and get cleaned up too. I was going to take care of it."

I wave him off. "It's no problem, I promise. I know from experience that the nastiness only gets worse the longer you wait. And trust me, you don't want that sort of stink to sink in."

"Well, thank you." Jace smiles at me and nods. "I really appreciate it."

"Don't mention it." I snap off the gloves and shove them in the cabinet under the sink before clicking the child lock back in place.

Tanner leans on Jace's shoulder, and I step closer. "You okay there, monkey? That probably didn't feel too good, huh?"

Instinct makes me lift my hand to rub his back, but I pull it back before touching him. Just in case. The last thing he or Jace need is a vomit speck on them.

Tanner shakes his head and yawns.

"Poor baby. Are you going to go and sleep some more? Hopefully, you'll feel better after a nap."

Tanner nods, his eyelids heavy as he blinks at me.

"Why don't you jump in the shower while I put him down?" Jace's voice is deep and incredibly close, making the hair on my back rise. In a delicious, and slightly forbidden, way.

"Sounds good." I don't look at Jace, too freaked out he

might see something in my expression that I don't want him to see. Instead, I focus on Tanner, who's now half-asleep on his dad. "Feel better, okay? I might not be here when you wake up, but I'll see you tomorrow."

He waves a tired hand at me before letting it drop on Jace's arm.

Jace chuckles. "I better put him down. This whole ordeal tired him out even more."

"I'm going to try and get this terrible smell off me."

"Good luck." With that, he turns and walks away.

That leaves me standing here like the weirdo I am, staring after him as my heart turns into goo at the sight of this father-son duo, especially at the way Jace protectively holds Tanner against his broad chest with his long, muscular arms surrounding him like a cage.

The quick flicker of my gaze further south is completely unintentional, yet just as mesmerizing. Those sweats do something mighty fine to his butt. It's round and firm and makes my fingers tingle with the need to—

No, no, no.

I think the vomit fumes have made me delirious.

Shower time. Right. Now.

Jace's butt follows me into the shower—not literally, of course—and I try to distract myself by singing songs from *Moana*. I keep my voice down but still hit all the high notes as if I'm performing in front of a sold-out auditorium.

My falsetto has never been as sharp, but the acoustics in the bathroom give it an extra edge.

Sadly, Jace's butt is still front and center of my brain, and I let out a frustrated shriek.

A few seconds later, the bathroom door slams open, and I yell in surprise.

Jace fills the doorframe, eyes wide open, his gaze frantically looking around before fixating on me. "I heard you yell. What happened?"

Neither one of us says a word as we stare at each other, the situation slowly sinking in.

Then, Jace's gaze flickers down my body in a slow perusal.

Because shit ... glass door.

My hands fly up, unsuccessfully trying to be in too many places at the same time, giving him more of a wet nude show than successfully covering up my private parts.

My mouth opens. I should say something. Do something. But I'm utterly speechless.

Jace finally snaps out of it and clears his throat. If I'm not totally wrong, his cheeks look flushed.

He turns away from me, rubbing his hands over his face and neck. "I'm so sorry. I heard you yell and thought something happened. I shouldn't have ... I should have ... I'm so sorry."

With that, he leaves, closing the door quietly behind him.

My mind struggles to process what just happened. Because Jace didn't just burst into the bathroom while I was taking a shower, right? It's impossible that my *boss* just saw me naked.

Floor, please swallow me up. Now.

Maybe we can just laugh it off.

I can tell him I was ogling his firm backside earlier, and we're even.

On second thought, that might not be the best idea after all.

The biggest question of all is, why is this low and pleasant hum spreading through my body at the knowledge that Jace just saw me naked?

And how on earth can I get rid of it?

EIGHT

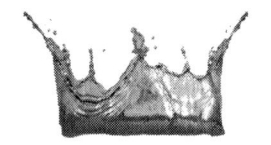

JACE

Fucking shit on a cracker.

Pacing the living room, I wait for Emilia to come out of the bedroom. On second thought, maybe I should pull a disappearing act and be gone before she comes out. But . . . it's her day off, so I can't do that.

This must be a lot worse for her than me.

There's a layer of guilt tugging on all sides of me, but it's not even close enough to penetrate the wall of pure desire that filled me the second I laid eyes on her naked skin.

After all, I'm not a monk, and that woman's beauty is literally skin-deep.

The way her wet skin glistened with the light shining through the window, subdued enough through the milky glass to highlight her stunning looks rather than overshadowing them.

It's like the glimmering rays knew to not even try and outshine her.

I feel like I got punched in the gut. But instead of pain,

there's this buzzing sense of electricity in my body. Every skin cell tingles; every neuron fires.

I'm suddenly strung so tight, I'm aware of everything going on inside my body. My heartbeat. The sensation of being flooded by flames that keep burning brighter with each passing second.

One thing's for sure, I need to chill the fuck down.

Rubbing my hands over my face in agitation, I practice my deep breaths.

This is what I excel at, calming myself down enough to shut out the entire world around me. This is my strength and why I'm such a fierce competitor in the water.

It takes me longer than I'd like, but I finally get to a point where I have both my body and mind under control. At least, mostly.

My phone buzzes in my pocket, and after getting it out, I swipe the screen to answer it at the same moment Emilia walks around the corner of the hallway.

Her hair is wet, red waves falling down her shoulders and back. As expected, she avoids my gaze, and I feel equally relieved and disappointed.

"Dude, are you there?" I pull away the phone at the intruding noise.

Putting it back to my ear, I breathe out. "Yeah, sorry. What's up?"

"It's Sunday." Hunter says it like it's self-explanatory, and in a way it is.

If we can, we usually hang out on Sundays—Hunter, Noah, Ryan, and me—even though it's been a few weeks with everything going on.

He chuckles. "We're on for later?"

My eyes are trained on Emilia. "Everyone?"

"Nah, just me. Ryan and Harper are busy, and Noah is still out of town."

"If you want to be around Tanner coughing, and possibly throwing up, then sure. Come on over." While I wait for Hunter to reply, Emilia's gaze flickers to mine. It's such a brief moment that I would have missed it had I blinked.

Hunter's chuckle doesn't sound as upbeat anymore as before. "Oh no, poor dude. I'll bring something to cheer him up. Be over in a couple hours?"

"Sure. See you then."

"Bye."

I'll appreciate the fact later on that my best friend doesn't recoil from the reality that my boy is sick. Right now, I'm distracted by the flurry of motion that is Emilia. She went back and forth between the kitchen and the hallway a few times, now holding a trash bag with what looks like her clothes in it.

My breath catches in my chest as my mind races through the different ways of how to best handle this situation. Should we talk about this or pretend like nothing happened? I'm not sure it's possible to tell what option Emilia would prefer without asking her. From the looks of it, she's about ready to bolt, which is an answer in itself, I suppose.

Disappointment settles over me like a heavy blanket as I watch her put on her shoes. Her bag is next, carelessly thrown over her shoulder.

She clears her throat but doesn't look at me. "I have to go home to get ready for my . . . my meeting."

Her *meeting*. Of course.

"Your Vespa." I totally forgot that we left it at the hospital last night. I'm such an ass.

"Don't worry. I called an Uber. I don't want to wake up Tanner." She shuffles her feet, her flushed cheeks a bright contrast to her white shirt.

Tight black leggings complete the look. Seems like she had more than one outfit stored away. Smart woman.

"Just let me know how much it is so I can reimburse you." I push my hands in my pockets, slowly getting impatient about this situation.

I don't want her to go.

I want to address the elephant in the room, but she seems to shy away more with each passing second, slowly inching toward the front door.

She lifts a hand and waves me off. "Not necessary, Jace."

"Not up for discussion. You're only here because I needed your help, so it's the least I can do." My voice is steady, my hands tightening into fists inside my pockets.

Her lips flatten into a thin line, and I know she's going to fight me on this.

Her gaze finally locks on mine, the vibrant combination of her green eyes and red hair hitting me like a punch in the gut. It reminds me of hope and new beginnings, like when the dead brown soil gives way to new life in the spring, opening itself up to a beauty that's incomparable to anything else.

Transcendent.

I want to step closer, get a better look at her face that mesmerizes me more every time I see her. And to think I initially cast her aside as a simple kids' entertainer who wears a silly getup.

That joke's definitely on me.

Her phone vibrates and she looks at the screen. "My car's here. I'll see you tomorrow morning."

Without more than a quick glance at me, she's out the door before I can utter another word.

Needless to say, she's left behind a whirlwind of chaos in my mind, and I'm not sure what to do with any of it.

"What is going on with you? You've been fidgeting ever since I walked through your door." Hunter's gaze is burning a hole in the side of my head as we're both spread out on the couch.

As far away from the earlier vomit crime scene as possible. Even though Emilia was an angel for cleaning it up, it'll probably take until tomorrow to fully dry.

"It's nothing. Just a long couple of days." A yawn pulls through my body, a wave of exhaustion right on its heels. I should have told him not to come and taken a nap instead.

Now, Tanner will wake up any moment, and it's too late to lie down. With training waiting in the morning, I will definitely have to turn in extra early tonight.

"Are you sure?" His eyes are still on me, studying me in a way that he would a competitor. Calculated. "You seem, I don't know . . . *flustered*?"

A nervous chuckle escapes my mouth, and I want to punch my fist into his spreading grin.

Thank goodness, Tanner chooses that moment to wake up, his coughs echoing through the baby monitor.

"Be right back." I almost run toward the bedroom, unable

to get away fast enough from Hunter's questions and appraising gazes.

Opening Tanner's room—which was painted and decorated in a jungle theme he seems to love—I keep the light off as I walk over to his crib. He's still lying down—on his back, of course—coughing his little heart out.

I don't understand why they don't switch positions when they're so uncomfortable. Halfway coughing up a lung sounds like a pretty good indicator to me that it's time to flip over, or to sit up. But then, I'm not a toddler.

"Hey, buddy." Due to the blackout curtains, the room is mostly dark when I reach out and brush over Tanner's hair. He's woken me up more than enough nights, and I quickly had to learn how to navigate in the dark. "Come here. Let's get you something to drink."

He snuggles on my shoulder the second I pick him up. I feel his warm cheek through my shirt as I gently pat his back, inching toward the door so his eyes can adjust to the brighter light from the hallway. At least the upright position seems to help with his cough.

I grab his water bottle from the shelf, my gaze automatically flickering to the framed picture of Tanner and his mom. Lila has her arms tight around Tanner as they laugh at the camera. They look so happy, and Tanner deserves to remember her exactly like that.

I'm not in the position to give him any memories of her, so the least I can do, is provide him with the few pictures of her existence. Lila's neighbor, Bette, was kind enough to pack them for me.

Tanner holds his cup at an angle, and the straw makes a

loud noise when it hits air. He must have drunk at least half of it. Poor guy.

"Let's get you out of your diaper and go potty, okay?"

We use the bathroom across the hall, and I'm glad to see his diaper is dry when I take it off. "Good job, buddy. Let's go potty in the toilet."

He steps on the stool on still wobbly legs and I help him turn around and sit on his small potty seat that's on top of the regular toilet seat. "There you go. Push it all out. You're doing so good. Just a few more weeks of dry diapers and you can wear underwear to bed too."

At least, that's what Millie said because what do I know? It took me several days and nights of cussing and wanting to rip my hair out until Millie finally saved my sanity. When she started working for me, she asked if Tanner's still wearing pull-ups when he sleeps. Man, I felt so stupid. At that point, I'd changed about a gazillion wet sheets, sleepsacks, and pajamas.

How was I supposed to know that he's only potty trained when he's awake and that the rest would come later?

Tanner starts singing, or rather babble-singing, and when I recognize the melody of "ABC", I quietly sing with him like I've seen Emilia do before.

"Now I know my abc's..."

His face lights up, and we keep singing until he's done in the bathroom and dressed in underwear and pants.

I grab all his things and hold out my hand for him to take.

His little one grabs my bigger one and nothing has ever felt like it.

Even though we were all small at some point, it's a strange concept that a peanut like Tanner puts his trust in someone as big as me. You're literally responsible for their life, which makes it equally special but also stressful.

Especially the way he's blown into my life.

I know that wasn't his doing of course, or his choice, but normally you have months to prepare for such a change. And then you grow and learn with them as they do. Our situation is so different, and has had such a big impact on my life, that I'm still not sure how to handle it all. Or if I'm even doing a good job at it.

But I'm trying, pushing down the frustration and irritation that wants to bubble up so often. At least, I'm attempting to do so, knowing I don't always succeed. When I don't, I do my best to not let Tanner see any of it and letting it out in the pool or at the gym instead.

When he sees Hunter in the living room, he immediately perks up, pointing at him and smiling. Then he stops and looks at me, babbling something that sounds like a question. Right before trying to fingerspell some gibberish.

It's fast and messy, but I can see the distinct letter *m*, where three fingers of his right hand—pointer, middle finger, and ring finger—are draped over his thumb.

I know what he wants before he starts scanning the room, or rather *who* he wants.

Millie.

The only thing he can fingerspell, or at least tries to.

"Did he . . . did he just ask for Millie?" Hunter leans forward on the couch, his eyes focused on me.

I blink at him. "How would you know?"

He shrugs and chuckles, immediately leaning back on the cushion. "I told you I watched a few of her shows."

Like there's nothing abnormal about a full-grown man watching a kids' show for the lady chick.

I groan. "Hunt, I don't even know what to say right now."

Tanner pokes my leg. When I look at him, he signs *Millie*. Again.

"Are you asking about Millie, buddy?"

Tanner smiles.

I barely manage to hold back another groan, not wanting Tanner to think there's any sort of beef going on with his nanny. "Millie had to go bye-bye."

His mouth turns downward, and I hate it. I had no idea that having a child meant opening yourself up to a vulnerability like you've never experienced before. The pain cuts deep, like we have an invisible connection, and what hurts him, hurts me too.

It's overwhelming and terrifying.

At least the same can be said for the other side. Seeing him happy makes me happy. One of his smiles is an instant mood boost for me.

"I knew it."

I startle at Hunter's abrupt outburst, shaking my head at him. "What now?"

"She was here, wasn't she?" He gets up from his spot and walks over to us.

"Yes."

Tilting his head to the side, he goes back to sending me inquisitive looks. Like he can magically make me spill whatever he's after. "Isn't it her day off?"

"Yes." I bite the inside of my cheek to keep from laughing. Instead, I quietly enjoy giving him these monosyllable answers, knowing it drives him crazy.

Deserves him right, the curious bastard.

Hunter surprises me when he holds out his arms to Tanner instead of throwing more questions at me. "Your daddy isn't any fun, T. But Uncle Hunter is awesome and brought you some presents. Want to see?"

If there was any man that would win over kids quickly and easily, it's Hunter. We didn't get to hang out like we usually would last Sunday, but he did spend hours with us, just playing on the floor with Tanner.

Together they go to the couch and sit down. Hunter hands him something he stashed in a bag under the table. It's something . . . yellow?

I walk over to get a better look and stop short when Tanner squeals, his babbling so high-pitched, my ears ring for a second. And he's back to signing *Millie*.

Millie? Yellow? No fucking way.

When I sit down next to Tanner, my suspicions are confirmed. A doll that looks like Millie.

My head snaps up to Hunter and I mouth *what the fuck?*

He only shrugs and chuckles before focusing back on Tanner's excited face. "Is that Millie, buddy? Isn't she awesome?"

What an asshole. Unbelievable.

Hunter's hand disappears in the bag once more and he gets out some pretzel sticks, handing Tanner one after opening the bag. "Let's see if your tummy's okay with one first."

Since Tanner's now happily occupied, Hunter's back to trying to burn a hole in my head.

After a moment, I give in because I know how relentless

he can be. The last thing I need right now is him being constantly on my ass.

I brush my hand through my hair. "Tanner's cough got really bad last night, so I called her. She met us at the ER, and since it was late, and I didn't want her to drive home on her freaking moped, she stayed the night."

"So you got some . . . *naked* time with her? Saw her birthday suit and all?"

I shake my head and lift my hands, palms up. "How on earth did you come to that conclusion after what I just told you?"

He sighs dramatically, like I'm the one who's clearly missing something. "Wishful thinking?"

I let my head fall back and stare at the ceiling for a moment.

"So is that a no then?" Of course, he's still at it.

My problem is that I hate lying. Absolutely detest it.

Maybe it stems from that one time when my mom knew I was lying about my high school project, but instead of helping me fix the problem, she left me to fend for myself and I ended up embarrassing myself in front of the whole class. Scarred me for life.

I rub my hand over my forehead and down my face, exhaustion still rushing through my veins. "Just drop it, Hunt."

"Shut the—"

"Shush."

"Calm down. I was gonna say shut the front door."

I can't help myself and chuckle. I guess I should give him some more credit. He's Super Uncle Hunter to a lot of nephews and nieces, after all.

He reaches over Tanner, who's munching and playing between us, and punches my shoulder. "Dude, for real. Spill."

"There's nothing to spill. It was an accident." Since I know that doesn't explain anything, I tell him what happened, watching his eyes look like they're dangerously close to popping out.

"Lucky duck." Hunter's kid-friendly vocabulary is turning out to be rather entertaining, and judging by the way the corners of his lips twitch, he knows it too.

"Like I said, it was an accident."

"Uh-huh. Sure, sure." He wiggles his eyebrows like the lunatic he is. "Like one of those accidents you don't mind happening again?"

I pick up one of the pretzel sticks and throw it at him. Of course, he catches it, throwing it happily in his mouth.

"Don't even pretend like you don't want a repeat. It's written all over your face." He holds out his hand in front of Tanner, who's still marveling at his Millie doll. "Am I right, T? High five."

Tanner beams and slaps his palm against Hunter's and they both laugh like they know something I don't.

But that's where they're wrong. Because, fuck yes, I'd like a repeat even when I know I really shouldn't want one.

NINE

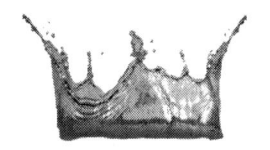

EMILIA

"Emilia, are you listening to me?" My mother's exasperated sigh blasts my brain with a magnitude only she can achieve. No one else I know can put this much disappointment in one sigh.

"Yes, Mom. I'll be there on Sunday. Prim and proper, as always." Four more days of dread for me until then. I can't remember the last time I missed our monthly family dinner.

"Wonderful." She sneezes, and it's so delicate, it could be mistaken for a kitten sneeze. But kittens are adorable, my mother *isn't*. She's more like the evil queen who eats cute kittens for breakfast. "I'm guessing you're coming alone?"

If I continue to bite my lip to keep from groaning, I might draw blood. This woman loves to play mind games with me and has done so her whole life. I'm equally terrified and thrilled to see what happens if I can pull an "in your face" one day. *If* that will ever happen.

I still haven't had the guts to take anyone with me to dinner at my parents' house. Not that I've had a lot of candidates over the years—I had my last boyfriend a few years ago—but I'm also not that mean.

"Yes, Mom." I say what she expects me to say, knowing it will make this phone conversation be over that much quicker.

"I thought so." Another exasperated sigh. "Just know that one of your dad's business partners will join us, so let's keep quiet about your unfortunate job situation right now. That's nothing anyone needs to know."

I count to five, inhaling deeply every time.

Every single time.

She's your mom, the person who gave you life.

I can't remember the last time we had a conversation that didn't demand every ounce of patience from me.

It's exhausting.

"There's nothing wrong with my job, *Mother*." She hates it when I call her that, and I take full advantage of it right now, even though I'll probably pay for it next week when she'll nitpick even more than usual. "It pays the bills, and I enjoy it."

"Your father needs something. I'll see you next week, Emilia. Be on time." She doesn't wait until I reply to hang up. It's her standard line she uses whenever she's reached her limit and is too "tired" to talk more.

If there's one thing she doesn't like, it's disagreements aimed at her. She only likes to dish it out but can't take it.

"Ugh." I let myself plop back on the couch and throw my fists and feet in the air like I could punch it. I probably look like a struggling insect that's stranded on its back, but I couldn't care less. It feels too good.

Until someone clears their throat.

Loudly. Deeply.

All male sexiness-ly.

I close my eyes and blindly grab one of the throw pillows to pull over my face.

How embarrassing someone actually watched me behave like this, and not just any someone either. Of course, it has to be Jace.

It was supposed to be one of those meltdowns that was just mine. Where I could be one hundred percent my crazy self, lost marbles and all.

And all of that only a few days after he saw me naked.

This is clearly not my week.

"What are you doing here?" I don't take the pillow off, so my words come out muffled. I'm actually not sure if he can understand me—and I'm aware it's not very polite or possibly socially unacceptable—but I don't care.

My face and neck are impossibly hot, and my earlier irritation is still making me all twitchy too. It's not a good mix, and I'm sure not very pretty either.

Since my ears aren't covered by the pillow, I hear his low chuckle just fine.

"Well, I just happen to live here."

His footsteps come closer, and I mentally calculate the chances of him not coming in my direction. Or maybe I could make a run for it? I mean, after our disastrous shower run-in, and my humiliating bug-imitation just now, how much worse could it possibly get?

A weight settles next to my hip, making the couch dip toward the edge.

I'm so startled he'd sit right next to me, basically gluing

his hip to mine, that I push the pillow far enough aside to peek at him.

"Hey, ladybug." The corners of his mouth twitch, and I let out a loud groan, pulling the pillow right back over my face.

So he *definitely* witnessed my meltdown. Every second of it.

"Wanna talk about it?" His voice is gentle, making me want to pour my heart out.

Then he pokes my arm.

I shriek, the sound thankfully swallowed by the pillow. Well, mostly at least. Wanting to breathe better, I pull it aside the tiniest bit. I also use the chance to hiss around the corner. "Did you seriously just poke me?"

"I had to make sure you're still alive. Maybe that was an "I'm dying" bug dance that I walked in on. Can't be too sure around here." The humor is easy to detect in his voice in the way it's slightly wavering, like he's trying hard to hold on to his control and not laugh.

"Ugh. Why, oh why? Because my mom wasn't bad enough today?" I realize what I just said and shut my mouth.

"That was your mom?" He's quiet for a moment, and I'm dying to see what he's doing. "Is she trying to set you up for a date?"

"Huh?" Playing dumb, another one of my favorite methods to use on people. His question pretty much crushed any hope that he didn't listen to the whole conversation. *Great.*

"Your answer sounded like she's been hounding you about bringing a date."

"Not just *any* date." I grind my teeth so hard the words barely make it out of my mouth.

"What?"

Before I have a chance to repeat my sentence, he tugs at the pillow. Not hard enough to make it fly off my face, just enough for me to lock gazes with him. He leans over the pillow to get a better look at me, suddenly *very* close, and holy moly.

Those eyes.

Those beautiful blue eyes.

This isn't the first time I find it ironic that he's a swimmer and his eyes are the exact blue that most people associate with swimming pools.

They're so vibrant, the light touch of turquoise making me want to lean closer to get an even better look. They're also the same eyes I get to look into almost every day when I'm with his boy.

"Much better." The corners of his eyes lift when he grins. "Now what did you say about your mom and dates?"

My mood deflates quicker than a popped balloon. "I don't think you want to know."

"Try me." He grabs my ankles and lifts my legs enough to sit properly on the couch, with my calves across his thighs.

I gulp, for so many reasons.

His body heat seeps through my clothes.

Why is this man so hot? Literally *and* figuratively.

I swallow, trying my best to look completely and utterly unaffected and inconspicuous.

Or maybe I just look constipated. That's always a possibility. My mom actually said that to me once, and now it's ingrained in my brain for all eternity.

I sigh. "My family meets once a month for a mandatory dinner. It's always the first Sunday of the month, and we're all required to attend. Well, all as in my sister and I. Partners and children included. Usually, at least one of my dad's business partners attends too since my parents like to show we're a tight family. They think it will help with my dad's investment company."

The words pop out of my mouth at an alarming speed, and I'm quite terrified I admitted all of that out loud.

When I glance at Jace, his eyebrows are raised. "Wow."

"Pretty much." I pull the pillow back over my face, just to have it taken away five seconds later.

"I'm not sure what to say, to be honest."

I blindly wave a hand around in his general direction. "You don't have to say anything. They're crazy. I don't even know why I bother."

"They're you're family." The way he says it, it's a statement. A fact. "So . . . your mom isn't happy when you arrive alone?"

"Not really. Sometimes she invites someone as my date. I'm not even sure where she finds these guys. There's always some business association." I think about it for a moment before shooting up into a sitting position. "Maybe she blackmails them. Poor fellas need to sit next to me for a few hours to be able to survive another day at the company."

Jace chuckles and gives my shoulder a gentle nudge. I fall back on the soft cushion, ready to wallow some more.

Usually, I give myself half an hour after these phone calls with my mom. They stress me out, and I ask myself for most of those thirty minutes why I was born into this specific family instead of one that actually loves me for who I am. Most days, I don't even think they like me.

"I could go with you." Jace's voice is so soft and quiet that it takes a moment for his words to penetrate my brain.

"What?" I sit up again, almost knocking into him, my reply coming out in a screech. "Why on earth would you willingly do something like that after everything I just told you?"

"Because I want to help." He shrugs as much as he can in his position. "And because I owe you."

My eyebrows furrow as I stare at him. "No, you don't."

"I do."

What on earth is he talking about?

"Why would you think that?"

"You helped me with Tanner."

I move around so I can sit normal, next to him, biting my lip to keep from wincing—or moaning—when my leg brushes along Jace's hand for a nanosecond. Totally accidentally, of course.

When I feel like I've got my composure back, I turn his way again. "Jace, you don't owe me a thing. I would never expect anything in return for helping you, least of all when it's related to Tanner."

"I know." His gaze is alert, his jaw set.

It's the same look I've seen on him plenty of times over the last two weeks when he leaves for his training. It's like a mask, a mental preparation for whatever battle is coming his way, even if it's against himself.

He turns so he's facing me as well, our legs touching in several places. "Unless you want to take the guy you saw the other night."

"Huh?"

"Didn't you say you had a meeting on Sunday?"

Did I say that? Dang it. "I . . . I did." Goodness, I sound like one smart cookie today.

"Since it was Sunday, and you were acting a bit odd, I thought it was code for date."

Sunday. The day he saw me naked. The day that I've been trying really hard to erase from my memory, at least that part of it.

I brush my hand along my chin, avoiding his gaze. Crap. Why did I mention that? I don't have any recollection about saying anything about my meeting. And of course, I was acting weird. I can barely tell my boss that I'm meeting with some tech guy who could help me with my project. The same project I hope to present if I get an invitation to audition for my dream job.

Would he fire me if he knew?

This is not good. I really like this job, I like him and Tanner, and don't want him to fire me.

I give him a smile I hope screams honesty and shake my head. "Nope, no date. I really was meeting up with someone who's going to help me with a music project I've been working on."

There, that's the truth.

The baby monitor turns on with Tanner's babbling.

"Well, maybe you can tell me more about that during our family dinner date. I'll ask my mom to babysit Sunday." Jace takes the baby monitor and stands up before I can get in a word. "I'm glad that's settled. I'll get Tanner."

With my mouth slightly open, I stare after Jace. *What the hell just happened?*

How on earth did I end up with a date for my family's Sunday dinner? With my boss, of all people.

I do not have a good feeling about this at all.

It's actually so bad that I'm not sure what's worse. The fact that my boss saw me naked, or the fact that my boss is going to be my pity date to appease my mother.

Maybe it would be better to turn up alone, after all.

TEN

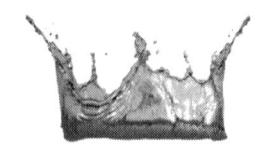

JACE

This week has been busier than usual, and when I park the car in front of my house on Saturday night, I'm beyond exhausted. It's just after six, and I'm ready to pass out after my grueling afternoon training session in the pool.

Lately, my sessions have been more straining even though we haven't changed anything. Coach has been giving me the side-eye all week for my poor performances.

But I know what's causing it. This fatigue.

My new life as a dad.

Without Emilia or my mom I wouldn't function at all. Thank goodness, for their help and constant advice. I think I called my mom about three hundred times the first few days alone. She stayed with me that first weekend, but then she had to go back to work too.

She's an English professor at Hawkins university, which she loves. She's never said anything but I think she's lonely, and the long hours fill that void.

But she stops by whenever she can to see Tanner, either

with Emilia or me. Tanner loves it when his grandma stops by for a visit, no matter how short they are.

I don't want her to overdo it either. It's bad enough if one of us is exhausted.

As it is, it's been a lot more taxing on my body than I thought it would be. Missing naps and having to get up in the middle of the night when Tanner isn't feeling well or has a nightmare has taken its toll.

Nationals are coming up next month, and I need to get my head back in the game before my times plummet. Coach would have my ass if I dropped out this late.

When I step into the house, I pause, savoring the lavender scent permeating the air.

Emilia.

She loves that stuff and diffuses it whenever she has the chance to. I'm pretty sure she's stashed it away in some secret spots too because it always smells like it now, no matter if she's here or not. At least I'm used to it after coming home to it for almost three weeks now.

Maybe I'm even looking forward to it, not that I'd openly admit to it.

Another thing I've been anticipating is getting to know her better. After everything that happened this last week—especially the ER visit, and the revelation about her parents and my subsequent demand to accompany her—I've been curious about her.

I'm still not sure what I was thinking, offering my company, but the strong surge of protectiveness that ran through me was impossible to ignore. I wanted to make sure her family treated her the way she should be treated. From the bits and pieces I heard of their phone conversation, that might not be the case.

Which doesn't make any sense.

Yes, I had my reservations about her at first, but my opinion changed quickly after spending some time with her. It's undeniable that there's a fascinating woman under the crazy exterior.

Maybe I shouldn't care about her private life. Maybe this is overstepping my employer-employee boundary, but I feel like we might have crossed that line when we started spending time together outside of her working hours.

This week, I started asking her questions every night. If I'm going to chaperone her to her parents, I *should* know her better.

"Is that Daddy?" Emilia's soft voice carries through the house, and not a second later, Tanner sprints around the corner to stop in front of me.

With his hands behind his back, he looks at me from beneath his eyelashes, swaying back and forth.

He's been with me for almost a month, but we still have our awkward moments.

Moments where he pushes me away, or acts all shy like he isn't sure if I like or want him.

Those are usually the times where I feel like someone jammed a fist into my chest and sucker-punched me.

Things have definitely gotten better since Emilia's been around. She's our glue, the missing ingredient that helps us stick together in a way I'm not sure we'd fit without her, at least not at this point.

"Hey buddy." I drop my duffel bag, crouch down, and open my arms. "Can Daddy have a hug?"

It's still weird to be called or call myself Daddy, but it's my new reality, and I'm slowly getting used to it.

Tanner shuffles forward, putting his hands around my neck. When I close my arms around his small body and gently pat his back, he mimics me, patting my back too.

"He started doing that today. It's adorable." Emilia's leaning against the wall, her hands crossed under her chest.

Don't look at her boobs.

I focus on her face. *Hard.* Her beautiful face and the way her relaxed posture softens her look. It also makes it seem like she's comfortable here, which . . . pleases me.

Tanner squirms in my arms, and after one more squeeze, I put him down. Instead of running off, he grabs my hand and pulls.

I stare at his mop of brown waves. "Where are we going?"

Still holding my hand, he turns around and puts the fingers of his other hand together with his thumb to tap his mouth.

"Ooooh. Are we going to *eat?*" I repeat his gesture but also say the word, just like Emilia does it. Repetition and more repetition, hoping it pays off eventually. We saw the pediatrician who wasn't too concerned and thinks he'll catch up, and if there isn't any progress by his birthday, we'll re-evaluate.

Tanner nods and says something but it's not an actual word. His big eyes are expectant and proud as he gazes up at me, like he actually just said the right thing.

This kid.

"All right. Let's get some food. Daddy is super hungry." I rub my belly for emphasis before I stop. "On second thought, maybe I'll need a snack first."

Without warning, I snatch Tanner around the waist and pull him up to me, pretending to eat him. His neck, chubby cheeks, belly, and whatever else I can reach.

He flops around, his giggles filling the room. It's music to my ears and not like anything I ever expected it to feel like. The deep satisfaction that comes from seeing him happy makes me feel weightless and . . . content.

It's incomparable to anything else I've ever experienced. It's almost like there was a place in my heart that was untouched until he entered my life, a spot that was reserved for him alone.

Tanner keeps pulling on the back of my neck, trying to pull my face back to his belly, wanting to be tickled more.

Once we're both out of breath, and Tanner's face is red from laughing, we make our way to the kitchen. When I put him on the floor and look back up, Emilia's watching us with a gigantic smile on her face.

I soak up the elation she radiates because I can't help myself. It's like a drug.

She's addictive, and no matter if I think it might be better to keep this a normal boss-employee relationship, I can't deny that she's getting under my skin. Her company, her role in my life, has added something that wasn't there before.

I enjoy having her around. I enjoy our conversations and spending time together, no matter if we watch a movie or sit on the floor and build blocks with Tanner.

It's easy, effortless, and so contrary to any of my previous interactions with women that mostly seemed like work. Even though that might have mainly been my fault for picking the wrong dates.

Tanner runs to Emilia and she scoops him up. They

bounce to the dining room table where she gives him a coloring book and crayons after securing him in his seat. It all looks so natural, as if it's been this way for years. Yet, it's only been weeks. Hard to believe that a month ago, there were no highchairs, no building blocks, no sippy cups or bowls with sucking things on the bottom. Surreal.

When she joins me in the kitchen, I can't help but notice the lingering smile on her face. Those pink lips turned up at the corners. They look absolutely del—

"Jace?"

"Huh?"

Emilia pokes my upper arm and laughs. "You zoned out. Are you tired?"

Man, she almost caught me staring at her lips, or maybe she did. I'm sure I looked like I'm starving and she's the most delectable piece of food I've seen in decades. Which pretty much sounds like how I feel.

What is going on all of a sudden?

This must be my tired brain playing tricks on me. Right?

Since she's still waiting for an answer, I try to focus on her eyes and forget about those delicious-looking lips.

"Yeah, I'm spent. It's been a long week." I rub my hand over my eyes, my eyelids feeling like they're loaded with fifty-pound weights.

After studying me, her eyebrows draw together. "Are you sure you want to go to dinner with me tomorrow? It's totally okay if you change your mind and don't want to go. You deserve a day off. You should be relaxing instead of wasting it on me and my dramatic family."

I stand straighter at her question. "Nope. Definitely going."

"Okay."

"I'll make sure to relax too, no worries. I was thinking of taking Tanner to the Bay Trail in the morning for a walk. You think he's going to like it there?"

Her eyes light up. "He's going to love it. I wanted to take him last week, but then he got sick. He's going to be excited to get outside and run around, even if it's just a trail. It's such a beautiful spot with the whole bay in the background."

Doubts infiltrate my mind like so often lately. Should I ask her or just figure it out on my own? Ah, screw this. "Is it best to go in the morning? During the time I usually have training?"

Emilia's gaze softens as she nods. "Yes, that would probably be easiest for both of you. That way you can be back by ten or eleven and feed him before his nap."

Her statement is so simple, but emotions tighten my throat. I shouldn't have to ask her simple questions like this. He's my son, for crying out loud. I should know everything there is to know about him. My mouth feels dry. "You could come with us?"

We stare at each other, my words hanging in the air between us. Why did I ask her that? I hope she doesn't feel like she has to because I'm her boss, invading on her Sunday for a second time in a row.

I rub my shoulder, willing the awkwardness away. "You don't have to of course. I shouldn't have—"

"I'd love to." The words rush out of her mouth at the same time mine do, and we grin like the awkward duo we are.

We're snatched out of our bubble when Tanner lets out a whine and starts throwing his crayons.

"No, Tanner. We don't throw crayons." Emilia's voice is

stern as she grabs his pasta bowl from the counter and walks to him.

But not before looking over her shoulder and shooting me another grin.

I jump into action, getting my meal out of the fridge and popping it into the microwave. Emilia comes back and rummages around, getting her own pasta. Her hair is pulled back into a high ponytail, her shirt extra wide and hanging halfway off one shoulder.

I don't think I've ever seen her neck exposed like that. Her porcelain skin looks soft and creamy, a few freckles splattered across her collarbone and shoulders.

Where else might she have freckles? Is her whole body covered in them?

When we're both seated at the table, she looks up at me. "No burning question for me today?"

Oh I have a few . . .

She winks, and I'm momentarily frozen. Is she trying to flirt with me, or am I that out of it that I read something into this that isn't there?

"Oh, I do. Are you ready?" She nods, and if my assumption is correct, she's enjoying this as much as I do. "What's the worst job you could have?"

The smile on her face falls for a moment before she fixes it, but the spark in her eyes isn't the same anymore.

"Depends on who you ask." Her voice is quiet as she stabs her fork into the pasta like it did something to offend her.

"Why's that?" I pause, not wanting to miss a moment of her expressions, knowing how much more I sometimes learn from her non-verbal clues.

Her answering sigh is somber, like this topic has been heavily weighing on her for some time.

When I think she might not answer at all, she clears her throat and looks out the window. "For me, having an office job where I stare at a computer and deal with paperwork all day long is the worst possible job. Just imagining doing that for the rest of my life . . . I'd feel like a caged animal that should roam around unrestricted and happy instead."

Tanner hums next to us, pushing his pasta away and trying to reach his applesauce. I push it closer to him so he can get it, and he completely ignores me, happily digging into his food.

Turning back to Emilia, a small smile has returned to her lips as she watches us.

Maybe I should leave it at that, but tonight, I feel like pushing.

Maybe it's because I'm going to meet her family tomorrow, or pure curiosity, but I want to know as much as I can. "I'm guessing your parents don't agree?"

She lets out a humorless laugh. "You could say that. They think it's one of the most sanctioned ways to earn not only a living but also respect in life. Any sort of creative *work* is a joke in their eyes."

She puts down her fork and leans back in her chair, her expression a sad mask of her usually happy self. "It's the equivalent of child's play to them, something they've never known how to engage in either. They don't work and play. They work and exist. In a rather miserable way, if you ask me."

I don't know what to say.

This is clearly a touchy subject for her, and I'm all the

happier I'm accompanying her tomorrow. Even though I have a bad feeling about how this is going to go down.

At the same time, I'm also more than ready to have her back in all aspects.

After asking her questions all week and paying more attention, things have changed between us. The way I see her has changed.

I've learned that Emilia is the absolutely perfect person to work with children. She genuinely enjoys being with them, even if it means she needs to make a fool out of herself. And I've witnessed before that Tanner doesn't always make it easy for her. That child can flip a switch like no one else when he doesn't get what he wants, even worse when he's tired or hungry.

I also know that she's not a morning person. She's usually still half-asleep when she gets here, and I have to admit, I like her sleepy face. It makes her look younger than she is, and a bit more vulnerable, but also more real. Even when she's grumpy, which I've only ever witnessed in the morning.

She tries not to eat refined sugar, usually putting some natural sweetener in her drinks and food.

She got her bachelor's degree in business—which I'm guessing wasn't her idea—*and* music with a minor in dance.

Another thing I've noticed is that she reads slowly and often uses read-aloud apps. Something she mostly does when she thinks I'm not there. I've never said anything, but it makes me wonder if she has trouble reading.

I've considered asking her but refrain from it every time, because I don't want to make her uncomfortable.

Would I appreciate it if someone asked me a question like that?

Probably not.

Stubborn Emilia, always putting up a tough front and wanting to appear perfect. That probably is a huge reason for my apprehension and the feeling that I'm in for a show tomorrow at her parents' house.

The question is, how well will I take to watching that show go down? Just thinking about it not going well makes my body tense up, my flight-or-fight sense kicking in.

But I've never been one to flee from anything, and I'm not going to start now.

Especially not when it comes to making things right by Emilia.

ELEVEN

EMILIA

Jace and I decided to meet at the Berkeley Pier parking lot. It's a beautiful morning, the North California summer temperatures warm enough to wear leggings and a T-shirt. I spot Jace and Tanner right away on the paved trail, both guys clad in sweatpants and hoodies.

Jace is carrying a tricycle and running after Tanner, who's apparently made it his mission to take off, trying to leave his dad in the dust.

The scene is so comical, the joy on Tanner's face so palpable in the way his chubby cheeks almost meet his eyes, that I stay in the car a moment longer, laughing at the scene like a school girl.

Jace finally snatches Tanner, and they both make their way into my direction. Tanner's happily paddling on his tricycle, or rather trying to keep up with the paddles while Jace pushes him. I get out of my car, pulling the knot of the long-sleeved shirt tighter around my waist before making my way to them.

Tanner lets out a tiny squeal when he sees me, trying to

scramble off the bike faster than he's capable of and landing on his knees. I pause for a moment, holding my breath while I wait for his reaction, happy to see he's still wearing the same cheerful smile when he gets up and runs toward me.

I automatically quicken my step, trying to reach him before he tumbles to the ground again in his excitement. I easily catch him when he flings himself at me, feeling his familiar weight in my arms as he snuggles in to my neck.

He makes an elongated "mmmm" sound, and even though it doesn't sound like much, I'm convinced he's trying to say my name. Which turns my insides to mush, absolute gooey-and-feeling-all-soft-in-the-knees mush.

"You made it." Jace walks up to us, his casual stride confident and full of swagger.

There's no better way to describe it, and gosh, it's sexy as hell.

With one hand in his gray sweats, the other one holding the tricycle, he smiles at me. It's a real smile, not one of the polite ones he used to give me when I first started working for him.

I'm pretty sure he either wasn't my biggest fan back then, or he thought I was crazy. Something I've gotten used to over the years, especially when I'm in my tutu-and-bow ensemble.

But things have changed. So much. It's like he fits right into my life, both of them actually. Taking care of Tanner is my job, but it doesn't feel like it. This whole experience isn't even comparable to any of the previous nanny jobs I had. Those definitely felt like work.

I actually look forward to seeing these two guys, even though I wouldn't mind sleeping in for an extra hour or two in the morning. I'm slowly adjusting to that too though.

Looking at him now, with that devilish smile aimed my way, and the sun illuminating his handsome face and brown hair, one thing becomes crystal clear.

Jace Atwood might just be the sexiest man I've ever seen.

When I realize I'm still staring, I nod. "I did. Couldn't miss this fun hangout today. Especially on such a beautiful day."

"Very beautiful." His gaze is intense as we have a mini-staredown. I suddenly feel like we're playing a game I don't know the rules of.

I'm pretty sure he's winning too since I'm the first one to look away, biting my lip to keep from grinning like a fool. Meeting with him today—with both of them—on my day off without an emergency, feels different.

There's a lightness in my chest that wasn't there before, one that's usually absent on the first Sunday of every month. Knowing it's time for family dinner takes care of that, normally leaving me with a roiling stomach more than anything.

But I don't want to think about the inevitable family dinner yet. We still have several hours before that disaster is going to go down, and I plan on enjoying every single minute of it.

With a smile on my face, I look first at Jace and then Tanner—tickling his side—pointing toward the trail that leads to the Berkeley Pier. "Shall we?"

Tanner nods right away, wiggling both pointer fingers into the same direction, signing *Go*.

"Let's do this." Jace sets the tricycle on the ground. "Do you want to get back up here, buddy, or walk instead?"

He makes a pedaling motion with his hands, immediately

jumping on the tricycle when I let him down. Grabbing the handles, he gives us a big grin and babbles.

"Looks like he's ready to go." I chuckle, because listening to Tanner babbling never gets old. There isn't really a word in there we can understand, but sometimes it sounds like a mix of Chinese and French, which is equally hilarious and cute.

Jace pushes the bike, and we fall into a wordlessly, leisurely walk.

The sun warms my skin as awareness spreads through my veins at the close proximity of our bodies. There's almost no room between us that I could easily reach out and grab his hand.

Why am I thinking of grabbing his hand?

Having this dinner later today, and knowing he'll have to endure time with my family—somewhat willingly—is harder to ignore than I thought. Because why would he do that? It doesn't make sense. He said he wants to help because I helped him last week, but it's really not necessary.

Meeting my family, and having to spend time with them, seems more like a punishment than anything else.

One *I* might owe *him* for once it's over. Most likely, for the rest of my life.

Jace's fingers touch mine for a moment, and my gaze snaps over to his.

"What are you thinking about so hard?"

I sigh, not even wanting to know how he knows. "Dinner."

He nods as if he understands. And maybe he does. After all, he witnessed that awful phone conversation I had with my mom. That should have given him some indication. "Why do you go?"

And there it is.

The real question.

I expected him to ask me eventually.

Because why do I?

The way he says it, combined with the way he studies me, it's not as uncomfortable as I thought it would be. Because he doesn't judge me. He seems genuinely curious. And I don't blame him since it's a legitimate question. One I've asked myself a million times over.

And truthfully, I still don't have an answer. At least not one that makes sense.

So I shrug. "Because they're my family."

He seems to think that over for a moment before he nods. "Well, I can't wait to meet them."

I laugh at that. It's pretty easy to tell by the deep frown on his face that there are probably a million other things he'd rather do. And not for a second do I blame him for feeling like that. I share that dreadful sensation through and through, just for other reasons.

"You're one strange woman, Emilia." He shakes his head but can't keep the corners of his mouth from lifting.

"Thank you." I wink at him as we reach the closed pier. The Golden Gate Bridge serves as a beautiful background in the distance, and I take a moment to enjoy the view before focusing back on the trail ahead of us. "Let's get him out so he can walk for a bit."

Jace stops, and I unbuckle Tanner, who's already trying to get off the tricycle.

With Tanner's hand securely tucked in mine, we keep going at a slow pace, Tanner's footsteps comically loud for such a small body. We walk for a while, Tanner stopping every few feet to look out over the water.

It's relatively quiet today, and the water's gently lapping against the rocks at the shore. Tanner excitedly points in all directions as if this is the coolest thing he's ever seen.

When we stop once more, and Tanner is enthralled in watching a man throw a stick for his dog, I peek at Jace. He hasn't said much for the last few minutes, mostly staying a step or two behind us. His head is turned toward the water, his chest rising and falling in slow succession.

His eyes are closed, his face relaxed, and I wonder what this must feel like to him. Does he get out like this very often? From the looks of it, my guess would be no, but he certainly seems to enjoy today's outing.

My attention zeroes in on Tanner when he pulls on my hand, and we continue to walk a few more feet until we reach the end of this loop before circling back around. There's still time before lunch and his nap, but the first signs of tiredness are already taking over his features. As if to confirm my thoughts, he rubs his eye with his free hand.

Jace must notice it too as he nods in the direction we came from. "Looks like it's time to head back, huh?"

"Yeah." I smile down at Tanner, who's happily trotting along, once more stopping every few feet to gaze at the water. "I don't blame him. I could use a nap too."

Jace waits for us to fall into step beside him. "Are you tired?"

"A little. Didn't get a good sleep last night." I'm not about to tell him that I'm getting my period and one of my PMS-symptoms is crappy sleep.

"Maybe you should take a nap when you get home." He's

still carrying the tricycle, softly swinging it next to his body like it doesn't weigh a thing. "That's what I plan on doing once Tanner's out."

"You sleep a lot, do you know that?" I chuckle and without thinking about it, I nudge him with my shoulder.

He doesn't react, just goes along with it like it was nothing out of the ordinary. And maybe it's not. Maybe women nudge him all the time, who knows? Even though I wouldn't know when he has time to meet up with one seeing how incredibly crazy his schedule is. He barely has time to spend with Tanner as it is.

"I love to sleep, and know that sleep is a very important part of my training. I need my body to be well rested so it can perform at its best, especially with the strenuous training sessions we do twice a day."

"I can't imagine training that much. Does it not get old doing the same thing all the time?" I know I get bored with my workout quickly, and I'm not doing half as much as he does.

"It does sometimes, but I also love it. My . . . my dad was the one who introduced me to swimming, and I fell in love with it from the first moment. We shared our passion for it. There's just something about the water that . . . I don't know, speaks to me I guess."

"Your dad?"

He's quiet for a moment, brushing a hand through his wind-tousled hair. "He passed away when I was a teenager. I think of him every time I'm in the water. It's my element and where I thrive to be my best. My dad always said I could be the best, have the most medals, and I believed him . . ."

The wind, Tanner's footsteps, and his squeals, are the

only noise until Jace lets out a deep breath. "I still want to make him proud and achieve that goal, even though I could have retired after the last Olympics."

I watch him, trying to wrap my head around this new info of Jace and his father when my hand jerks away.

Tanner's on the ground on all fours, his shoulders shaking as the first wail rips out of his throat. He must have tripped, and I lost my grip on him. Dang it.

"All good, monkey. Come here." I bend down and lift him up into my arms.

Like I hoped, he doesn't seem to be hurt badly and calms down within a couple minutes of me rubbing his back. When I try to put him back down, he tightens his arms and legs around me.

"Do you want me to take him?" Jace's voice is mostly calm and collected, but he can't hide the small leftover of worry in it.

"I'm okay, thanks." I tighten my grip on Tanner and fall in step next to Jace.

The parking lot comes into view in the distance as my eyes land on a couple on the trail ahead of us. They're a tangle of limbs, apparently trying to suck off each other's faces. I squint, my heartbeat picking up speed as I try to make sense of what I'm seeing.

"Emilia, you okay there? You look a little pale."

Shit.

This can't be happening.

I bite back the cuss words on the tip of my tongue.

Instead, I switch Tanner over to one hip while grabbing Jace's hand with the other, pulling with all my might.

Walking as fast as I can, I turn away from the couple until I pull us behind the nearest tree.

Blowing out a shaky breath, I push Jace against the thick trunk, begging him with a pleading look to be quiet. Using the tree as cover, I slowly peek around him, hoping I imagined the whole situation.

Nope.

My brother-in-law is still tightly wrapped around the blonde gazelle that is most definitely *not* my sister.

Shit, shit, shit.

Tanner giggles into my shoulder, probably thinking we're playing a fun game of hide-and-seek. Thank goodness.

My brain is spinning, trying to figure out what's going on. How can he do this to her? And for how long? Does she know? Gosh, I hate him. Ashley has always been the perfect daughter, and I've envied that. She has the right job, the right husband, the perfect children . . . but even still, no one deserves this.

When I look again, they aren't in the same spot but now in the parking lot. Is this where they always hook up? Where does Ashley think Shane is right now? That scumbag. Shane and his lady friend bid each other farewell—after more disgusting lip-locking—and leave in separate cars.

I wait until they're both gone for sure before I sag against Jace.

Holy moly.

And I'm pressed against Jace from top to bottom.

I close my eyes and take a few deep breaths, trying to calm my still-racing heart.

"What's going on, Emilia?" Jace's voice is full of concern, his brows drawn together tightly.

I draw back, suddenly having the strong urge to leave. Even though it's highly unlikely they'll come back, I'd rather not be here either way. "I'll explain later, okay? Let's just get out of here. I need to . . . I need to get home."

This will be another check mark on Emilia's craziness list I'm sure Jace keeps. I'm a lost cause.

Tanner giggles into my shoulder before pulling back to look around the tree trunk.

I practically sprint back to the car—much to Tanner's delight—and after handing him off to a still-bewildered Jace, I promise once more to explain later when he picks me up. That's if he's still going to dinner with me. I wouldn't blame him if he makes an excuse about not going.

Then I take off like a rabbit being chased by a lion.

I need to be alone so I can think clearly. I need to figure out what to do with this information. My head feels like it's about to explode from seeing my brother-in-law cheat on my sister.

And now I have to face her in a few hours, and him probably too.

With Jace in tow.

Why does this feel like a total clusterfuck about to happen?

TWELVE

JACE

One thing is blatantly clear when it comes to Emilia. Whether it's her extravagant clothing choices, her eccentric behavior, or the fact that she pretty much fondled me against that tree trunk earlier with her delicious curves, things are never boring when she's around.

Now we can add another one to that list.

Family drama.

From the sounds of it, shit might just go down at dinner today.

Possibly even worse than either of us imagined.

After I picked her up from her place—searching for the right words to tell her how stunning she looks, even though words could never do it justice—she clued me in on what happened this morning.

To say I'm speechless is an understatement.

The biggest part of my life, I've been an only child with a mom, and most of it has been devoted to swimming. Sure, sometimes there's drama in the swim community or with the press, but I've always been able to avoid it.

Family drama is on a whole different level, and definitely nothing that's averted easily.

From the sounds of it, my mom couldn't be more opposite of Emilia's. From the second she learned about Tanner—after the initial shock wore off—she welcomed him with open arms, adjusting her busy professor schedule however she could to get to know her grandson. And they adore each other. When she came over to babysit Tanner tonight, it was hard to tell who was more excited.

What would my life have been like without that kind of love and support growing up?

I can't even begin to imagine what Emilia's childhood must have been like.

She's been quiet for most of the short drive to her family home, not that I blame her after the bomb she dropped on me.

Regardless of what's going on, I'm unable to keep from looking at her. Not just to make sure she's okay, but also because she looks incredibly beautiful. She always does in her own way, but tonight, she looks like she stepped straight out of a dream.

Her copper hair falls over her shoulders in soft waves, and my fingers have been itching to touch it, to see if it's as silky as it looks. Her makeup is heavier than usual without being overdone. She paired her black slacks with a golden blouse.

The outfit is formal, proper even, the total opposite of everything I've seen her in so far, as far as clothing or behavior goes. It's undeniably sexy.

One reason is because it's formfitting, accentuating both the mouthwatering curve of her breasts and the delicious curve of her ass. But more than that, she looks like a badass, like she's ready to face whatever is going to go down at dinner.

From the glimpses I've witnessed of her family life so far, it might just feel exactly like that.

Thank fuck I had the sense to dress in slacks and a button-down shirt, throwing my suit jacket in the car as almost an afterthought.

Emilia has been fidgeting this whole time, but it gets worse the closer we get to our destination. Does she go through this every month?

When we roll up the driveway, she looks like she's ready to jump out of her skin. I turn off the car and get out to walk over to Emilia's side. Of course, she's already out, brushing over her outfit in a measured motion.

I'm battling between wanting to push her back into the car and get her out of here and pulling her into my arms to tell her it'll be all right. Not that I'm sure it actually will be.

Both options fly out the window when the front door of the decent-sized two-story house opens, and an elegantly dressed woman pauses in the doorway.

At the woman's appearance, Emilia snaps into action, straightening her back and putting on a smile. It almost looks like a real smile—almost—but it doesn't reach her eyes. Those gorgeous green eyes look dull and unhappy, making a hardness form in my stomach at the sight of it.

I don't like it at all. I fight my instinct, trying to be a good friend and follow her lead.

Since I'm here as a favor to her, I swallow my own judgement and opinions, and put up the front I've perfected over the years. I've had to attend plenty of sponsors events I could have cared less about. But that's part of the big game. And boy, am I ever ready to play.

At first, I thought the woman looked like an older version of Emilia with dark hair, but the closer we get, the more obvious it is how wrong I was.

Even though it's obvious they share some similarities in their features, the older woman looks like a sad caricature of Emilia, the woman I've seen more of in the last three weeks than any other woman in the whole last year, including my mom probably.

"Hey, Mom." Emilia sounds like she has to force the words out of her mouth, and the urge to pick her up and run comes back with a vengeance.

"Emilia."

Her daughter's name flows from her thin lips like a verbal whipping, and reminds me of the moment Emilia said only her family calls her by her full name.

Until now, I didn't understand why she'd prefer Millie since Emilia is a beautiful name. After witnessing this, I'm beginning to understand why.

And I kept insisting on calling her Emilia this whole time. I'm such an idiot.

"Mrs. Davis, it's so nice to meet you. I'm Jace Atwood." I stretch out my hand and shake her delicate one. "Emilia's told me so much about you."

She gives me a tight-lipped smile, her gaze bouncing back and forth between me and her daughter. "Mr. Atwood, please come inside. Everyone's already waiting in the dining hall."

The atmosphere has dropped about twenty degrees, and

the welcome couldn't have been much more unpleasant had she tried.

The accusation is also easy to read between the lines, but I know that we're on time. A few minutes early, actually. From the looks of it, that's considered late in this household.

"Of course." I take a step forward and practically push Emilia inside with me.

We quietly follow her mother as she leads the way, her head held high, not a hair out of place.

When we enter the dining room, Emilia stops so abruptly, I run into her. My hand goes around her waist on instinct, wanting to keep her steady before she topples over from the impact. All eyes snap in our direction, particularly on my hand still securely around her midsection.

"Emilia brought company." The words come out of Emilia's mother's mouth like an accusation, sharp and short.

Emilia's body tenses under my fingers. "I told you I was bringing Jace."

"I'll let Amy know we need another place setting." Her mother turns on her heels without another glance and leaves the room.

Since I haven't let go of Emilia, I feel rather than hear her deep inhale before she clears her voice. "Everyone, this is Jace Atwood. Jace, my dad Jeff, my sister Ashley, and my brother-in-law Shane"—she stumbles on that introduction for a moment but I don't blame her—"and... Marcus? What are you doing here?"

A snooty-looking guy, who seems to be in his mid-to-late thirties, rakes his eyes up and down Emilia's body like she's a tasty treat. Who the hell's this guy?

Emilia clearly knows him, and from the way his nostrils

flare and his gaze keeps flickering to my hand, I'm not sure I actually want to know.

I already felt tense when we arrived, knowing I'd have to deal with her difficult family. Also having to deal with a potential ex, and/or admirer, puts my teeth grinding to a whole new level.

Of course, Marcus has to be the first to jump out of his seat, making a show of straightening to his full height—which I'm guessing is close to my six four—extending his hand toward me, and therefore, forcing me to let go of Emilia.

That seems to immediately lift his spirits, because he can't contain his smirk.

Fucker.

"Marcus Smith. A pleasure to meet you." He shakes my hand, trying to make ground meat of it. Classic. Just like I expected. "What was your name again? I was distracted by this beautiful lady." He lets go of my hand and bends down to kiss Emilia on the cheek.

No. I will *not* smash his face in. I will *not* stoop to his level of idiocy.

Fucking asshole.

Emilia's mom chooses that moment to re-enter the room, a red-faced woman chasing after her with a place setting in her hands. She gives Emilia a big smile before catching herself by placing everything on the table.

That must be the woman who helped raise Emilia. Talking about Amy was the only time Emilia smiled when she told me about her family.

"Thanks, Amy." Emilia reaches out and squeezes the middle-aged woman's arm before she scurries out the room.

Emilia's mom calls out after her. "Amy, make sure the children stay in the kitchen and do not disturb our meal."

I think I can hear a faint, "Yes, ma'am," as the tension in the room settles like a dark rain cloud.

She seems . . . lovely.

Emilia's mom, Regina, gestures to the table. "Emilia, we saved you a seat next to Marcus." Pointing to the other side of her daughter, and also directly next to her dickhead of a son-in-law, she gives me a look down her nose. "Mr. Atwood, please take a seat."

Emilia shoots me an apologetic side glance as we both lower ourselves onto the plush dining chairs. I grab her hand under the table, wanting to reassure her that I'm here. With her. For her. She's not alone in this mess, and never should have been in the first place, but that's a whole other issue.

Her father clears his throat. "Mr. Atwood, I'm not sure I'm familiar with your name. What do you do for a living?"

Wow. Straight to the point.

Depending on which way this conversation goes, I can respect that.

I intertwine my fingers with Emilia's under the table and place them on my knee. "I swim."

His crystal tumbler pauses halfway to this mouth. "As a hobby?"

"No, as a job."

"Oh. I've worked with a few football and baseball players before. Does swimming pay a lot?"

Emilia's hand tenses in mine. "Dad."

He doesn't look at her, and I squeeze her hand in reassurance to let her know it's okay.

Rude, but okay.

I bite the inside of my cheek to keep from laughing at the absurdity that this conversation has leapt to in less than two minutes. Not only do they seem clueless about my field of sport, which is not a big deal, of course, but they clearly don't have their priorities straight either.

And I do not feel like playing into their hands.

Not one bit.

Everyone's eyes are on me, clearly trying to gauge if I might be worth their time and attention.

How those people could have ever raised someone so bubbly and warm like Emilia is beyond me.

I shrug. "It pays okay. Puts food on the table, clothes on my body, et cetera."

"I see." He lifts his glass to his lips and guzzles the contents.

Emilia squeezes my hand so hard I barely keep from wincing.

That woman could crush Marcus in a fight. Somehow that thought satisfies me greatly.

My interrogation seems to be over with my unsatisfying comment. It looks like I didn't pass the first question. Too bad.

I'm quickly forgotten as conversations around me pick up, us excluded. Emilia's father and brother-in-law talk about possible investment partners while Marcus keeps trying to get Emilia's attention, disregarding the fact that she ignores him.

Emilia's sister keeps shooting me curious glances around her husband's body, and I'm oddly fascinated with the way he's affectionate toward her. Putting his arm around the back of her chair, absentmindedly rubbing up and down her back.

The urge to make a snide comment about seeing him on the Bay Trail this morning is hard to ignore, but it's not my place. As if Emilia knows my struggle, she intervenes my thoughts by pinching my thigh.

My gaze zooms in on hers and she gives me the faintest head shake I've ever seen, her eyes pleading with me.

I don't know why she wouldn't just bring it up, out him in front of everyone. That douchebag deserves that and much more.

Emilia must have her reasons though, and I will respect them, even if it leaves a sour taste in my mouth.

One thing's for sure though. I won't be watching her family stomp all over her all evening. If it gets too much, I'm out of here. And I sure as hell won't leave without her. Not a chance.

THIRTEEN

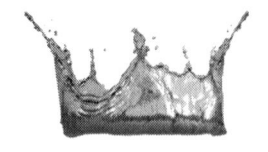

EMILIA

This might just go down as the worst day in history, and I'm not sure I can ever look Jace in the eye again.

Maybe I should quit my job right now and save both of us from further pain that's surely waiting around the next corner after this debacle.

Never before have I been this embarrassed about my family. I'm not delusional and know how dysfunctional they are—*we* are—but today has definitely taken it to a whole new level. The blunt refusal to acknowledge Jace beyond the point of asking for his income, and the immediate dismissal thereafter, was only the start of this humiliating dinner.

We're not even through the main course, and my mom has already had several meltdowns, and even more glasses of wine. The moment when my sister's kids "escaped" from the kitchen, and my mom tried to herd them back in like they're cattle, screeching at everyone to help her, was so over-the-top ridiculous it was comical.

If I wasn't so embarrassed about this whole evening, I might have burst into laughter until I cried.

Jace has been a trooper through it all, squeezing my hand or thigh reassuringly every few moments. Or at least he pretends to be. For all I know, he's here out of some wrong sense of obligation and is going to fire me the second we leave the premises. Or worse, he might just up and leave me alone with this crazy bunch.

Marcus has been an absolute pain in the ass too, poking at Jace whenever he gets a chance, and I'm about to push his face into the fancy mashed potatoes like it's no one's business.

Why on earth my parents think we'd be a good fit is beyond me. This is the third time they've invited him to dinner as my quasi-date, and he gets slimier and more obtuse every time.

No idea what his issue is that he keeps coming back. He's good-looking, has money, and isn't super old either. Is this a challenge for him?

And there he goes again, leaning around me to look at Jace. "So, Jace, I'm guessing your professional *career* will be over soon too like most other athletic ones when you hit a certain age. Have you put any thought into what you'll *attempt* to do after?"

Oh, I hate his face. So much.

He might have slight resemblances to a young Adonis, but there's no outward beauty that could ever rectify his inner ugliness.

And then there's Jace . . . *Jace*. I could kiss his face. Not only because he's still sitting next to me, like he promised, but also because he's been simply amazing. Pushing his way through one ridiculous and offensive question after the other, and all of that with a smile on his face.

If I didn't know any better, I'd say he's enjoying this.

He places his fork and knife on his plate, much to my mother's wide-eyed surprise at exactly the "twenty-after" mark, and picks up the ironed linen napkin to wipe his mouth.

Those lips. Full and so delectable, I might just promise to abstain from chocolate if I could nibble on them instead.

And there goes my brain again. This day has officially short-circuited it, and it's been all over the place.

Jace puts on a polite smile and looks Marcus straight in the eye. "Not really. I have a few ideas, maybe doing some training camps, you know, teaching young ones, but I haven't decided yet. Hopefully, I have a few more good years in me, building up my investments during that time."

Marcus doesn't waste time to let the smugness take over his face. "Well, if you ever need help with those investments, let me know. I don't normally handle small accounts, but I'd make an exception since you're Emilia's friend."

The dig couldn't be more obvious had he tried. The whole room falls quiet, even my sister and my brother-in-law —who were happily ignoring us, as usual—perk up and stare at us.

That's the moment when I'm sure Jace is going to have enough and leave.

And I'm going to punch asshole Marcus in the face. Straight in the mouth. I'm pulling my hand out of Jace's, or rather, I'm trying to, but he doesn't let go of me.

I close my eyes, waiting to wake up, and all of this has just been a bad dream.

Instead, Jace—freaking Jace Atwood—starts to laugh. Loud, unrestrained laughter flows out of his mouth. The world could have ended outside, and I wouldn't have noticed.

There was only one thing my brain could focus on right now, and that was this incredible man beside me. I don't give a damn that my mouth is hanging open or that I probably look like a total idiot, because I'm enthralled.

Utterly mesmerized.

This moment.

This is, without a doubt, the moment I become infatuated with Jace Atwood. I'm ready to have all his babies, the whole shebang, and I can't even put into words why.

Placing a hand on his chest, he takes several deep breaths and wipes at the corners of his eyes before looking at a stunned Marcus, who's wearing the stupidest expression I've ever seen on his face. "Thanks for the offer, man, but I think I'm good. I'm happy with my team of financial advisors and investment managers."

It takes Marcus several moments to regain his composure before he clears his throat. "Of course. No problem. I didn't . . . I didn't realize you already have someone."

"I do. And word has it, they're the best too." Jace picks up his water glass and takes a long drink.

Marcus wouldn't be dumbass Marcus if he didn't take the bait. "Oh? Someone I might have heard of in passing?"

The audacity of this man knows no bounds.

Normally, I would have had enough and said something to him, and I know I'll replay this conversation later in my head when I'm in bed, but right now, I can't take my eyes off Jace. He's absolutely brilliant.

This verbal volley captivating.

He winks at me, freaking *winks* at me, before he nods at Marcus. "You know, you just might have." He squeezes my thigh, and my breath gets stuck in my throat. "I'm with Schneider and Chase."

Marcus swallows audibly while a row of gasps erupt on the other side of the table when the rest of my family finally catches on. Jace *isn't* as small a fish in the water as they thought he was.

After enduring these types of dinners for as long as I can remember, and having the unfortunate displeasure of ninety percent of conversations being work-related, even I know that Schneider and Chase only take on big clients.

The atmosphere in the room changes in a nanosecond.

Instead of turning away from Jace, everyone—especially my dad and brother-in-law—turns toward Jace, leaning in his direction with real interest for the first time tonight.

It's hideous to watch and only adds to the long list of things I wish I never had to witness tonight.

I knew my family didn't think I was the smartest in the room. I knew they didn't think my career choices have been the best.

But I didn't expect them to think that I wasn't a good catch for someone.

I thought all their attempts to set me up with a constant stream of my dad's and brother-in-law's business partners was their twisted way of setting me up with someone good. That they actually thought I was worthy of being with someone they admire and accept.

What just transpired changes everything, and I'm not ready for the wave of sadness to hit me.

Time seems to slow down as the fact that my family assumed I'd never find anyone special or decent on my own hits my system.

Shock and somberness floods me, weighing down my limbs to the extent that breathing becomes difficult.

I'm not sure why I was still holding on to that last piece of hope that my family might accept me for who I am one day, that they'd actually *love* me for who I am one day.

Awareness spreads through my veins like the most potent poison. It's cruel, out to cause utter devastation. Clawing at my flesh like it wants to rip it straight off my bones.

"Em." Jace's voice cuts through the fog in my brain and I look at him, trying to focus on him.

On the way his brown waves fall across his forehead, how his blue eyes are so beautiful, and his clean-cut features so handsome. I want to smile, I try to, but my facial muscles don't want to work.

They're broken, just like the huge realization is still tearing me up on the inside. Relentlessly and unforgiving.

His hand comes up to touch my face. "You okay there, ladybug?"

My brain is slowly starting back up, trying to stand up proud and loud, pushing away the darkness and doubt that momentarily pulled me under.

I inhale and exhale. Inhale, exhale.

Focusing on Jace helps.

Focusing on the fact he didn't call me Emilia for the first time but *Em*. Followed by *ladybug*.

In front of my family. In front of the people who not only once, but several times in these past few hours have shown him how superficial and pretentious they are, trying to put him in a place they assumed he belongs after their quick dismissal.

He's all I can see to not fall apart.

He's my center, inadvertently helping me get my equilibrium back. Just by being here. By being him. By seeing *me*.

Then he leans in and gently touches my cheek with his lips. "Let me get you out of here."

Not *let's get out of here*, but let *me* get *you* out of here.

Like none of what they did to him mattered, like he's doing this for *me*.

I was wrong before. I did not become infatuated with Jace tonight. I jumped off that cliff a while ago, and I'm still falling.

I'm so stunned, completely floored by his behavior and my realizations, that my body isn't capable of blushing at his obvious affection in front of the people that just hurt me deeply.

Without waiting for a reply, he grabs my hand and stands, pulling me up with him. "Well, it's time for us to go. Thanks for the meal, it was delicious. I'd say it was fun but I think we all know it wasn't."

My mother's mouth falls open as she shoots me a glare like this is all my fault. "*Emilia*."

She might as well have slapped me across the face for the way my name sounded on her lips.

It adds another drop to my already overfilled patience tank, and red-hot anger surges to the surface. "No, *Mother*. I think we've had enough for tonight."

Mr. Dickwad-cheater pushes his chair back and glares at us. I'm not sure if he's trying to be intimidating, if his actions are supposed to be a warning. Who knows? But he's at the very top of my shit list.

I point a finger at him. "Don't."

His eyes form small slits as he huffs and stands up, propping his fists on the table to lean forward. "I can do whatever the fuck I want. I certainly don't need permission from *you,* so watch your mouth."

That's it. He didn't just add another drop to my tank, he pushed the whole dang thing over. I'm used to having my feelings trampled on by those people—purposefully or not—but then everyone's been incredibly disrespectful to Jace tonight too. And now Shane's being extra assholish.

My fingers tingle as I squeeze them into a fist next to my body.

I've never hit anyone in my life before, but I'm so incredibly angry that I pull back my hand.

Jace snatches me around the waist and pulls me back several feet, not letting go.

He points a finger at Shane. "If I ever hear you talk to her like that again, *we'll* have a talk. Right now, how about you tell your wife why we saw you at Berkeley Pier this morning."

Jace spins us around and starts walking, and somehow, I manage to put one foot in front of the other without tripping.

Absolute chaos erupts behind us, my sister's angry voice loud and clear as she tells her husband that he promised to not meet up with his *women* in public places anymore.

Disgust turns my stomach into a sour mess, and dinner is starting to make its way up as we stumble out of the house and into the fresh air.

She knows. My sister freaking *knows* her husband is cheating, and all she asks of him is to do it behind closed doors? What the ever-loving hell? How is this my family?

I try to pull in a few lungfuls of air but Jace doesn't slow down.

And I get it. The urge to get distance between us and everyone else is impossible to resist.

Jace unlocks the car and opens my door.

I don't look at him, I can't, not ready yet to appraise his reaction to this mess now that we're away from the crime scene.

He closes the car door after I slip into the seat before getting in himself, zooming out of my parents' driveway like it's no one's business.

It will take me a while to work through what went down tonight and what it actually means for me and my life.

Now, I keep my eyes ahead, unwilling to look back at the mess we left behind.

Neither of us attempts conversation, and Jace stops the car a few minutes later on the side of the road, turning on the blinker.

He shifts my way. "Em, talk to me."

Em. Again.

My eyes stay trained on my lap. "I don't know what to say."

And I really don't. Even though there weren't a lot of words spoken tonight—especially not with me—so much happened. More than I can wrap my head around at this point. Too much to even begin dissecting it.

"That's okay." His voice is soft, gentle. "Do you want to go somewhere else? You barely ate anything."

I shake my head. "I don't think I could stomach anything, so just home please. If it's not a bother."

"Of course not." This time, the softness is gone from Jace's voice, replaced by a grit I haven't heard before. "And just so we're clear, you're never a bother. *Never.*"

I swallow hard when his hand reaches for mine across the middle console.

"Em, look at me. Do you understand that?"

My eyes flicker to his, burning from the suppressed emotions slowly clawing their way to the surface. I need to get home and be alone, get away from him before I have a meltdown. I don't think I could take him witnessing that today.

So I bite my tongue and push everything back down for a while longer and nod. "Yes."

That's all I manage to squeeze out.

"Good."

I turn my face and look out the window, grateful when he gets back on the road. His hand stays interlocked with mine, and I pull strength from that connection, even when it comes from a point of sadness.

If tonight has brought out one of the darker parts of my family, it has also brought out one of Jace's good ones.

He was there for me, defending and supporting me when I needed it the most.

I know I'll be okay, even if it'll take some time to lick my wounds, but I'm more glad than ever that life has brought Jace and me together.

From the looks of it, this man is in my corner.

He *chose* to be in my corner.

And I'm not sure how to handle that.

Because, and this is even more horrible, it's the first time I know what that's like.

FOURTEEN

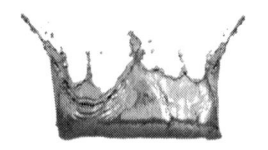

JACE

The music blasts in my ears—thanks to my waterproof earbuds—as I enter the last few laps of one of my equally most-loved and most-hated training sessions: my freestyle and individual medley swim. It's four thousand meters long, lasts almost an hour, and mixes speed and endurance.

My muscles burn, and I can barely feel my body anymore. Every motion, every movement of my arms and legs is one hundred percent muscle memory at this point, proving how resilient we are as humans, and that when pushed, we're truly made for greatness. To reach goals we ourselves didn't know we were capable of.

When the music stops, and I hit the wall, I practically throw myself on the line divider, putting every ounce of my weight on the small plastic buoys. I'm spent, absolutely spent. Maybe even more than usual.

"You look like you're going to pass out." Coach Martin crouches down with a huff on the pool edge, and I tilt my head his way with the speed of a turtle.

"I feel like it." My heart is hammering like crackling thunder as I lift the tight cap from my head and pull it off along with my goggles and headphones.

Coach reaches out, and I sigh in relief as I hand everything over. "You okay?"

I snort, unable to do much else at this point. He waits until my lungs have recovered enough for me to push out some words. "Was my time that bad?"

"It wasn't your best, that's for sure. But that's not why I'm asking, and you know it."

"I know."

"Sharon's worried about you too."

"Tell her I'm okay." Sharon and Bill Martin have taken it upon themselves to smother me with attention ever since I started training with Bill when I was younger.

Bill saw something in me that motivated both of us, and he was there every step of the way, even more so when my dad unexpectedly died. Bill and my dad grew close over my years of training with him. Which turned my life into even more swimming when our families hung out together outside of training. But I was okay with that since it's always been my happy place.

Sharon, on the other hand, likes to play mother hen number two when my mom isn't around.

"You know we're here for you if you need help, right? You've had a lot going on. It's normal that you need some time to adjust to all the life changes." He leans in and gives me a pat on the shoulder. "Now cool down and get your ass out of here, so I can go home too. And get your head back in the game for Nationals. You ain't gonna win anything like this."

A genuine chuckle comes out of my mouth at Bill's way of showing affection.

"Will do, old man."

"I can kick your ass any day, son. Any day." With that, he slowly pushes back to standing and brushes through his salt and pepper hair. "I still have some paperwork to do at the office. I'll see you tomorrow. Try and get some rest tonight. You look like you could use it."

"Duly noted."

Of course, he's right. I feel like I could sleep for a week straight, but how's that supposed to work with my new life? But worse than that, Coach is right about my times. I've been training to win at Nationals to keep me sharp for the Olympics next year. Right now, I'd say it's a blurry mess.

Even though I've been doing this for years and have plenty of national and international wins under my belt, I hate to lose. I absolutely detest it.

But how the hell am I going to perform at my best under these conditions?

The conversation with Coach, and an extra-long shower, caused enough of a delay to throw me straight into rush-hour traffic. I make it home almost an hour later than usual, grateful for the extra protein bars in my bag. Otherwise, my stomach would have eaten itself on the drive over.

Em—or Millie, or ladybug, since Emilia is officially banned from my memory—already texted me saying that Tanner was extra tired after a short nap and went down early tonight.

Which suits me just fine. Even though I'm sad I didn't get to say goodnight to him, I did see him earlier today before his nap. With my own exhaustion, I rather not have to bring up the energy to deal with a toddler right now.

When I get home, I'm quiet, not wanting to wake Tanner. I enter the living room and hear Em cussing in the kitchen.

"You stupid computer. I can't read this shitty caption, okay? It's the worst thing ever for someone like me, why don't you understand that? *Ugh.*" She growls the last bit, and I bite back a grin.

Even though it's easy to tell she's frustrated, it's also cute as hell.

Seeing someone like her, who is remarkably cheery and pleasant by nature—which is even more extraordinary considering how fucked-up her family is—acting a little rough around the edges is somehow refreshing, and I respect that.

Walking around the corner, I stop and lean against the wall to watch her.

She squints at the screen before typing on the keyboard of her laptop, nearly stabbing the keys. Two seconds pass before she throws her hands in the air in small fists. "Ah, I hate you, you stupid . . . you stupid *thing.*"

"Tell it how you really feel." I push off the wall and walk to the kitchen island where she's set up shop.

Her hand flies to her chest as she glares at me. Then she points a shaky finger at me. "Oh my goodness, you scared me. Don't do that."

"Sorry, I was trying to be quiet because of Tanner."

This is the first time I get a good look at her today. Last night when I dropped her off at her place, she practically sprinted out of the car. And when I saw her during my lunch break today, she kept busy, avoiding me.

Her red hair is piled into a messy bun on top of her head, and her skin looks extra pale today, her freckles standing out more than usual.

Since she's back to staring at her computer screen, I walk up next to her and look over her shoulder. "Can I help?"

She hesitates for a moment before her shoulders droop. "I guess . . . if you don't mind. I want to sign up for this website, and the captcha test is making that incredibly difficult today."

"Yeah, I hate those."

"Normally, I use the read aloud function, but for some reason, it's not working. None of the functions on the right side are. I already refreshed the site but it stays frozen."

"Want me to give it a try?" I keep my comments and suspicions about her issues to myself.

"Sure."

"Okay. It's 6GI ME3."

A moment passes without her doing anything, and I take another small step closer. "You want me to repeat it?"

"Yes, please. Mmm . . . could you do it slower, please?" Her voice is barely above a whisper, and I'm close enough to see her neck flush. I stare at it for a moment, focused on her pulse beating wildly in her throat.

"Sure. 6 . . . G . . . I . . . M . . . E . . . 3." I take my time, waiting for her fingers to circle over the keyboard until she's hit all the numbers and letters.

Her cheeks puff out before she blows the air through her puckered lips.

It's fascinating to watch her this close.

With the captcha test finished, there's no reason to be this close behind her, but I can't seem to move.

Shit, I don't *want* to move.

The smell of her skin and hair is intoxicating, and I haven't had my fill yet.

"Thanks, Jace." She does a half-turn, peeking over her shoulder at me, stopping when she realizes how close I am.

I'd placed my hands on the countertop next to her to be able to lean in closer, yet refrain from pushing my whole body against hers. It's obvious now that I've practically caged her in. How is that hot? "No problem."

We study each other in silence. "You know there's nothing wrong with asking for help, right? We all struggle with something."

Her head tilts downward as her eyes close. "I know. It's a habit, I guess, and a hard one to shake."

"I'm here for you."

"Thank you."

She's still avoiding my gaze, and it makes my stomach churn.

"Em?"

Her gaze snaps up to mine, and I get a total kick out of the glimmer in her eyes at my new name for her. "Hmm?"

A satisfied hum builds in my chest at the sight of her beautiful eyes up close. They look earthier under the artificial kitchen light, the burst of gold radiating around the pupil more pronounced than I've ever seen it before.

The need to have her confide in me overrides everything else for a moment. "Tell me what you're struggling with."

This time, even though the shimmer in her eyes loses

some of its brightness, her gaze stays locked with mine. "Dyslexia."

I bend down to her eye level. "Nothing to be ashamed of, you hear me?"

After having met her family, I'm pretty sure I know where her desire to hide it comes from.

"Okay."

"I mean it." Her face is only a few inches away, her breath sweet and inviting.

My gaze flickers to her lips.

"I know you do." She licks her lips. "Otherwise I wouldn't have told you."

Fuck.

I'm not sure what's sexier. Her damn mouth or her trust.

The computer *dings* behind her, effectively breaking whatever moment we had, as she spins around to look at the screen before quickly shutting the lid.

But I saw the open chat window. A dude called Brandon, asking if they were still on for tonight.

I straighten to my full height and walk over to the fridge to get one of my prepped meals. "Hot date tonight?"

"What?"

I point at the laptop she's currently shoving in her bag like it offended her. "Brandon."

Maybe I'm an asshole for calling her out, but I'm too tired for games. And a bit frustrated.

"Oh no." She shakes her head. "It's business related."

"Same business meeting as the other week?"

Her eyes widen before she nods. "Uh . . . actually, yeah."

I nod like I have a clue what she's talking about. I'm sure

there's more to it she isn't telling me, but I believe her when she says it's only business.

With that, my plans to ask her if she wants to hang out tonight are out the window, but I guess I should be happy. At least it looks like I'll be able to get an early sleep, after all.

If I'll be able to stop thinking about her that is. Lately, she seems to be taking over more and more of my brain space, especially when I'm in bed by myself.

The images of her in the shower have been permanently burned into my mind, keeping me from sleep more than I'd like to admit, replaying in my head and making me harder than anything else has in a long time until I take care of business.

I watch her grab her things and pretty much flee the house after our slightly awkward situation, leaving me alone in my exhausted and confused state.

I have no doubt she was telling the truth, but when it comes down to it, why does it matter to me if this Brandon guy was her date for the night?

It's not like I have any claim on her.

Or is that something I want?

FIFTEEN

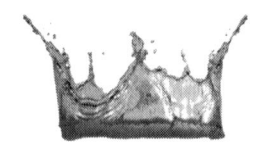

EMILIA

Nothing can bring down my mood today. My meeting with Brandon last night went better than expected, and we've made huge progress with my music program. Even though I haven't received an invitation to the audition yet, I still want to get this done. It's been a dream of mine for several years now, and I'm excited to see it finished soon.

Watching the program come together has been absolutely magical, and I'm more in love with it than before. The thought alone of being able to teach music to any kid with something I created makes me giddy.

Then there's Jace. So much has happened in the last few days, and I'm still trying to process it all, glad for the distraction. It allows me to push my family matters to the back of my mind, because I'm not ready to deal with *that* yet.

Things have been a bit awkward between Jace and me, but what did I expect?

In the span of a few days he was subjected to the embarrassing behavior of my family *after* witnessing my brother-in-law cheat and *before* watching me practically check out mentally, fleeing from his car.

And all of that after he was the sweetest—not to mention hottest—guy ever, kissing my cheek right before dragging me out of my parents' house like a personal bodyguard.

Then yesterday he more or less forced me—in a nice way—to confess my learning disability to him, just so he can be super accepting of that too.

Now, he's home for the rest of the day working out at his gym in the basement, and I might or might not be keeping my eyes on the stairs so I won't miss when he drags his sweaty—and delectable—ass back up.

It's a sight I'm exposed to several times a week, and it never gets old.

That brings back that moment in the kitchen last night.

Where I thought he might kiss me.

He was so close that I could smell his minty breath, and I was ready to offer myself to him. I'm not even that desperate, but this man does things to me. Hot, sparking, exciting things.

My phone vibrates, and I startle. A text from Nicole. As if she can sense my inner turmoil.

Nicole: Just checking in. You okay over there? Anything new since we talked yesterday?

It's been difficult to get together now that we both have busy jobs and Nicole's with her boyfriend almost every free minute she has. But we promised to talk on the phone or text as often as we can.

Emilia: Not really. No peep from anyone since my mom gave me her disappointment speech in the voicemail she left and Ashley texted me to mind my own business. They're all acting like I'm the bad guy. Because I just live for the drama.

Nicole: I'm sorry, sweets. They don't deserve you and clearly don't know you either if they think that. Never have, never will, so don't listen to a word they say.

Emilia: Thanks, Nic.

Nicole: Of course, babe. And tell that man of yours he deserves a gold star for what he did. I haven't been able to stop thinking about it.

My face heats up at the implication.

Emilia: He's not my man.

Nicole: Sure. Are you blushing yet? ;)

Emilia: Whatever.

Nicole: Thought so. Anyway, I stand by my point. Your family deserved far worse

than that. And anyone who stands up for you the way he did is pure gold in my eyes.

Emilia: It felt good.

Nicole: It was long overdue.

Emilia: I'm sure my family thinks otherwise.

Nicole: Who cares? Not everything's about them, and Jace clearly thought the same. Like I said, gold star. I would have done the same a long time ago had you ever taken me to them.

Emilia: I know. Thank you.

Nicole: Always. My break is up. Have a good day, okay? Love you.

Emilia: Love you too.

I smile as Tanner starts humming along to a kids' music station. He's also squeezing the heck out of the Play-Doh ball on the dining room table in front of him. Jace ordered a ton of different sets online in a panic when he wasn't sure which one to buy. Apparently, he thought he could solve the problem by ordering half of what the store had. So cute.

Tanner shoves the plastic mold with his pretend cupcake in my face.

I act as if I'm eating while he giggles. "Mmm, delicious. Thank you."

"That good, huh?"

That deep voice. That rumble.

Jace is only a few feet away, sneaking up on me like the other times before. I swear that guy's a freaking ninja.

"Oh my gosh. Could you stop doing that please?"

He chuckles and wipes his face with the towel hanging around his neck. "I'm not trying to, sorry."

"Like I believe you." I grin at him before remembering where we are and what we're doing. Turning back to Tanner, I collect the leftover pieces of Play-Doh and squeeze them together for him. "Do you want to make a cupcake for Daddy? I bet he'd love one."

Tanner gazes up at his dad—who gives him a reassuring smile—before nodding. He babbles excitedly and attacks the doughy mass in front of him with a newfound enthusiasm. His tongue pokes out of the corner of his mouth as he shapes and molds, and it might just be the most adorable thing I've ever seen.

Except when Jace plays with him. Nothing can top that. I bet there isn't a single woman on earth who could keep her hormones under control when seeing this sexy dad play with his darling son.

There go my thoughts again like so often lately when Jace is around.

I watch him out of the corner of my eye as he walks to the fridge to get an electrolyte drink. He comes back over and gulps down that whole bottle like it's nothing. I'm mesmerized by the way his Adam's apple moves with every swallow and the way beads of sweat run steadily down his temples and neck, disappearing behind the collar of his workout shirt.

With his arms on full display, it's easy to get a good peek at the arrow tattoos on his left bicep. They point downward, and even though I cannot figure out why, I think arrows are my new favorite thing. There's something about that tattoo that makes me want to trace it over and over. Preferably with my tongue.

I pull my lip into my mouth to keep from groaning at my own ridiculousness, just as Jace pulls out the chair next to his son and winks at me.

I have absolutely no chance to keep heat from flooding my cheeks. Did he see me ogling his arms? Just another thing to add to my things-Jace-Atwood-did-not-need-to-know-about-me list.

Tanner is beside himself with excitement, giggling as he hands his dad his pretend cupcake and Jace generously takes his time to devour it.

After another minute of pretend eating he hands it back to a beaming Tanner before ruffling his hair. Then he leans closer to give his forehead a kiss. "Thanks, buddy. That was the best cupcake I've ever had."

My heart. My poor freaking heart. It never had a chance.

My ovaries seem to be in agreement with that as well.

Tanner's smile is so wide, his face might split in two soon.

Jace smiles at him and gets up. "Daddy's going to jump in the shower, okay? But I'll be back soon."

Tanner nods, already focused back on his Play-Doh. "Otay."

Jace and I both freeze, our gazes clashing.

"Was that—?"

"Did he just—?"

We both talk at the same time, neither one of us finishing our sentence.

"Wow." That's all I get out, and Jace nods in a daze. "Go. Hurry up."

I'm not sure why I say it, but he seems to get the urgency because he nods again. If we didn't just imagine Tanner saying okay, neither one of us wants to miss the possibility of it happening again. Not if we can help it.

Naturally, Tanner doesn't try to say anything else as we clean up, just in time for Jace to get back to us with a hurried expression.

"Hey, buddy." He picks him up when Tanner reaches for him. "Did you have fun playing with your Play-Doh?"

Tanner grins and babbles excitedly like he's telling Jace the most amazing story. By now, Jace is really good at mimicking the excitement, ooh-ing and aah-ing when Tanner expects a reaction.

"You're good with him, Jace? I'm going to start with dinner."

Jace looks at me over Tanner's shoulder and gives me one of his crooked smiles. "Sure."

Okay then.

At least I know my hormones are still working, because my body is positively tingling in all the right places. From one dang smile. And a sexy arrow tattoo that's imprinted in my brain.

The open floor plan allows me to watch them in the

living room while I'm by the sink, and I do that more often than I probably have a reason for.

It's why I see Tanner running around and screaming in a high-pitched voice that's filled with pure joy. My heart bounces around happily in my chest, because it's so dang adorable. He runs in a circle before launching himself on the couch where Jace sits, ready to play Tanner's favorite game: tickling.

The squeals and laughter echo around the room, and Tanner does it over and over, never tiring of playing the same game.

I'm telling myself I'll only be watching one more time before I continue cooking.

But this time, Tanner doesn't quite make it to the couch. He jumps too early, and instead of landing on the couch, he hits the corner of it with his chest and falls back on the floor, immediately starting to cry.

Jace picks him up and softly rubs his back as Tanner takes another deep breath, getting ready for another loud wail.

But the wail never comes, and it takes me a moment to realize that. A cold chill coats my body at the absence as I race around the island, hating the fact that it makes me lose sight of them for even a second. "Jace."

My feet are heavy, feeling like cement on my body as I drag them forward. "Jace." I'm yelling now, my heart pounding relentlessly. "Why isn't he crying anymore?"

When they enter my field of vision again, my heart feels like it's free-falling, hitting my stomach with such a force that nausea immediately travels up my throat at the sight in front of me.

Tanner's motionless in Jace's arms, too still, and I immediately see his limp face. It's pale, so pale, having lost all its color in seconds. "Oh my gosh. Jace. He isn't breathing." My throat feels like it's swelling, a cold sweat breaking out across my skin.

The words have finally registered with Jace and he pulls Tanner's body away from him. "Fuck."

His wild eyes meet mine as he jumps into action and places Tanner on the floor, bending down to press his ear to his nose and mouth.

My chest feels like it's constricting, a weight pressing on it that's so heavy, it doesn't allow me to get the oxygen I need. When I finally reach them, I sink to the floor in a heap.

My hands feel numb as they flutter around, unable to figure out what to do as I watch the scene unfold in front of me. *I should know what to do.*

Dizziness overtakes my body as spots appear in my vision, and I barely register that I'm back on my feet, racing to the kitchen and my phone at the same time Jace's yell reaches me.

"Call 9-1-1."

My hands shake so badly, it takes me several tries to get my phone to work. My brain is racing, still trying to make sense of the situation when the dispatcher comes on the line.

I can barely make out the questions as I explain what happened and rattle off our address, walking back over to Jace to watch with absolute horror as he's bending over Tanner's body, giving him CPR.

Tanner's lifeless body.

With his eyes rolled back in his head, his face now blue.

Sirens sound in the distance as Tanner abruptly starts moving, just to fall back limply again.

He does this several more times before he starts crying.

Jace picks him up and Tanner sobs against his chest.

The sirens get louder and I race to the door, opening it just as the ambulance and police car enter the property, Tanner's loud wails echoing through the otherwise quiet house.

SIXTEEN

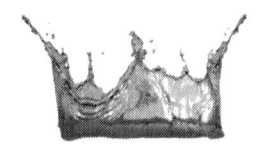

JACE

THIS HAS BEEN, WITHOUT A DOUBT, THE LONGEST DAY OF my life. We just got back from the pediatrician who said Tanner looks and sounds all good. Just like the EMTs had told us after they were done checking on him. They did a thorough assessment, including hooking him to a defibrillator, but they didn't think it was necessary to take him to the hospital.

They must have seen the terror on both Em's and my faces and quickly added that we could take him to the pediatrician if we'd like.

As if that was even a question at that point.

Since I like to be rather safe than sorry, I'm going to set up an appointment with the cardiologist at the children's hospital to make sure we aren't missing anything. Considering how suddenly his mom died, extra precautions are the only way to calm my worried mind.

But that's it. Nothing else, which seems almost comical after the almost-heart attack I suffered only a few hours ago.

It was weird, to say the least, to take a smiling child to the doctor after what happened. While I retold what happened, reliving the horrible moment when I thought I might have lost Tanner, my son was jumping around like he didn't have a care in the world.

All the while, I still feel like I just survived a catastrophe.

From what the EMTs and the doctor explained, Tanner had the wind knocked out of him, which isn't anything abnormal. But instead of continuing to breathe afterwards, his body went into some sort of shock, a breath-holding episode, from experiencing intense pain.

Apparently, this can happen sometimes and is most common with younger children. In most cases, they grow out of it around age four or five. It's not anything you can control, but rather lie them on their side and simply wait.

Well, shit.

I really hope this won't happen again, because these last few hours took a good ten years off my life. At least.

And I don't see that being any different if this ever happens again.

Even now that we're home, and Tanner is back to his normal self, I still feel like I'm having an out-of-body experience, my limbs weak and shaky.

Em doesn't seem to fair any better, only putting on a smile when Tanner's looking at her, but even then it isn't anywhere near her normal one.

We're both shaken up.

Since it's way beyond Tanner's bedtime, we go through the motions of getting him ready. Em's been off the clock for hours, but I'm not stupid to point that out. If she wants to stay, she can stay however the hell long she wants. I definitely don't want her to go, that's for sure.

What if something happens to Tanner again?

I would have lost my mind had I experienced this accident by myself. Just having her close by, knowing she was right there with me every step of the way, helped me keep my cool enough to not freak the fuck out. At least not more than I did. No matter how much I wanted to.

Thankfully, Tanner doesn't give us any issues, his exhaustion evident when his eyelids get heavier with each second.

By the time he hits the mattress, he's passed out.

Em and I stand in the doorway of his room for a long time, neither one of us saying a word as we stare at the crib, the dim night light bright enough to illuminate his angelic face.

When I shift around, Em's gaze finds mine. Her face is red and puffy from all the crying earlier. Fatigue is deeply carved in her features, and I'm positive I look the same.

Without a doubt, this evening left a mark on both of us. The visible one will be gone by tomorrow or whenever we're able to get a good sleep.

The invisible one probably not.

I have a feeling this horror, this terror-clawing panic in my chest, will stay with me for a very long time.

Looking at her, seeing her in this much pain, cracks a piece of my heart.

When her eyes appear overly shiny, and she starts blinking rapidly, I open my arms for her. She doesn't hesitate, stepping right into my embrace, and I'm not planning on letting go of her anytime soon. I need this contact just as much.

Somehow I manage to get us into the living room and to

the couch without letting go of her. She's a quiet crier, her shoulders gently shaking as the tension in her body slowly leaves her.

When I sit down, it feels natural to pull her onto my lap. And that's where she finally comes to rest, her body calming down, softening in my arms. Quiet sniffles the only noise, except for the baby monitor that's yanked up to the max volume, gentle rain sounds creating harmonious background music.

With my chin on Em's head, I inhale deeply and close my eyes, willing away the pictures sure to haunt me for days if not weeks or months.

Seeing my child in a lifeless heap on the floor, his innocent face turning blue, is nothing I'll be able to forget anytime soon.

It has changed *me*.

Especially since we haven't been able to get Lila's medical records, but my lawyer is working on that. Privacy laws are complex, but hopefully, we can find a way around them. It would be helpful to have them now particularly.

Em tries to draw back, to pull out of my arms, but I'm having a hard time allowing her to do so.

Right now, I don't ever want to let go, needing this contact to feel alive. To confirm that everything is truly okay.

She wiggles again, and I loosen my hold on her. Marginally. "I wasn't planning on snotting all over you, sorry."

Her eyes are puffy, her face flushed, but she's still beautiful.

Her beauty is bone deep and surpasses her outer layer in a way that's indescribable. There's this shimmering piece of personality in her eyes, visible in the way they flash all-encompassing. It's captivating, and I've never witnessed anything like this before.

"I'd say you can snot all over me, but that sounds all sorts of wrong." My voice is gravelly, my throat dry, like I haven't used it in weeks.

At least my comment brings a smile to her lips. It's small, and only lasts about two seconds, but it was there.

And *I* put it there.

This is the first happy moment since the accident, and warmth spreads throughout my chest at the realization. I needed that. I needed a glimpse of hope, of normalcy, knowing we'll be able to get back to a *normal* life, whatever that means after a day like today.

"Thanks. That felt good after everything. I'm still trying to process what happened."

I nod. "I know exactly what you mean. My brain keeps replaying the scene on an endless loop, and it's driving me crazy. At this point, I'm not sure how I'm ever going to sleep."

Her eyes widen at my words, and her lower lip trembles. "Me too. I . . . would you mind if I stayed a little longer? My roommate is with her boyfriend, and I don't want to be alone."

Before I have a chance to respond, she opens her mouth again.

"Maybe we could watch a movie or something?"

Her voice is soft, a hint of uncertainty in it, but her eyes . . . they're still on me, strong and inquiring like they're trying to figure me out. Or maybe she's searching for that same connection I am? That need to connect too loud to ignore?

Another part of my brain snaps to life, noticing how close

we are, how good and right she feels in my arms. My gaze flickers to her mouth, and Em doesn't miss my wandering eyes, her lips parting on a soft inhale that makes my heart pick up speed.

I'm about to lean in—pushing aside all questioning thoughts—when the baby monitor comes to life on the coffee table.

Em is off my lap, and I'm off the couch in a nanosecond, both of us on the floor and leaning over the screen.

"He's snoring." Em chuckles softly and lets her head fall back against the couch. "I think I just had a heart attack. Another one."

Brushing a hand over my face, I stare at the monitor for another moment, watching Tanner move around and settling in another sleeping position. "Fuck, I know."

I lean back and stare at the ceiling before facing her.

Her eyes are already waiting for me, pulling me right back under like every time our gazes meet.

She tilts her head. "So . . . you want to watch a movie?"

"Sure." I don't have to think about it. I know I'd say yes to pretty much anything right now to ensure she won't leave.

Neither one of us moves though. Instead, we keep staring at each other like the connection between us is the only thing keeping us grounded at this point.

"What do you want to watch?" My gaze flickers to her lips and my newfound fascination with them.

I think I'm on my way of turning them into an obsession. Because those lips aren't just kissable. They're fucking perfect. Waiting to be devoured like they've never been devoured before.

The urge to kiss her in a way that erases all memories of

any man who's ever even looked at her grows in my chest, surging through me with a strength that almost makes me growl.

Either she's oblivious to the fire burning within me, or she ignores it. "Do you want to pick something? I need to use the bathroom."

My brain's foggy but somehow I manage to push through it. "Okay."

"Do you want something from the kitchen?"

"Maybe a drink from the fridge?"

"Okay."

"Thanks."

She nods. "Of course."

After hesitating for a moment, she walks across the living room, leaving me to my mixed thoughts and emotions.

What a day.

Who would have thought that it would end not only with a heart-attack inducing accident but also with a movie night that seems to screw with my mind even more.

One look at her, one look at that gorgeous face, and that sexy ass swaying like leaves in the wind, makes one thing blatantly clear.

I want her.

I want Em with my whole being.

SEVENTEEN

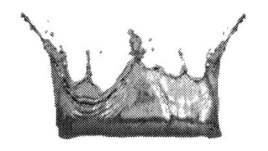

EMILIA

Warmth surrounds me like a blanket, and I sigh happily, snuggling deeper into this cocoon of comfort. Until it moves.

It freaking *moves*.

I freeze, still as a statue, as I try to find my way through my fuzzy brain, willing away the clouds of sleep that cling to me like an unwelcome fungus.

When something squeezes my boob, it does the trick.

My eyes fly open, immediately zooming in on the hand on my chest. A big, broad, and very manly hand. One that I immediately recognize as Jace's because well, I might have noticed his long . . . fingers before.

Now that my brain's awake, and my senses have come to life, I also feel his breath on my neck. It's slow and even, hopefully meaning he's still sleeping.

Looks like Jace enjoys squeezing boobs in his sleep. I'll make sure to remember that.

I continue to lie there like a weirdo, face smooshed halfway in the couch, my brain replaying images of yesterday.

First, the terrible accident. Those memories squeeze my heart in a paralyzing way every time I think about it, making it hard to breathe. Like someone's trying to choke me with their bare hands.

And then, images of last night.

Once the terror gave way to the sweet relief of knowing that Tanner's okay, a reprieve so powerful, I wanted to sink to my knees and cry like a baby. I had never felt anything like that before.

After feeling like I barely escaped a tragedy, I don't know how people do it. I don't know how people get over that void.

I thought for only a few minutes I'd lost someone who'd securely planted himself into my heart in the short time I've known him.

Because how could I not love this boy? Despite the hardships Tanner had to endure, and the changes he's had to go through, he's adjusted so well. It's probably a good thing he's so young and doesn't always understand what's going on around him.

As if summoned, the screen of the baby monitor turns on, showing Tanner moving in his crib. Not sure what sound triggered the camera, but it looks like he's still sleeping, probably adjusting his position.

Sweet, adorable Tanner.

The thought of losing him was absolutely incapacitating. To see the life leave his normally happy face drained me of everything. For a while there, when I thought we might have lost him, I couldn't feel anything. I was numb, utterly empty.

And then the pain slammed into me with a brutality I wouldn't wish on my worst enemy. It scared me, took away some of my positivity and hope, leaving a dark, vast space behind. It hurts to think about and I press my eyes closed, wanting to escape this terrible feeling.

My lip trembles as I blow out a breath, trying to control my emotions that try to bubble to the surface.

"Shh. It's okay. He's okay." Jace's voice is rough, but also displays a tenderness I didn't know about until last night.

The same tenderness he showed me when he soothed my bleeding heart, holding me so close to him as if he was afraid I'd break apart otherwise. And I might have. No, I'm sure I would have.

I still broke down, but Jace was the reason I didn't break apart.

This man who still has the occasional unsure moment around his son showed me a kindness I'll never be able to forget and also hope I'll never have to repay in a similar situation. Even though I would. In an instant. Without a single doubt.

For him, I would because his heart is pure, and his intentions are good.

His hand moves away from my breast to my collarbone, adding pressure to my body to pull me back, to pull me closer to his body. His other hand finds its way up the length of my body to push a few loose strands of hair out of my face. Since my mane of hair is piled on top of my head in a messy bun, they must have fallen out.

Another "Shh" in that seductive low voice.

I can't hold back the shiver rippling through my body, successfully distracting me from the mini-meltdown I just had.

"You okay?" His lips are so close to my shoulder, they brush my skin.

Maybe it's wrong, but I have to close my eyes and bite my lip to contain the moan that wants to escape. The contact was miniscule, innocent, yet it lit a flame inside my body that's been on a low simmer ever since I've gotten to know Jace better.

"Mm-hmm." I hope he can't detect the squeakiness in my voice, my telltale sign when I'm fibbing.

Am I really lying? I'm still shaken over yesterday's events, and probably will be for a while, but I *am* okay. Unsure of what any of the new developments of last night mean for *us*, but it sure feels okay to be in his arms.

More than okay.

"Good." A satisfied grumbling sound comes from his chest after a deep inhale.

Yet, he still doesn't move.

He's awake, talking to me, and still holding me to him.

Like it's the most natural thing to watch a movie together, fall asleep next to each other, and somehow wake up in a tight embrace.

Like he needs this as much as I do.

Maybe it holds him together too.

We didn't really talk much about what happened. Both of us too shocked to put into words what almost happened. Too distraught to put labels on the turmoil going on inside of us.

"I could get used to this." His nose runs up and down my neck. "You smell so good. Like lavender and sunshine."

He inhales deeply, his nose tickling my skin, and that's when I feel it. His hard length pressing into my butt.

Holy crap on a cracker.

Is he still half-asleep and that's why he hasn't pulled back yet?

No, he just talked about Tanner and asked if I was okay. Or can people who talk in their sleep have conversations like this?

His chuckle, the low rumble at my back, pulls me out of my thoughts. "Sorry, it's morning."

"Huh?" Way to go, Millie. Yes, let's play dumb.

Another chuckle from behind, a movement that pushes his erection even more into my butt.

Or did I push back? No, I didn't, right?

I'd die from embarrassment, that's for sure.

"I can feel you tense up, Em." This sexy voice. "Not to mention, I wouldn't—"

The monitor flashes to life once more, but this time with a babbling Tanner.

Pressing my eyelids together, I inhale deeply, trying not to finish his sentence. Because what good thing could have possibly followed his statement?

I wouldn't get an erection because of you? I wouldn't push it into your ass and make you all hot and bothered? I wouldn't act on it because I'm your boss, even though I just snuggled you like you actually mean something to me?

Talk about all my fears coming out to play.

Goodness.

I'm not sure about his intentions, but my skin is tingling everywhere, my heart giddy behind my ribcage, excited at the possibility of playing, momentarily shutting my worried brain.

What is this man doing to me?

It's one thing to find him attractive, and then to start liking him after spending so much time together, but now . . . things have changed.

He's quickly become a huge part of my everyday life—which is to be expected when I spend most of my time on *and* off the job with him. We've just kind of fallen in to a natural rhythm with our schedules. I take care of Tanner when Jace isn't home, and when he is here, we take care of him together.

Almost like a *family*.

This is how I know these two guys, as a double deal.

Two for one.

And I think about them constantly when I'm not with them, which isn't often these days.

They even distract me from my side project and my possible audition, even though I should be thinking about that all the time.

My life's dream.

Getting the job that will finally prove to my family that I can do something great too. That I can achieve big things outside the corporate world, and without their help.

And with Jace allowing me to use the spare room when Tanner is sleeping, I've already recorded most of the videos for my project, my very own music program for kids.

Jace's lips are traveling down the back of my neck, pulling me successfully out of my thoughts and throwing me into a bout of lust instead. A sound vibrates in my throat that can only be described as a purr, and I'm not even embarrassed about it.

His hands feel right on me, his lips like they belong on my skin.

When he follows the curve of my neck to my shoulder, my toes curl, and I'm ready to beg him. For what exactly I'm not sure, but I'm willing to find out. I *want* to find out.

His hands are on the move, inching towards my chest

once more when the monitor comes to life again, presenting us with a clapping and babble-singing Tanner, who's clearly enjoying the new songs we've been practicing.

Jace groans, his hands falling off my body as he rolls onto his back. "He sure has the worst timing."

I chuckle, attempting to get my pounding heart under control.

Tanner lets out a choking cough, and Jace and I scramble to our feet, hurrying to his room like our behinds are on fire. Of course, Tanner greets us with a big grin and a friendly wave.

My poor heart. Between the two of them, it's in for a wild ride.

Jace gets Tanner out of his crib and snuggles with him, a sight that will never get old.

They walk over to me, and I plant a kiss on Tanner's outstretched hand, making him giggle.

Jace bends down with his mouth close to my ear. "Don't think we're done yet, sweet Em. We've only just gotten started."

With that, he drags his lips over to my cheek and kisses it, his mouth grazing the very edge of mine.

I close my eyes, giving my body a moment to recover from this moment and this *man*.

I'm not sure I'm ready for whatever he has in store for me, or if it's a good idea. But I know that nothing has ever felt this good, so *right* before, and that I'm incapable of resisting Jace's touch.

EIGHTEEN

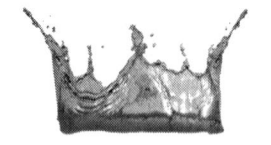

JACE

I barely see Em the next few days, and I hate it.

I miss her. It's plain and simple.

But Coach is also having my ass because of my poor performance lately, and I know he's right. My focus hasn't been the same, and I haven't been taking good care of my body lately either. How could I have?

Nationals should be a walk in the park compared to what's waiting for me next year at the Olympics. But what are the chances of achieving my dream if I fail at this upcoming competition?

I know that if I want to reach my goal of beating the only record that stands between me and being the most adorned Olympic swimmer of all times, I need to get my head back in the game.

Right now.

That means making sure I give my body the rest it needs since that's always played a huge part in my routine, and why I've been capable of pushing myself the way I did all these years.

If that means I get to spend less time with Tanner and Em, then that's just what it needs to be right now. Instead, I'll have to make the time we have together count more, schedule them in my busy calendar like everything else.

I'm sure they'll understand. Plus, I want to make them proud too.

For the first time in my life, I want to make someone else other than my parents proud.

Of course, I'm having this pep talk today of all days.

My dad's birthday. He would have turned sixty.

He's the reason I love the water so much. He's the reason I started swimming.

He's the reason I want to succeed.

I usually spend this day in the pool, and today is no different. It's the one day my coach lets me be, knowing I need to deal with this my way. Work through it.

Chase that relief, that feeling where the pain of losing him so early in my life eases slightly.

The blackness that usually pulls at the edges of my whole being weaker than normal though. The pain that's usually right in the middle of my torso is duller today. For the first time. Ever.

It's all still there but it's fading, and I'm not sure that's a good thing. It scares me.

Instead of the never-ending library of pictures of my dad rotating in my brain, there's now also Tanner. Which causes the pain to shift into a different beast, something unfamiliar yet powerful. The extra loss of my dad never meeting my son. Tanner never meeting his grandpa.

A void that's impossible to fill, no matter how much I try.

A sudden motion in front of me makes me slow down until I come to a stop at the end of the lane.

Hunter, Ryan, and Noah stand in a half circle at the edge of the pool. All in swim trunks and a towel wrapped around their shoulders.

There's a moment of silence between us before Hunter crouches down. "Hey, dude. We thought you might want some competition today."

They all know about my dad and how I normally spend this day, but no one says a word about it.

Ryan takes a step forward, one side of his mouth lifted the slightest bit. "We thought we could show you how it's done right."

Despite my gloomy mood, I chuckle. "You think you got it in you, old man?"

He grins in return, never caring if anyone mentions that he has several years on us, almost ten on Hunter, which in swimmer years basically turns him in to a senior. "I *know* I do."

Noah stays quiet like so often, giving me his signature nod, his expression relaxed.

My friends are here, for *me*. To help me through this tough day.

I swallow back the emotions, looking at each of them for a long moment, my chin raised. "Bring it."

"You've got it."

"Get ready to have your ass handed to you."

"Cocky bastard."

The voices all blend together as they put away their towels and go through their own rituals of getting ready.

Hunter jumps up and down a few times while shaking

his arms, looking like a monkey performing a rain dance more than anything. Ryan clenches and unclenches his fists several times before rolling his neck and clapping his hands.

Noah stretches his body, his long arms extending far above his head, making his reach seem almost unnatural, before he brushes off his shoulders.

I observe the three men for a moment, my friends, the people that know me as well as anyone, even though we all lead busy lives and aren't able to spend a ton of time together.

Hunter gets in my line of vision. "Are you going to get out of there at some point today so we can get started or continue to stare at us like a lovesick puppy?"

Only he gets away with shit like this.

"Fuck you, Hunt."

"Gladly." He extends an arm and holds out his hand, helping me out of the water in one swift move. "Let's do this, you pussies."

Everyone glares at Hunter, but he only laughs. Like I said, only he gets away with shit like this.

We get on the blocks, the tension between us friendly but present, as we get in our positions.

"Ready?" Hunter yells, and we all grunt in response.

My focus is laser-sharp when Hunter gives us the signal with a loud whistle. With my gaze trained ahead of me, I dive into the water, my fingertips entering the liquid body first before my shoulders, torso and legs follow.

I hold my streamline and start kicking right before I lose my momentum. As I near the surface, I take a powerful stroke to propel myself to the top of the water.

My body takes over, completely on autopilot. My flutter

kick moves my body forward, my hands cutting in and out of the water in alternating strokes.

After going almost non-stop all day, my muscles are on fire, but it also feels so damn good to push myself one more time.

This is exactly what I needed, giving me that last push to get my head back in the right place.

I don't know how long we go, losing track of time as my body goes through the familiar motions. But at some point, we all stop, like a well-trained team.

Since no one's there to referee, we all claim to have won.

We swim several laps to cool down. No need to store that excess lactic acid and be sore as hell tomorrow.

When we get out of the water and grab our towels, Hunter's next to me, brushing a hand through his wet hair. "Go grab your stuff, we're going out to eat. I'm starving."

His gaze is on me, his chin slightly lifted as he studies me, waiting for me to decline.

"Okay."

"Okay?" His eyes widen for a moment, and he's unable to keep the hint of surprise out of his voice.

"Yup, let's go." I grab my duffel and head to the showers before anyone else asks questions. I'm glad the guys are here, but I'm not sure I'm ready for a full-on conversation yet.

When I'm showered and changed, I get in my car and pull out my phone.

Jace: Things go okay today with Tanner?

Em: Yes. He had a fun tantrum at the store,

but that's nothing new. And your mom picked him up earlier like we talked about. They were both pretty excited. I think they took half of Tanner's toys with them.

For some reason, today is easier to deal with for my mom than me. Since she knew how hard it would be for me, she offered—or rather insisted—on having Tanner over for a sleepover. She's got a whole room made up for him at her house and they love spending time together, so I thought why not.

I'm still staring at my phone when another message pops up.

Em: You doing okay? I can still cancel my plans for tonight and meet you at your place.

I want to say "Hell, yes," but I can't. She's got plans for tonight, and it's Saturday after all, and I don't want to pull her down with my funky mood either.

Jace: No, you're all good. I'm heading out with the guys to eat.

Em: Oh, okay. That's great. Have fun.

Jace: Thanks. You too.

Just not too much fun, but I don't say that. I have no right to tell her what to do, no matter how much I want to.

And boy, do I want to.

I want to claim her.

Tell everyone she's mine.

A knock at the window makes my gaze snap up. Hunter's peering in my car like a lunatic, and I put my phone away. No point in dwelling over Em right now.

Hunter makes a "let's go" motion with his thumb over his shoulder, and I nod.

Our favorite Italian restaurant is only a short drive away, the chef expecting us after one of the guys called in earlier. We're greeted with big platters of appetizers, and the waiter then advises that our chicken pasta will be done shortly.

Ryan groans. "Damn, this is still some of the best food out there. Harper's probably salivating, knowing I'll take some home for her."

Hunter nods before shoving more tortillas loaded with spinach-artichoke dip in his mouth. "She doing alright?"

Ryan wipes his mouth and nods. "Most of the time, yeah. She's starting to get uncomfortable, but we still have a good two months ahead of us, so she's hanging in there."

Noah puts down his glass. "My sister was always miserable in the last few weeks. She'd bite everyone's head off over nothing."

Ryan groans while Hunter laughs.

"How's Daisy doing?" All heads turn my way, probably because I've been quiet.

Noah lifts one shoulder. "She's doing okay. The divorce has been civil enough I guess, even though my parents are still in shock. Just shows that you never truly know what's going on behind closed doors."

"True." My thoughts immediately flash to Em and her family. Noah's words couldn't have been more true.

Ryan elbows me. "How's Tanner doing? You know we're here to help, right?"

"I know, thanks." How are things with my son? "Things are okay. I definitely thought it would be easier, I can tell you that much, but we manage. I couldn't do it without Em though. Or my mom."

I shake my head and brush my hand over my face. "Actually, I'd be completely fucked without them. Half the time I don't know what the hell I'm doing, but I'm trying."

My friends' eyes are on me, no form of judgement or disapproval in their expression, and I feel lighter. Even though nothing has changed about my situation, it feels good to be honest about it with the guys.

Ryan is the first to speak up. "You've got this. You need help, you call, you hear me?"

I nod, emotion clogging up my throat as the other guys chime in their agreement.

Ryan picks up his fork. "I can't wait to meet him. Harper already got some presents for him."

I chuckle. "She's really getting into this."

He sends me an amused look before stabbing his pasta. "You have no idea."

We finish our meal with companionable talk, and my thoughts keep wandering to Em.

I enjoy my evening with the guys, but I do wish I told her to cancel her plans. I surely wouldn't mind going home and having a repeat of yesterday. To hold her while watching a movie, to fall asleep with her cradled to my chest, and to wake up with her in my arms.

Maybe more.

How could I not wish for that after this morning? To feel her sexy curves was absolute heaven. And even though fondling her boob was a total accident, I definitely don't regret it. She felt perfect in my hands in every possible way, and I want more of that. I want to feel more of *her*, preferably without barriers of clothing between us.

The guys are probably aware I spaced out, and when my mom FaceTimes me for Tanner's bedtime, I use that to excuse myself and make a hasty exit out of the restaurant and into my car.

A smiling Tanner greets me on the screen, my mom's voice right beside him. He waves at me, a timid "Hi" leaving his mouth before he touches his thumb to his forehead to sign Daddy.

"Hey, buddy. Are you having a great time with Grandma?" I sign grandma with my thumb on my chin before pulling it away, trying to sign as many words with him as possible even though he knows most of them by heart.

"You want to tell Daddy that you just took the biggest bubble bath ever?" My mom's voice is excited, and I'm so grateful to have her in my life. The way she's accepted Tanner right away like he's been there all along has made me appreciate her strength even more.

Tanner's eyes go wide as he nods frantically, forming small circles with his hands and letting them *pop* in the air. *Bubbles.*

"A bubble bath? Wow. That sounds like a fun time. And now you're going to bed?"

He nods again before waving, his chubby finger already on the way toward the screen. The brain of a toddler.

My mom laughs. "I didn't know anyone could love pushing that red hang-up button as much as he does."

I snort. "Yeah. I'm lucky I got more than five seconds with him."

Tanner's eyebrows draw together as he frowns, still trying to reach the screen.

Oh boy.

"Okay, Mom. Better hang up before he throws a fit. Let me know if anything's going on."

My mom shifts the phone so she's half on the screen too. "Don't worry about us, I've got this. Try and get some good rest tonight though, okay? I know you've been tired lately."

She has no idea how tired.

"Will do. Thanks, Mom."

"Of course." She turns the camera back to Tanner. "Say bye to Daddy."

Tanner waves, once more back to happy now that the phone call is about to end.

"Bye, Tanner. Be good for Grandma, okay? I'll see you tomorrow. Love you, buddy."

My mom gets in a quick, "Love you, sweetheart," before Tanner's finger pushes the end button.

Leaning my head back, I inhale deeply before starting the car and driving home, feeling lighter than before.

My focus should be completely set on my training, yet I know I want more of Em. I want her in my arms. In my bed.

NINETEEN

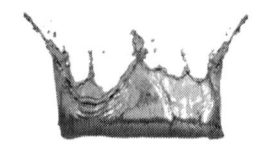

EMILIA

Jace: I'm about to pass out. Did you have a great night?

This man.

My night was incredibly productive, and I finally got some technical difficulties figured out with Brandon that I discovered after our meeting last week.

Whereas I handle the program itself, like coming up with the music lessons and exercises, I'm not tech savvy enough to handle the program. That's where Brandon has been a life saver, ironing it all out to get us exactly where we're at now. Smooth sailing into completion. Or at least as close to it as possible.

I'm beyond thrilled to finally see the end in sight, but I do regret not being able to spend tonight with Jace.

Especially knowing what day it is today for him.

His mom clued me in when I saw her earlier, explaining how down Jace usually is on the birthday of his late father. Which was also one of the reasons she planned this sleepover with Tanner.

He seemed a bit off this morning when I showed up at his place, but then I haven't seen more than a quick "Hello" and "Goodbye" of him when he comes home or leaves the house. He's been training more than usual, making up for the time he lost with Tanner's accident.

But tomorrow is Sunday, and besides a quick trip to the grocery store, I have nothing else planned. Hopefully, that means I'll be able to see Jace on his day off.

I climb into bed, my phone tightly in my hand as I get comfortable and ready to text him back. Giddy about the knowledge that I'm on his mind too.

Em: Get some good rest. I had a great evening, thank you. Hope you did too.

I wait for a moment, and when nothing comes back, I put my phone on my nightstand, lying down on my pillow.

I'm just about to close my eyes and do my current favorite thing—daydream about Jace—when my phone lights up.

Jace: It would have been a lot better had I seen you tonight.

My face flushes, immediately reacting to his words.

Relief rushes through me, because I feel the same.

We don't see a ton of each other, but we make every minute count, our connection growing daily, like vines tightly wrapping around a trellis. Searching for that support, needing that strength from the very beginning to be able to flourish and grow to its full potential.

My fingers hover over the keyboard.

There are so many things I want to say, so many things I want to ask but am afraid of. I don't want to say anything stupid and jeopardize what we have, or rather where it looks like we're headed.

Praying my autocorrect won't wrong me too bad tonight, I sort my thoughts. It's not doing me any good to worry about even more stuff tonight. At least it makes it easier that Jace knows about my dyslexia. The way he accepted it was mind-boggling. It's sad that I'm still surprised when people don't laugh about it or react condescendingly, but old habits die hard.

Em: I told you I could reschedule my plans and come over.

I know for a fact, Brandon was all jumpy to get back to his new girlfriend too. Not that I'm Jace's girlfriend. At least, we haven't talked about it. Maybe I should ask him before this turns into something more.

All I know is that I'm not looking for a hookup. If I was, my roommate would have dates lined up for me every week.

"To get back in the game," she always told me before I started refusing to go on any more dates. Because it's not a game for me. It's also ironic seeing that she and her boyfriend have been together for over a year now. I want that too.

Regardless, Jace would be the last prospect for a hookup anyway, with him being my boss and all.

Jace: I knew you had plans and your project is important to you.

I told him about my music program last week when he walked in on me filming a segment of it in the guest room. He doesn't know anything about the audition but he knows how important the program is to me.

Jace: But maybe tomorrow?

Em: I have to go grocery shopping in the morning, but after that I'm free.

Jace: Want to come over for lunch? I've got dessert covered.

Em: What's for dessert?

Jace: Me

Em: You?

Jace: Yes, me. Who else?

Em: You mean what else?

I'm lost. Was that supposed to be a joke?
I certainly wouldn't mind Jace for dessert.

Jace: No, who. Anyway. I'll cook us something.

Em: You can cook?

Jace: Of course I can cook.

Em: Huh. Interesting.

Jace: Why did you think I couldn't cook?

Em: Maybe because you have the whole fridge stocked with chef-made meals?

Jace: I do.

Jace: So you assumed I couldn't cook?

Em: I guess I did.

Jace: Never judge a book by its cover, ladybug. ;)

I chuckle. Only Jace would come up with such an uncorrelated comparison.

Em: Touché.

Jace: So, what are you up to?

Em: Nothing. I'm in bed.

Jace: Interesting. Me too. What are you wearing?

I burst out laughing, a huge lovesick-teenager perma-grin firmly planted on my face.

Em: Go to sleep, Jace.

Jace: Ouch.

I can't remember the last time I've been this giddy talking to a guy. Even though he's this talented athlete with a laser focus on his career, he also makes me laugh like no one else.

I know, without a doubt, that I could chat with him for hours on end, but he really needs to sleep. Between spending time with Tanner and me, I know his routine has suffered tremendously in the last few weeks. It's written all over his face and in the dark circles under his eyes.

And I want to be there for him too, even if it's as a silent supporter, making sure he gets the rest he needs to function better. Not every support needs to be loud and fierce.

My phone lights up with Jace's picture, and I smile like an idiot when I answer it. "Didn't I tell you to go to sleep?"

"You did." His voice is husky. It's incredibly sexy and does something funny to my insides. "I just wanted to hear your voice before I pass out."

"That's acceptable." I cuddle deeper into my blanket, wishing I was cuddled up with him instead. "You okay?"

"Yeah." He lets out a long breath. "The guys helped."

"I'm glad they did."

"Me too." He pauses. "Hey, Em?"

I doubt I'll ever get over how much I love it when he calls me that. It's *ours*. "Mmm?"

"I miss you." The confession comes out quietly and quickly.

I don't think everyone would have understood his whispered words, but I did.

Tragedies connect people in a way that isn't possible otherwise. The bond is instant and deep, cutting straight through layers that otherwise might never be penetrated or would take a much longer time to work through.

Tanner's incident did this for us.

It's like he got this instant line to my heart, an express line, and boy, is he cashing in.

Now I can only hope there won't be any obstacles in the way to get that bridge between us built more solidly. Even though it's already built, it's still new and fragile and needs to be treated with caution and care.

I'm also a big believer in honesty, which sounds incredibly hypocritical considering I haven't told Jace about the audition yet.

Even though I'm suddenly not as excited about the possibility to move away for the show. Because how would this work out?

"I miss you too." It's easy to say the words back when they're true.

"Lunch tomorrow?"

"Lunch tomorrow." My confirmation fills me with

anticipation of seeing him soon and being able to spend more than just a few minutes with him.

"Sweet dreams, ladybug."

"Sweet dreams, Jace."

With that we hang up, and it doesn't take me long to fall asleep afterward, my heart happy and full.

Sometimes, all it takes is one mistake.

My mistake today was to run to the boutique mall next to the grocery store to get that shea body butter I like so much.

Major error on my part.

I didn't expect to run into my mom when I walked out of the store.

Even worse, she's not alone.

Her *friend* Clara—I use the term friend very loosely when it comes to my family since I'm not sure they're capable of real friendships—is with her, their chins tilted in a way that always makes it seem like they're looking down on you, even when you're taller than them.

Sadly, I don't have enough time to hide, and they spot me right away. Eye contact is made, which makes it impossible to pretend I didn't see them.

"Hey, Mom. Clara." I air-kiss them the way they prefer it, feeling stupid, as always.

"Hello, Emilia." My mother looks pristine in one of her beloved blouse and pantsuit combination.

"Emilia." Clara's voice is just as nasally as I remember it, but I give her a big smile nonetheless.

Not because that's how I was raised—maybe a courteous

smile, yes, but not a real, genuine one—but because that's who I am.

I've always tried to appease my parents, hoping they'd one day look at me with approval in their gazes like they do with my sister. Maybe I could have gotten there had I completely submitted to them, but I'm incapable of it. Instead, I usually did double loads like when I majored in business *and* music. It's exhausting.

I'm exhausted.

My major contributor to our family drama is my occupation, of course. Everyone wants me to join the family business, which would pretty much be the equivalent of a death by boredom to me.

How they cannot understand that I would never fit into their world is beyond me. Not to mention, they don't even seem to *like* me.

Clara's gaze is stuck on my shirt, and I stiffen when I realize what she's looking at. My *Kinder Street* shirt. My dream show. My dream job. I've been in love with that show for as long as I can remember.

Our housekeeper Amy, who doubled as a nanny when I grew up, let me watch it in the kitchen every morning before school when my parents were doing their "important" things.

My mom must have caught on to what Clara's staring at, or it could be the elbow that Clara's jabbing into my mother's side.

Both their noses wrinkle identically, and it's almost comical.

For a moment, I worry she might bring up our quick dinner departure, but then I remember it ended with my sister—who still hasn't said a peep after telling me to mind my own business—and her cheating dick of a husband, and I know she would never air that dirty laundry in front of her friend.

I expected my mom to be on my case for our rude departure and the fact that she wasn't impressed with Jace. Possibly some other insults thrown in for good measure. Usually, she doesn't waste a chance to criticize me, but there's been . . . nothing more. Clearly, I still don't rate on their radar. *Why do I care?*

My mom sighs heavily, in that exaggerated way she likes to do so often when dealing with me and points at my shirt. "Do you have to wear shirts like this in public? Don't you find that rather inappropriate for your age?"

"Why?" I swallow the acid burning in my throat at the tone she's using with me. "You know I love that show. It's got great content and is incredibly reputable in the industry."

"Do you work there?" Clara's voice reaches new levels of nasality.

My mom waves her away. "Oh please, Clara, don't be ridiculous. Emilia's done playing childish games after finally finishing that job at that other obnoxious kids' show. She's going to get a *real* job now."

Clara hangs on to my mother's words and nods enthusiastically before they both turn their gazes back on me. Like I'm a doll they can play with as they please.

I feel like a million stadium lights are directed my way. I start sweating, and the weight of this whole situation, the words my mother just uttered, pushes down on me with such a force, I feel dizzy.

Especially since I finally received my invitation to audition for *Kinder Street* this morning. I'd checked my email one more time before I left the house in a blissful bubble, now one step closer to my dream job, just to have these two trample on my joy like it's nothing.

"Isn't that so, Emilia?" My mother's brow is raised as much as her cosmetic procedures allow. Her gaze is impatient, like she's trying to talk to a child that doesn't understand what she's saying.

I continue to stare at her, trying to focus on my breathing before I lose my shit. I will not break down in front of these two and give them even more ammunition.

"I've got to go." The voice that comes out of my mouth sounds far away, but I'm relieved to hear that the words sound strong and confident, not weak and crushed like I feel on the inside.

I turn on my heel and walk as fast as my feet can carry me without breaking into a sprint, my sandals slapping against the polished mall floors.

When I'm finally in the confines of my car—thank goodness I didn't come on my moped today—I have to focus on my breaths for several minutes before I'm calm enough to start the car and get out of here.

With one goal in mind.

Jace.

Because I can't think about what just happened or it will ruin my time with him.

Instead, I want to forget.

I want a distraction.

And what better distraction is there than a six-foot-four, blue-eyed hottie whose smile is always on my mind?

TWENTY

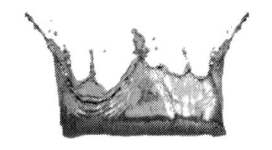

JACE

I'm just getting the lasagna out of the oven when a car door slams outside.

Perfect timing.

After placing the baking form on the stove, I take off the oven mittens, and make my way to the door.

A thrill of anticipation tickles my neck as I swing the door wide open, staring straight into Em's beautiful eyes.

But something's off. They're duller than when I last saw her. She's smiling at me, but the spark never makes it to her eyes.

Taking her by the hand, I pull her inside. "What's going on?"

Her eyes widen for a brief moment before she shakes her head. "It's nothing."

Which means something.

"Nothing?"

Another shake of her head. "I don't want to talk or even think about it. I want to forget."

"You want to forget?" Apparently, I'm just going to

repeat everything like a damn parrot, my brain busy trying to figure out what could have happened that's made her so distraught. It must have been bad enough, or big enough, that she doesn't want to tell me.

"Yes." Something changes in her expression as she takes a step toward me. "Make me forget, Jace. Please."

With my back at the door, I have no place to go when she closes the distance between us, not that I really want to.

A part of me rebels inside, demanding to know what happened to her before we take this any further.

But that part is quickly shoved away when her body presses against mine and her arms brush up my chest and loop around my neck.

I'm still a little dumbfounded when she goes up on her toes. A second later, her mouth crashes on mine.

Fuck, yes.

Her lips are soft and warm, and it only takes me a moment before instinct takes over. My arms move around her body, one hand pressing into her lower back to pull her closer, the other circling around her neck, my fingertips gently massaging her silky skin.

Her mouth opens on a whimper, and I don't need another invitation. I dive in, ready to explore. Ready to claim what I've wanted for so long. I suck on her tongue and bite her lip, and she meets me stroke for stroke, nib for nib. If I had to guess, I'd say she's been as desperate for this as I am.

The sensation, the pure lust, is so overwhelming that I don't even notice her hands have left my neck and instead found their way under my shirt until she lightly scrapes her fingernails across my stomach.

Shit.

My hard-on strains behind the fly of my jeans, painfully so, and I already regret putting them on in the first place.

Even though it goes against everything I want right now, we need to slow this down, or I'm going to take her right here on the floor.

Her hands on me, especially on my bare skin, it's too much, more than my body can take.

But I'm selfish and can't stop yet. I'm not even close to being done with her.

Taking things in my hands, literally, I pull her fingers away from my skin and spin us around, pressing her back into the door, with her arms pinned by her sides.

Her breathing is heavy, her chest rising and falling against my own as I peer down at her. With her lust-filled eyes, and flushed cheeks, she's even more beautiful.

So damn hot.

Neither one of us says a word, and when I bend toward her, she tilts her head back eagerly, those swollen lips reaching for me until they get what they want.

This time, I try to turn it down a notch, keeping it slow and steady. Exploratory, deep, and sensual.

If her moans and whimpering noises are anything to go by, she's enjoying it too. I let go of her hands, silently hoping she'll behave this time.

A minute later, they're on my ass, and I can't help myself and chuckle.

Pulling back, I look down at her. "You've got some wandering hands there, ladybug."

"Sorry." She gives me a sheepish look, and I take her cheeks into my hands, cupping the contours of her gorgeous face.

"So beautiful." I don't give her a chance to say anything because I'm already busy devouring her mouth again.

When she pulls my bottom lip into her mouth and gently nibbles on it, I almost throw my earlier resolve out the window.

Who says I can't have sex right here on the floor?

I groan, my cock pushing unhappily against the back of my fly.

When she whispers a demanding "Touch me" against my mouth, I know I either have to pull the brake right now or there will be no going back from this.

After one small taste, I know she's like a drug to me. She's already infiltrated my system, potent but so damn good. This is one addiction I can sign up for, one I want every damn day for the rest of my life.

Because this woman is worth it.

She might be a little odd and crazy, but I've come to like her odd and crazy. A lot. I've been craving her so badly that I *have* to look at her when she's in the same room as me. She's like a rare natural phenomenon—impossible to ignore, absolutely breathtaking, and one of a kind.

And . . . I can't do this with her right now.

As much as I want this—and shit, I want to bury myself deep within her—this isn't like her. I have no doubt she can turn into a sex kitten like this, but not today. Not the way she attacked me when I opened the door.

Make me forget, Jace.

Her whispered words from earlier slam into me like a sledgehammer, and I want to bang my head into the wall. I'm such an asshole.

There was obviously something wrong, something

happened, and I wasn't even able to turn off my dick for two seconds to figure it out first. Taking her excuse with merely a shoulder shrug.

That realization pushes through the lust fog, and I pull back.

I lean my forehead against hers, not ready to break all contact with her. Our labored breathing is the only sound in the house, and I close my eyes, trying to override my body's wants and needs with doing the right thing.

Reaching down, I take one of her hands and interlace my fingers with hers before straightening.

"Let's go eat." I ignore her shocked expression and pull her with me to the kitchen.

While she's still too stunned to say a word, I hand her a plate and start dishing out the lasagna. After placing a fork on both of our plates, I grab mine with one hand and use the other to gently push her to the table.

We're quiet as we eat, and Em is doing her best to avoid my gaze. Using her hair as a shield, she hides most of her face from me, but I still notice the glances she throws my way when she thinks I'm not looking.

Whenever I catch one, her face flushes, color rising in those delectable cheeks that I want to hold in my hands, preferably while kissing her.

Let's face it, I might be sitting here, casual as fuck, eating my lasagna.

But on the inside, I'm still hung up on that kiss.

Because it was one of the hottest kisses of my life. I'm not sure exactly why, but maybe it's because it was with Em, my slightly crazy nanny. And of all things, she was initiating it too, practically jumping me.

I'm ready for round two, and then some.

Time to push though, because I need to figure out what happened, what caused such a reaction in her.

"So, you want to tell me what happened before you got here?"

Her fork stops mid-air to her mouth and she grimaces. "Do we have to talk about it?"

The sigh she releases is heavy and filled with discomfort.

I stay quiet and give her time.

Just when I think she might not answer, she places her fork on the plate and leans back in her chair, fidgeting and squirming. "I ran into my mom."

I grunt, not trusting myself to refrain from saying something I might regret.

"She was with a friend. And let's just say, the conversation didn't go very well." She blows out a puff of air, the hair near her face lifting from the airflow.

"I'm sorry." I swallow everything else I want to say, because it's easy to tell by her slouched figure and the sad expression on her face how much this impacted her.

Family can be a real bitch sometimes.

I've gotten lucky in that department, but growing up, I saw enough times that family does not automatically equal a solid support system. It also doesn't equal respect, kindness, or love. And it's hard to let go of that ideal. It's written all over Em's face.

But there will be a breaking point when everyone hits

their personal rock bottom depending on how much they can or want to take. Maybe she's reached that today.

Secretly, I hope she did, because she deserves so much more than what she gets from her family. She deserves loyalty, compassion, and affection thrown her way en masse, just like she gives it to others.

"They said some things about my shirt."

"Your shirt?"

"Yeah." She sits up straight and pulls on the bottom of her shirt to smoothen out the bumps and wrinkles so the writing is easier to see.

"*Kinder Street*? Isn't that the show you and Tanner love to watch?" Why on earth would they have something against a kids' show? Even though, from the way they seem to handle everything else, they'd have something against others breathing the same air as them.

I'd never felt so judged in my life. Admittedly, I hung around a lot of athletes and athlete's families, so my swimming profession has never been frowned upon. But to judge me presuming I didn't earn a lot? It truly was ridiculous and laughable.

It wasn't until I noticed the . . . shame and humiliation that crossed Em's face that I grew angry. At that point, I knew I had to get her out of there. Did her mother ream her out about our departure?

"My mom's friend asked if I worked at *Kinder Street*, and they made fun of it, saying that it's not a job for a grown-up and that I was going to get a *real* job soon."

I'm quiet, clenching and unclenching my fists under the table.

"It's my dream, you know? To work there. It always has been." Her voice is so quiet, I can barely make out the words.

I know you should respect your elders, but what a bunch of assholes. Those are the kind of people that kick you when you're already down. There's no excuse for that behavior. People like that get off hurting others. Putting them down, crushing their dreams, making them feel like less so they can feel like more. Pathetic.

Pushing back my chair, I get up and crouch down beside Em. "I'm so sorry. They don't deserve you. They don't see what's right in front of their eyes, and it's their loss." She gazes down at me, her eyes shimmering. "You're beautiful, funny, and so damn talented, and you have a heart of gold. They're blind and not worthy of it."

I push some of her hair behind her ear before cupping her cheeks. "This is your family, so it might not be any of my business, but maybe it's time to put your own happiness first, not theirs. If it's your dream to be part of that show, then do it. Fucking chase that dream like the devil's right on your heels because *you* deserve it. You deserve the world."

Then, since I'm unable to control myself where she's concerned, I lean in and kiss her.

A soft press of my lips to hers, reveling in the nearness this contact brings me.

If Em's relieved sigh is anything to go by, it means just as much to her.

For now, it's enough. More than enough.

It's everything I want and need, even though the burning need for her is growing inside of me, ready to be unleashed when she's ready.

TWENTY-ONE

EMILIA

Jace is all I see.

Jace is all I hear.

Jace is all I taste.

His handsome face, his sweet words, his lips.

His kindness and fierce speech have caused warmth to spread through my chest at a rapid speed, engulfing me in a blanket of comfort, soothing my soul.

It hasn't erased the run-in with my mom and all the million thoughts that have been racing through my head ever since, but it has eased the sting.

Being with Jace does that. It makes me feel safe and protected, like no one can hurt me when I'm with him.

"Hey." His hands are still on my face, cupping my jaw.

I already miss his lips on mine.

"Hey." I smile at him, sure he can see the timidity in it, but there's no point in hiding it.

He leans in and touches his lips to mine once more. "I love your mouth."

"Thank you."

I try to tilt my head to escape his intense gaze but there's no going anywhere with his hold on me.

"Where did my ferocious ladybug go that attacked me the second she stepped foot into the house?"

Heat travels from my chest to my cheeks, and I want to hide from Jace. Badly. But since I can't, I go with the truth. "I'm so embarrassed. I've never done anything like that before."

He chuckles and grabs my hand to pull me up. We walk to the couch and sit down. Close to each other, *really* close. I like it.

"You can jump me like that anytime you want. No questions asked. No complaints uttered. Trust me." He winks at me, he freaking *winks* at me, and I'm positive there's a firework going off behind my ribcage.

His eyes roam over me, like they're taking in every single inch of me, and he doesn't try to hide it. My body comes alive, firing up in all the right places at his open perusal.

I like his eyes on me. He makes me feel wanted . . . like I'm enough.

It's simple, yet powerful.

Without another thought, I close the distance between us and kiss him.

My fingers ache with the need to touch, to feel him, to explore. I want more, I need more of *everything*. The way this exciting hum circulates through my blood, warming me from the inside out, or the way my desire burns a hotspot in the pit of my belly.

It's all-consuming, addictive.

And he tastes like absolute perfection.

His mouth is smooth and warm, his lips and tongue

talented as they mold perfectly together with mine, exploring new corners, and re-learning old ones.

My heart pounds hard, but I welcome the sensation. It's been so long since I've felt this elated, this excited about anything, least of all a man. Maybe I've never felt this passionate before.

I've certainly never been the aggressor, even though I think Jace is only humoring me, quickly showing me who's really in control without suppressing my wants and needs.

His hands leave my hair and move to my waist. He grips me, and in one swift move, lifts me off the couch and over on his lap so I straddle him.

Well, who would have thought? If that wasn't hot as hell, I don't know what is.

With his hands behind me, he kneads my butt, gently massaging my flesh through my jeans, and I've officially gone off the rails.

Why does something so simple feel so good, even a little naughty?

Maybe it's because I can feel his erection pressing against my center every time he squeezes, every delicious time he pushes me the slightest bit toward him.

I hold back a moan and bite my lip instead.

With his gaze trained on my face, Jace doesn't miss it and smirks. "You like that?"

This time, a tiny whimper escapes my mouth as the contact is stronger, the responding buzz at my core more intense. I can't think straight when he sets off these sparks everywhere inside my body. "Kiss me."

It comes out as a half-stutter, and I couldn't care less. He drives me wild, and it's too much work to pretend otherwise.

Thankfully, Jace doesn't need to be asked twice. He pulls me as close to him as possible before pushing one hand into my hair, his fingertips gently pressing into my neck and scalp.

He nips on my bottom lip, gently sucking it into his mouth before tracing his tongue over it. He leans back into the cushions and takes me down with him, his hard length aligned with me so perfectly, I almost see stars.

I gasp in Jace's mouth and he changes the angle, diving in deeper, pushing up with his hips in a rhythm so hypnotic I can't help myself and rock against him. Heat travels over my skin, setting it afire everywhere we touch, while scorching flames threaten to burn me up from inside.

The kisses get more out of control, the rocking quicker as our moans and groans blend together in the air, creating their own sound of pleasure, as I'm racing toward something I'm not sure I'm ready for.

But I don't get a chance to even think about that as I fall over the edge, an orgasm ripping through me so strong that Jace has to hold me up by the arms to prevent me from falling off his lap like a limp noodle.

"So fucking sexy." Jace's mumbled words are a blur before he kisses me again.

When he lifts me off his lap, I want to protest at first, but then he lies both of us down on the cushions, our limbs entangled as he brushes the hair out of my face.

We stare at each other like it's the first time we catch sight of the other one.

It's a mix of wonder, fascination, and undeniable attraction that runs deep in my veins, humming steadily and growing by the second.

I'm lost in him, a free-falling sensation taking over my

body, and I hope like hell Jace will be on the other side to catch me.

We both freeze when the front door opens and two sets of footsteps enter a few seconds later, reaching the living room before either one of us can react.

"Oh . . . ooooooh." Patricia's voice doesn't do a thing to hide her surprise. "Tanner, no, come here. Daddy and Millie are sleeping."

While she whispers, Tanner's babbling in all his loud toddler glory.

"Yes, sleeping. Let's get your ball and go to the park. Come on."

He babbles some more but his footsteps are retreating, and after a moment the front door shuts with a loud *click*.

I cover my face with my hands and lean in to Jace's chest. How embarrassing.

"Well, that was . . . something." Jace chuckles, a deep rumble vibrating through his body.

"This is so bad." I shake my head as much as my current position allows.

"No, it's not." His hand brushes over my hair. Front to back, front to back. It's soothing, and I cherish the contact. "You know my mom. She's cool."

He's right. She is cool. Very laid-back and likes to look at the good side of things. This won't be too bad, right?

"One thing's for sure, between you and your mom, I've had my embarrassment fill for today. Or probably the whole week. First, I jump you like a crazy person, and then your mom practically catches us red-handed." I peek at him through my fingers.

With a shake of his head, he goes for my hands, gently

prying off one finger after the other. "We already talked about you jumping me. It was the hottest thing, the absolute highlight of my life. And about my mom, I don't mind if she knows about us. Do you?"

That gets my attention. "Us?"

"Yes, Em. Us. You and me." He tilts his head to the side, studying me. "If it hasn't been obvious, I like you, and I'd like to see where this is going. Unless that's not what you want."

I push myself up on my elbows to see him better. "No, no. I mean yes, I'd like that too. A lot."

"Yeah?"

"Yeah." My cheeks are warm as he pulls me to him.

His lips find mine but this time he keeps it short. His warm touch lingers long after he pulled back, and I resist the urge to touch my lips to chase the lingering buzz.

Grinning at me, he touches the tip of my nose with his finger. "Want to go to the park?"

"I thought you'd never ask."

Thankfully, the park is only a few minutes away, or I'd feel even worse about sending Patricia scrambling off to it. Jace and I wear identical grins when we hear Tanner's happy squeal far before we can see him.

A few steps later and we round the corner to the park that's not much more than a playground with a small patch of grass next to it. In short, a dream come true for Tanner. It's also only a few minutes away from the university where Patricia works, and sometimes she meets us here when her schedule allows it. Or she drops by the house. She's been a wonderful grandma to Tanner, affectionate and loving.

She's at the top of the tall slide with Tanner on her lap.

When she sees us, she points her finger in our direction to get Tanner's attention.

He squeals again and waves, a big grin sporting his face.

Patricia grins too, her gaze flickering between Jace and me. At our hands. *We're holding hands.* Why on earth are we holding hands? Jace reached out for me when we left his house, and I took his without a second thought. It was so natural and felt good. I think my head was still in the clouds.

As inconspicuous as possible, I pull my hand out of Jace's and walk to the bottom of the slide.

"Are you going down the slide with Grandma? Let's see it."

Tanner's smile gets even bigger when Patricia tightens her grip on him with one arm and pushes off the top with the other. They both squeal as they slide down, slowing as the bottom levels out.

"Good job. Was that fun?" I grab Tanner so it's easier for Patricia to get off the slide.

Jace is next to me and takes Tanner from me to swing him around.

I stare at them as Patricia comes up next to me. "Looks like you guys had a great lunch?"

She says it like a question, and my cheeks are blazing hot in less than two seconds.

Ground, open up already please.

"Mmm, yes. The lasagna was delicious." Feigning innocence. Worth a try.

Patricia chuckles. So much about that. "I'm glad you enjoyed his cooking."

Is she trying to get at something? I'm not sure how much hotter my face can get before it explodes.

"He's a good guy." Patricia's eyes are on her two boys, but the words are clearly for me. "Some days I can't believe what an amazing man he's become. When my husband . . . when his dad passed away, I didn't know how to continue. But I had to be strong for Jace, I had to keep going for him, and there isn't a day where he doesn't make me proud."

The thought of having someone pass away who meant so much is almost impossible for me to imagine.

I touch Patricia's shoulder, giving it a gentle squeeze. "You did an amazing job raising him."

She puts her hand over mine, patting it a few times. "I'm so glad we found you, Millie. I can't imagine someone better than you."

The warmth flooding my chest is almost too much too bear.

How have I gotten this lucky to not only have an adorable boy and his amazing dad in my life, but also someone as wonderful as Patricia?

Nicole stands in the entryway of our house when I make it back home several hours later.

She greets me with a big smirk, her black curls gently framing her face. "Hey, roomie. I feel like I haven't seen you in forever."

Putting my keys in the bowl on the side table, I look at the duffel by her feet. "That's probably because it has been forever." I nod my chin to the floor. "Another round of one-of-us-is-coming-while-the-other-one-is-leaving?"

"I'm afraid so. Justin will be here in a minute." She looks

at the phone in her hand. "I thought you'd be back earlier so we could catch up."

Her voice is quiet, her smile a little less happy, and a sense of guilt washes over me. "I'm sorry. I've been a terrible friend. Patricia came back earlier than expected with Tanner, so we spent some time together at the park."

She shakes her head and holds up a hand. "No, don't apologize. I've barely been around either."

"That means things are still going well with Justin though, right? That's good."

The second I mention her boyfriend's name, the radiant smile is back full force. "They really are. I think he might be it, Millie."

A weight settles in my chest, and I swallow before speaking. "I'm so happy for you, Nic. Justin's a good guy, and you guys make an adorable couple."

"Thank you." She averts her gaze, looking at her feet. Something very untypical of her.

"What is it?" I take a step closer. "Everything okay?"

Her eyes snap back to mine, the smile on her face timid. "Yes, yes. But about Justin . . . He asked me to move in with him."

"That's awesome." I rush forward and hug her. "Unless that's not what you want, of course, but I thought you might."

"No, I do. Gosh, I really do." Her brown eyes shine with excitement.

"So what's the problem then?"

"Well, that would mean I'd have to, you know, move out."

Ah. It all clicks in place. "Oh, stop it. You're worried about me? I'd never stand in the way of this, you know that, right?"

"I know. I wasn't worried about that."

"Well, what is it then?" Time to get to the point of this.

"There's obviously the money situation, even though I'd pay my portion for the rest of our lease or until you find someone new. But if I move out, you'll be all alone, Millie. I don't want that."

Oh man. The backs of my eyes burn as I blink a few times. "Nic, stop being silly. I'll be fine. Look how busy I've been. I won't even have time to feel lonely."

"You have been rather busy. Spending most of your free time with your *boss*."

The implication is easy to hear, and I can't hold back my smile, my thoughts immediately going to what said boss and I just did several hours ago.

When I lose the fight with my body, and my cheeks turn hot, Nicole points her finger at me, a triumphant smile gracing her face.

"Ha. I told you. You're totally into him. When did this happen?"

"Just today." I mumble the words but know she heard them when she chuckles.

"He's gorgeous, Millie. And I'm not surprised he's into you."

"Really? But I'm . . . me, and he's—"

"Smart."

I smile. "I've missed you, Nicole."

"Oh hon. I've missed you too. So, you two are officially a thing?"

I nod. "He said he wants to see where this thing with us leads."

Nicole tilts her head to the side and reaches out to gently squeeze my arm. "That sounds very promising. As long as you're happy, and he treats you well, I'm thrilled for you. And after what happened at your parents', he sounds exactly like that. You deserve someone good in your life. Someone who puts you first and helps you achieve your dreams and goals."

Her words hit me right in the chest, my mind immediately reminding me of Jace's words.

Chase that dream like the devil's right on your heels because you deserve it. You deserve the world.

"I got the invitation for the audition."

Nicole's eyes go wide. "You did? *Yes.* I'm so happy you did. I knew they'd invite you, because you're absolutely perfect for the job. They'd be stupid not to take you."

Her words wash over me, cementing my resolve of doing this. I'm going to audition for *Kinder Street*. I'm *really* going to do it.

Nicole's phone vibrates in her hand. "Justin's here."

"Well, go already. Have fun."

"You too. I'm glad we got a minute to catch up. Let's get together soon, okay?" She gives me a hug, squeezing the life out of me for a moment. "Love you, Millie. I'm so happy things are going well for you. You deserve it."

"Love you too, Nic. Thank you. I'm super happy for you too."

I watch my best friend wave one more time before picking up her bag to meet with her boyfriend. The boyfriend she's going to move in with and possibly spend the rest of her life with.

And I'm happy for her, I really am.

The dull ache in my chest is there because I just realized I really want that too.

I want it all.

I want my dream job *and* my dream guy.

Is that too much to ask?

TWENTY-TWO

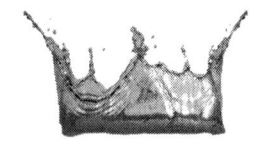

JACE

SWIMMING. TANNER. EM.

That's what my life has come down to.

The guys are giving me shit for having missed another Sunday with them, but I don't care.

My lunch and make-out sessions with Em were worth it. *Way* worth it.

And I can't wait for the next round.

Even though I'm training less due to my swimming taper, I've been busier than usual this week. Getting some extra relaxation sessions in, talking to Coach. Giving my body time to collect the energy it needs for the upcoming competition.

Despite everything, I feel like it has all just piled up, and I've barely seen Tanner when I get home, let alone spend time with Em.

All I want to do when my work day is finally done is go to sleep.

I'm still in the first phase of my taper where I feel sluggish. The accumulated fatigue is taking its sweet time to disappear despite me getting more rest. But I have to push through it so I can perform better at Nationals next week.

Tonight has been an extra late night, and the house is almost dark except for the stove light in the kitchen and the soft glow coming from Tanner's bedroom.

After putting my things on the kitchen counter, I make my way over to his room, stopping in the doorway.

Em is sitting in the oversized rocking chair in the corner of the room with Tanner on her chest. From the looks of it, they're both passed out.

Seeing them like this does something to me. They both entered my life at the same time, a double-deal that has changed my life drastically. It's hard to remember how it was when it was just me. Looking back now, it seems . . . empty.

Sure, my life has turned into a crazy show, my house now one big kid's showcase with drawings on the fridge, crayons and colored paper on the table, and toys wherever you look. But just like the objects have taken up space in the house, Tanner has taken up space in my heart I wasn't even aware of.

Add Em to the mix, and my heart doesn't know what to do with itself anymore. I wasn't lying when I told her I wanted to see where things are going with us. I'm not sure yet what this is between us, but I definitely want to explore it. Badly.

Even though I'm still not one hundred percent sure how all of this is supposed to work out. Or whether I'm stupid for even considering this right now. I need to focus on my job. Do I actually have anything left over for Em?

If my life was busy before these two entered, I'm in dire need of a clone or two by now. There just aren't enough hours in the day to give each area the proper attention it deserves.

Or at least that's what it seems like at this point.

I shift my weight on my other foot, and the floorboard underneath me creaks.

Crap.

I hold back a groan when Em moves her head, her eyes slowly opening. She blinks several times, her eyes still unfocused as she looks around. When her gaze settles on me, the corners of her mouth lift in to a small smile.

That's all it takes for my worries to disappear into thin air. At least, momentarily.

After adjusting her grip on Tanner, she stands up with him in her arms, and I take a few steps, meeting her by the crib. Em gives me a chance to kiss his forehead gently before she puts him in his bed and we leave the room with whispered "Good Nights" and "I love yous."

We quietly make our way to the dark living room, the dim light in the kitchen still the only light source. Em plops down on the couch, and I follow her wordlessly as she picks up the monitor from the coffee table to turn it on.

After checking the screen, and adjusting the volume, she places it on the table and leans back.

Straight into my waiting arms. "Hey."

She curls up sideways and snuggles into my chest. "I can't believe I dozed off. Tanner didn't want to go to sleep and kept crying. He's been extra clingy all day and chewing on his fingers, so I think he might be teething."

"You think he's okay?"

Her head moves up and down on my chest. "I think so. If

he's really bothered, we can give him something for the pain. At least, these are the last molars."

I have absolutely no clue about teething, so I nod. I didn't even know he doesn't have them all yet. Thank goodness, these are the last ones.

One of her hands is on my chest, softly grasping my shirt. I wonder if she's noticing my quickening heartbeat whenever she's around. Because I definitely do. To be fair though, that's not the only body part that reacts to her. Ever since she jumped me like a sex kitten last weekend, I've felt like a lovesick teenager around her, instant boner and all.

I shouldn't even be thinking about any of that right now.

Leaning my chin on her head, I kiss her head. "What about you? Are you okay?"

A loud yawn escapes her mouth. "Yeah. Just haven't been sleeping very well."

That gets my attention. "Because of what happened with Tanner last week?"

She tenses in my arms before pushing herself up on my chest, her gorgeous eyes shimmering in the near darkness.

"Do you have nightmares too?" Her words are so quiet, I can barely hear them.

But I do and immediately nod.

I haven't told anyone, but I've been having them almost every night since the accident.

Em squeezes her eyes shut for a moment before staring at me again. "I hate them. Every time I wake up, I think I might have a heart attack." Her voice can't mask the shakiness, and I know exactly how she feels.

"Same."

She exhales loudly before lying back on my chest,

holding on to me tighter than before. "I really hope they go away soon."

Holding her close to me, she feels like the one constant in my life that centers me right now. The one thing that allows me to be me. The person I can admit my weaknesses to without feeling less of a person. Not only does she get me, she's going through it too.

Lowering my head to hers, I press my mouth to her warm head once more. "I don't know if I'll ever be able to forget that day. The way he was . . . just . . . you know, lying there. With his eyes open, staring at the ceiling. And no life in him. Shit."

I squeeze my eyes shut and brush my hand over my face, trying to force the paralyzing pictures out of my mind.

Em sits up again. "I don't think we'll ever forget that day, but I hope it'll get easier to deal with it. We just have to make as many good memories as it takes to replace that bad one."

Brushing some hair from her face, I hold on to her cheek, caressing the soft skin with my thumb. "I like that idea."

"Me too."

Her words barely register as we stare at each other, the quiet confessions lightening the weight on my chest. Em unwillingly helps—providing the perfect distraction—as she pulls her bottom lip into her mouth before popping that luscious lip back out, something I'd very much like to do myself.

"Do you have anything going on tonight?" My brain's on autopilot, and I barely keep track of the conversation.

"I don't." Em watches me, her piercing gaze all-knowing. "Why? Do you?"

"I do now."

Her eyes widen, but I don't give her chance to react. I

close the distance between us and capture her mouth with mine, something I've wanted to do ever since I set eyes on her tonight.

Even when I don't see her, I *think* about her. About kissing her. And so much more. I catch myself daydreaming about her on a regular basis, the need to touch her, to feel her, consuming not just my body but also my mind.

Imagining what she looks like under me, what she looks like when I'm deep inside her has been one of my favorite pastimes this last week, whether I wanted it or not. My mind obviously has a thing for her and so does my body, so who am I to protest?

She leans against me, pressing her breasts to my side, her soft hands circling my neck to gently scrape along my hairline.

"Shit, that feels good." Her need to be close to me fuels me, urging my body to want more. To do more. To take more. "Stay the night with me."

I don't ask her because I don't want her to say no. I need this. I need *her*.

Even though I clearly want more from her than what we're doing right now, I'm also hopeful to get a better night's sleep with her here. Even if that wasn't the case, it would still be nice to have one another in case the night doesn't go as well.

She pulls back and tilts her head. "Okay."

"Yeah?" I can't keep the smug smile at bay. The ease with which she just agreed, not a single flash of doubt on her face, feels damn good. It shows me she's in this as deeply as I am.

Em's hand flies up to her face when a yawn overtakes it, and I chuckle.

"Come on, ladybug, let's get you to bed. Looks like you need some good sleep too."

After texting her roommate, she grabs her things from "her" room—she brought over a bunch of things after the incident with Tanner, just in case—and gets ready while I do the same.

I sit on the edge of the bed in a pair of pajama pants when she comes out of the bathroom, wearing a polka-dot tank top and sleep shorts.

She stops when she sees me, her eyes taking me in. And I let her. Her gaze feel good on me, and if the harsh swallow and the wide eyes are any indication, she likes what she sees.

Suppressing a chuckle, I crook my finger at her to get her attention. "Come here, Em."

I need another taste of her.

Now.

Tomorrow.

For as long as I can.

TWENTY-THREE

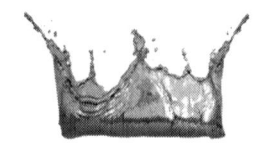

EMILIA

If it wasn't for my heart beating wildly in my chest, I might have thought I'd died. Jace is casually leaning against the bottom of his king-sized bed, his feet crossed at the ankles. And he's waiting for *me*.

In only his pajama bottoms.

Nothing else.

So simple, yet so incredibly hot.

Because holy moly, that body.

Maybe I've seen his body before when I watched a few videos of his races online. Maybe . . . Okay, I totally have. There was no way I couldn't look him up. Watching that tall, lean body do its magic is something else. Especially when he's only clad in a tight swimsuit.

Those videos are also the reason I know exactly what I want to see up close right now.

"Turn around for me, Jace." No clue where the confidence in my voice comes from, but Jace brings that out in me, especially in these moments.

It's a new feeling for me—contrary to my more passive

role in previous relationships—but I love it. It makes me feel strong and powerful, and oddly enough, desired. Because he clearly enjoys it.

"Yes, ma'am." The smirk on his face is sexy as hell, spurring me on even more, casting aside the tiredness that was clinging to the edges of my whole body.

He pushes off the bed but doesn't come closer. Taking his sweet time, he spins around in a slow circle, and I'm absolutely mesmerized. His body is a work of art, his skin tightly stretched over hard muscles that turn him into the beast he is in the water. Honed to perfection.

Once he's done with his spin, he looks at me with raised brows. The ball is back in my court, and I plan to play. And I'm definitely in it to win it.

My body buzzes with anticipation, wanting to touch him, wanting to take a closer look.

When I reach him, I lift my hand to trail my fingers up his left arm, stopping to trace the ink on his biceps.

What is it about arrow tattoos that makes them so damn sexy?

As if he knows where my thoughts are going, he flexes his muscles, and I can't help myself and give it a squeeze. I gaze up at him before continuing and halt at the expression in his eyes.

I've never understood what a smoldering look was because I've never had one directed at me. But goodness, this is it. His sole focus is on me, his eyes tracking my every movement. It's intense, and I've never seen anything sexier in my life.

My chest moves rapidly in response, my breasts feeling heavy and achy against the cotton of my tank.

Blinking out of the trance he's put me under, I smile at him before taking a step around him, my fingers moving up his arm and over his shoulder until I stare right between his shoulder blades.

The wave tattoo that adorns his skin is absolutely gorgeous, looking so real, the break of the water and the falling water drops at the peak of it so authentic, I almost expect to feel wetness on my fingers when I make contact.

Unable to help myself, I lean forward and press a gentle kiss to his skin, eliciting a shiver from Jace. Apart from that, he stays frozen in spot, gifting me this moment of unexpected intimacy.

"I got that on the morning of my eighteenth birthday. Got out of bed and went straight to the tattoo shop. My dad and I used to go the ocean whenever we could. It calmed us, helped us bond." The whispered words hang between us, his rib cage expanding and contracting under my touch.

"He was my biggest cheerleader, coming to every swim meet with me, getting up early to drive me to practice. Ever the optimist, he called every competition a new chance, and we started calling it fresh meet as a joke. Whatever I needed, he was there for me."

Closing my eyes, I slide my hands around his midsection and place my head on his warm skin. "I'm so sorry, Jace. It must have been hard to lose him. I can't even imagine."

"I miss him, you know? I *still* miss him." His voice is shaky, and my hands move with his deep breaths. The pain in his voice . . . "My mom's been pretty awesome, stepping up and turning into my number-one fan on steroids. Even though she's gone a bit overboard at times, I've always appreciated it."

"I'm sure she knows." I don't dare move, unsure if the only reason he's comfortable sharing this with me is because he can't see me. It's almost like confessing something in the dark. It's easier when you don't have to see the other person's reaction.

Some people might be able to control their facial features to hide their reaction, but it's pretty much impossible to hide it in your gaze. But there's safety in the darkness.

After a long moment of silence, I lift my head, pressing another kiss to the wave as he covers one of my hands with his and gently squeezes. Taking a step to the side, I pepper a trail of kisses to his right shoulder and around his arm to his chest, staring at his last tattoo.

Sink or swim in typewriter font right under his ribcage.

The words resonate with me on a deeper level, and I touch it with shaky fingers.

My family immediately comes to mind and the feeling of drowning, of being unable to breathe. The constant struggle of growing up in a household filled with unreachable expectations and conditional love.

And then it hits me. I've been swimming against a current I have no power of ever conquering when it comes to gaining their approval. My latest run-in with my mom and her friend pretty much sealed that deal.

The odds have never been in my favor, and it's a bitter pill to swallow. But I finally understand that it's a fight I'll never win.

I blow out a breath and rub over the words with my thumb. "It's so simple but so beautiful. Did it hurt?"

"Like a bitch."

My gaze snaps up at his matter-of-fact reply.

The corners of his lips twitch as he lifts his hand to rub at the spot between my eyebrows. "What's that frown for?"

"I was thinking of getting one. Maybe." I shrug. "I don't know. Probably not."

His lips widen into a full-on grin. "Oh yeah? What kind?"

I gasp when he grabs me by the hips and pulls me closer to him, his fingers digging into my flesh at the top of my waistband. It's a fantastic feeling.

I shake my head. "It's silly."

"Tell me." The command is unmistakable in his voice, yet it also soothes me. Paired with the insistent look in his eyes, I'm compelled to tell him whatever he wants to know.

"Dream big." My whispered confession hangs in the air between us as I wait for his reaction. Weirdly enough, I'm not worried. I know he won't make fun of me. He's the one who told me to go after my dreams, and I'll be forever grateful for that.

Besides Nicole, no one's ever been on my side like this before. It's like a rare gift that I want to treasure, wrapping it in bubble wrap to keep it safe from getting fractured.

I tilt my head back when he grabs my face in both of his large hands and stares into my eyes. And his reach goes much further than that. All the way into my heart, and into my soul.

"I don't think that's silly at all. It's perfect for you." Leaning in, he brushes his lips to mine briefly, the sparks zipping all the way down to the bottom of my soles.

"I'm not very good with pain." No need to hide that fact.

He shrugs. "If you're not set on a place, there are lots of other spots you could get it that hurt less."

"That's true." I nod, excited at the possibility of going through with this at some point. An idea sparks in my mind, instantly turning my insides into molten lava. "Maybe . . . maybe you can show me some good spots?"

Jace licks his lower lip. "Yeah?"

I nod. "I mean only if you want. I think it would be incredibly helpful to get help from someone more experienced." I can't believe I'm actually able to keep eye contact with him. He brings out this boldness in me that I didn't even know existed.

I've been with guys before, but no one's ever affected me the way Jace does. He makes me want it all. The love, the cuddles, the sex, the talking. All of it. The whole package.

"I'm always willing to help someone in need." He winks at me, and I giggle, because it looks hot when he does it.

My next breath is trapped in my throat when he kisses me. This one isn't timid either. It's burning my insides, like someone set my blood on fire. Jace does that to me. Before I can form another thought, his lips leave mine, trailing to my cheek and down my neck.

A shiver runs through me when he stops to suck on the curve of my collarbone.

Goodness, this feels good.

I blindly weave my hands in his hair, tugging at the strands because I need more. So much more. When he pushes the strap of my tank top aside to follow the path of his fingers with his tongue, I'm done for. Filled to the brim with a mixture of anticipation and lust that might as well be the end of me.

"You taste so fucking good." The words have barely left

his mouth before he nips at my skin, setting it ablaze as he steps around me.

Gathering my hair, he pushes it to the opposite side, allowing him access to my upper back and neck. His mouth is back on my skin, his hands under my shirt, gently massaging my lower back as he pulls me back against him, showing me how much this game arouses him.

My body temperature must have gone up by at least ten degrees; or at least that's how flushed I feel, ready to rip off my clothes, and offer myself to Jace. His hands move up farther, pushing my top up with it. When he reaches my shoulder blades, I wordlessly lift my arms, silently inviting him to take it off.

Who am I kidding, it's pretty much begging at this point.

My shirt hits the floor and his hands find my breasts a moment later, squeezing and massaging, playing with my nipples. Driving me absolutely insane.

And I love the feel of his warm chest on my naked back. The skin-to-skin connection feels so amazing, I drop my head against his shoulder in pure contentment.

He uses that moment to suck and nibble at my neck once more, extending his thorough caresses all the way to my ear. I gasp when he reaches the top part of it. I had no idea how sensitive it is, or that it's an erogenous zone for me.

A moan slips past my lips before I register the tingles between my legs. Holy crap.

"You like that, huh?" Jace chuckles into my ear while also pressing his hard-on further into me. Then he does it all again, making me arch into him, my breasts heavier and tighter than before.

He plays some more with my nipples, and the buzzing inside my body intensifies.

"I can't . . . I need . . . Jace, please." I turn around in his arms, pressing my breasts to his hard pecs. The need to find some form of release is growing stronger by the minute, and I'm close to rubbing myself all over him in desperation.

When he slowly walks me back to the bed, I pull him down with me, welcoming his weight on top of me. Somehow it makes this whole situation more real as I greedily paw at his back while also pushing my soles on his butt, urging him closer.

The contact is delicious, the pressure perfect, and I need more.

More of Jace.

I also know this won't be enough.

Right now, I can't see myself ever growing old of this intense connection between us that's about to pull me under, and I have a feeling it might take me to places I've never been before.

TWENTY-FOUR

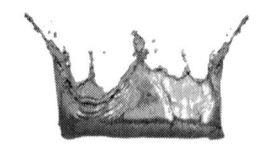

JACE

SAVORING THIS WOMAN IS OFFICIALLY ON MY LIST OF favorite things to do.

Her warm, soft skin welcomes me like it's been waiting for me its whole life. The noises she makes when I kiss her, nip and lick at her skin, are driving me wild. I feel like a fourteen-year-old, ready to shoot my load in my pants.

The buzz along my spine intensifies with each passing moment, my heart like I just finished a whole set of races. And my dick . . . he's never been this eager and desperate to be engulfed by warm flesh.

Even though he won't be happy once he figures out we won't be getting what we really want tonight. I'd die to sink into her this very second, but I don't want to rush into things either.

Usually, I don't think about things like this, but I want to do things right with Em. Not screwing this up by pushing too much too fast is important.

There's also the fact that she can't completely mask her

exhaustion, no matter how much she writhes and moans underneath my needy hands and mouth.

"You think my boobs are a good spot for a tattoo?" She giggles and pulls me closer by my hair at the same time.

Situated with my body between her spread legs, I've made it my mission to give her breasts the attention they deserve. They're a perfect handful, the nipples a beautiful rosy color, and I wouldn't mind spending the rest of the night playing with them.

"Hell no." I gaze at her, flicking her nipple with my tongue. "Is someone getting impatient?"

"Why would you think that?" She wiggles her pelvis against mine and we both groan. After closing her eyes for a moment, she opens her mouth slightly, fixating her gaze back on me before giving me a shy smile. "Maybe a little?"

Holy shit. This woman is so doing it for me.

"Well, let me continue my search then." After giving one of her nipples another twist, I move below her breasts, placing a kiss to the spot where the bottom of her breast meets her ribcage. "I have to admit, this would be an awesome spot."

Before she can say anything, I slide my tongue down the side of her belly. "But so would this." Over her navel and to the edge of her pajama shorts, pushing them down a couple of inches. "Or this."

"Jace." My name is a mixture of a plea and desperation on her lips, and it spurs me on.

She lifts her butt, making it abundantly clear what she wants. Where she wants me to go next. And even though it will test my restraint to the absolute max, there's no place else I'd like to go right now.

Her chest heaves when I put my fingers in the waistband of her shorts, slowly pulling them down inch by inch. My mouth waters as I expose more creamy skin and my balls tighten in my pants.

I toss the shorts behind me, and they land somewhere on the floor in a quiet *thud*. Time to devour this beauty in front of me. Her eyes are on me, her teeth tugging on her bottom lip.

Starting with her left leg, I grab her ankle, lifting it up to my mouth and kissing it. "This would be a great spot."

"Mm-hmm." She bites the tip of her pointer finger, and it's hot as fuck. Knowing this is driving her as wild as me almost snaps my willpower.

I lick my way up the inside of her leg, stopping a few inches below the spot we both want to give attention to so desperately. "I think this would be a fantastic spot."

I ignore her whimpering demands and move to her other side, latching on to the soft skin of her other inner thigh. "Or here."

Instead of making my way down that leg, I move up her pelvis and over her hipbone, all the while she continues to writhe underneath me like she's about to go off like a firecracker.

Her lower stomach. "Here."

Her other hip bone. "Here."

When I make it back between her legs, Em's quivering so much, I have to hold her down. "Shhh, baby. I've got you."

When my mouth finally touches her hot center, I'm done for. I tease her. Taste her. I could do this for hours. Over and over.

I've always enjoyed pleasuring women, but it feels different with Em. It's like the world is shifting underneath our feet, putting us in the position we need to be in for this to work. For this to be perfect. For this to feel better than any other encounter I've ever had. For this to be magical.

Pure fucking magic.

When I latch on to her bundle of nerves, while also entering her with two fingers, she goes off, flying to a place I hope we can soon visit together. She grabs at me blindly, trying to get a good grip on my hair but failing miserably. Her body spasms, clenching around my fingers so hard that I almost come.

Her moans are the sexiest thing I've ever heard, and I don't want it to stop. Em's gaze is on me, but I don't know if she can see me, her eyes glazed over with lust-filled ecstasy. I remove my fingers and mouth and crawl up her body.

The need to have her lips on mine, to feel that simple connection of our mouths together, is strong and impossible to ignore.

"That was the hottest thing I've ever seen. You are so fucking sexy, I can barely handle it." I don't give her a chance to say anything before I press my lips to hers, hungrily taking what I'm starving for. And she gives it back. Lick for lick. Bite for bite. Devouring me as much as I devour her.

When I pull back, both of our breathing is labored, and Em is openly gasping for air. "Oh my gosh, are you trying to kill me? I thought that orgasm was going to split me apart. I was sure I was on my way to explode into a million pieces of stardust, ready to float into the sky, carrying enough charge to illuminate the whole world."

I chuckle at her analogy but can't deny the burst of pride that fills me, making me want to pound my fists on my chest because I did well by this woman. I made her orgasm harder than she's ever had in her life. I can be cocky about that. I *want* to be cocky about that. "Glad to be of service."

She holds up a finger. "Just give me one moment. Just one second." Her chest expands in quick succession as she tries to calm her breathing.

I watch her, with her gorgeous red hair all over my pillow, and her beautiful body spread out on my bed. With a hand to her mouth, she tries to stifle a yawn, but she can't hide it.

Brushing a few strands of hair away from her forehead, I lean in and kiss the tip of her nose. "Let's go to sleep."

That gets her attention, her eyes widening as she tries, and fails, to lean up on her elbows. "What? No. We aren't done yet. I still want to . . . you know, return the favor."

"We'll have plenty of time for that. Right now, it's bedtime."

She pretends to pout. "Fine. I don't think I can move anyway."

With a laugh, I get up and grab her clothes. Together, we manage to put her top and shorts back on.

When I pull the blanket over us and cuddle next to her, she caresses my face. "I know it sounds lame, but thank you." Another big yawn escapes her. "And I'm sorry for ruining this evening with my exhaustion."

"Nothing to apologize for. I think this evening was pretty dang perfect."

She looks down and places her hands to her cheek. "It was perfect. Absolutely perfect."

"Come here." I pull her halfway on my chest, and she gets comfortable with her head on my shoulder, and her hand on my chest. I place my own on top of hers, wanting as much contact as I can.

"I love this." Her words are so quiet, I wonder if she meant to say them out loud.

But I heard them. And I felt them.

"I do too." I lean closer, kissing her head before leaning mine against hers.

She shifts around so she can look at me. "I feel bad about tonight. Are you sure you don't want to . . . I really don't mind. I want to."

"Nope. We're all good." I might have blue balls by tomorrow, but I mean it. Despite this slightly uncomfortable situation, I'm happy and content. Being around Em does that to me. That thought triggers something completely different. "You still want to go to Nationals next week with Tanner?"

"You bet. I've already thought of toys and activities to bring to keep Tanner happy."

"And my mom will be there too to help."

She chuckles. "I'm excited to see you in action."

"I like knowing you'll be there."

This time, I'm the one yawning, Em following two seconds later. "Let's go to sleep, ladybug. We both have a long week ahead of us."

"Sounds good."

I turn off the dimmed light on my nightstand and find her mouth one more time, kissing her lazily, yet thoroughly. Em's sigh sounds satisfied, and my heart pounds happily under her hand.

I might be miserable down south, but this is all worth it.

Holding her in my arms, listening to her fall asleep, and knowing she'll be by my side during one of the most stressful weeks of the year.

This week's already a success.

TWENTY-FIVE

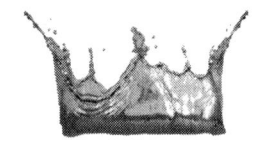

EMILIA

That wonderful night in Jace's arms feels like a distant memory even though it only happened last week. Jace had to focus on his training, and even more so on getting the rest he needs, and I couldn't stand in the way of that.

Jace, Patricia, and I sat down to talk about logistics, and together we came up with a plan. Jace stays at the hotel next to the aquatic center where the Nationals will be held, while Patricia and I will hold down the fort back home so to speak, taking care of Tanner while Jace focuses on his swims.

The few days before the event started, Jace and Tanner video chatted as much as they could, and I spent my evenings on the phone with Jace.

I miss him like crazy, but I try to push down those lonely feelings that arise often.

This isn't something to worry about, right? It's perfectly normal to support the people in your life, even if you take a backseat for a while. How would it feel like to be on the receiving end of this?

Thoughts like that usually end in a pity party, which is

why I've stayed busy with my program. My audition is happening next week, and I plan on wowing every single person of *Kinder Street*.

Today is the last day of Jace's five-day swim event, and it's been an interesting experience. Preliminaries are in the morning of each day, and finals are in the evening.

Jace has been extra busy, not only with training, racing, and meetings but also with interviews and meet and greets. He's certainly a popular guy, the crowd cheering louder when he's around.

So far, he's won gold medals in the 100m and 200m butterfly, and tonight is the final of the 200m individual medley, which is his strength, as his current world record indicates loud and clear to anyone in doubt.

Thankfully, our seating area is in the shade this afternoon. I've brought the whole arsenal of coloring books, Play-Doh, new books and small toys for Tanner, who's happily playing between Patricia and me, even though that usually only lasts for so long.

Toddlers certainly aren't meant to sit in the stands for hours on end, so Patricia and I have been occupying him as much as we can when Jace isn't racing.

Even though we drive back home every evening—to disrupt Tanner's routine as little as possible—Jace has rented an extra hotel room for us so we have a quiet and cool place for some downtime during the day and for Tanner's nap. It's not ideal, and Tanner's not always happy with it, but we've been managing okay and the event is almost over.

We're here to support Jace, and we're making do.

Speaking of the devil—an incredibly sexy one at that—he's in line with the other seven final swimmers, making his way to the pool. They all dispose of their things—tracksuits, sneakers, and headphones—and begin their various pre-race routines.

My eyes are on Jace. Even though I still don't know too much about this sport, I've become quite obsessed with it and Jace's performances this week. I'm usually on the edge of my uncomfortable plastic seat, wanting nothing more than to jump up and pace around in nerves and anticipation. I'm sure that wouldn't go too well with the other spectators though.

"Look, Tanner, there's Daddy." Patricia points her finger toward the pool, where Jace is getting on his starting block.

His swimsuit sits low on his hips, the compression shorts tight, leaving little room to the imagination. It's a pretty sweet sight to behold.

Jace swings his arms around his upper body, easily reaching his opposite shoulder blades. Talk about arm span.

After repeating it a few times, he presses the heels of his hands to his goggles before adjusting his cap one more time. I've seen him do the exact same thing a million times on video or live this week.

"Daddy." Tanner claps his hands excitedly when introductions are made and Jace pops up on the big screen. It sounds more like "Dead-ee" when Tanner says it, but he's been trying hard this week.

Of course, like so often with children, Jace has yet to hear it in person since Tanner acts like he's never said it before whenever Jace is around.

Thank goodness for phones and videos.

I finally got it on video this morning, and I'm not sure I've ever seen Jace smile so big before. Talk about a proud Dad moment.

I've been all emotional about it too. I think it's a big deal, so it makes it extra special to be a part of it.

Everyone around us quiets down as the swimmers settle on the starting blocks and take their mark.

My heart jumps when the start signal sounds, and the swimmers push off to glide into the water effortlessly. With their arms stretched ahead of them, their feet propel them forward as far as they can before they break the surface of the water, immediately going into the butterfly for the first lap.

Backstroke is next, followed by breaststroke. Jace started out in the lead, but the more laps swum, the easier it is to tell that he's struggling. The distance between him and his competitors keeps shrinking, and by the time he enters the last lap, freestyle, he's head to head with the swimmer from lane three.

My eyes flicker to the huge screen to get a better look now that it's such a tight race. They are only a few feet left from the wall and Jace's head pops out to look at his opponent.

They reach the wall. The crowd cheers as the results are announced.

The guy from lane number three won.

Not Jace.

It's *not* Jace.

Jace didn't win.

The guy from lane three also broke Jace's world record.

Tanner claps next to me. "Yaaaaaay."

When he looks at me expectantly, I join in and clap with him, trying my best to smile back. The second I can, my eyes find Patricia's, who still looks as shocked as I feel.

We take Tanner for a walk while the swimmers do their cool down and take a shower. I think we can all use a break before the medal ceremony.

The medal ceremony is a little underwhelming to me, but then I'm not an Olympic athlete..

But tonight's worse. It's definitely the hardest one to watch with Jace on the silver step. This was his race. It should be his gold. He's smiling, offering congratulations to the gold-medal winner, but the smile doesn't reach his eyes. Once it's over, we make our way to the spot outside the center where we always meet with Jace.

Normally we say goodbye at this point before Patricia, Tanner, and I make our way back home and Jace goes to his hotel room.

"There he is."

The man walking toward us has nothing in common with the man I FaceTimed an hour with last night, where Jace told me how much he missed me, how much he can't wait to fall asleep with me in his arms again.

And he couldn't be more opposite the man who's joined us after his gold-medal wins. I've gotten so used to his bright eyes and his boyish grin after his victories, that this is . . . heartbreaking.

"Hey, sweetheart." Patricia has snapped back into her cheery-mom mode, welcoming her son with open arms and squeezing him tightly when he walks into her embrace. "You did so well. Congratulations."

"Thanks, Mom." Jace steps back, placing his duffel bag on the floor so he can take a squirming Tanner from me. "Hey, buddy."

"Hi." Tanner throws his arms around Jace's neck and holds on tight.

Jace's arms wrap around his son's small body and he closes his eyes. When those beautiful eyes open again, they land on me. He looks at me but doesn't say anything, his face half-buried in Tanner's neck.

There's a sudden tension between us. His stare is vacant, his expression slack. Even his posture looks saggier than usual.

Is that regret in his eyes? Blame?

He's not blaming me for his loss, is he?

I'm trying to make sense of this, trying to calm down this overwhelming sensation inside of me, but without a lot of success.

I'm freaking out, but I don't want to show it. That probably wouldn't do me any good right now.

Instead, I swallow my feelings—something I'm used to—and force the corners of my mouth to lift. At least, a little bit. "You were amazing."

"Thanks." We both know he doesn't really mean it, but what else is there to say? Or I guess, it's less of him not meaning it, but more of him not believing I meant my statement. Even though I don't think it matters in the end.

I'm feeling more uncomfortable and out of place with each passing second, itching to get going. Back to our normal life, hoping our regular routine will help.

Gosh, what if it doesn't?

"We should probably get out of here before we hit traffic." Patricia gives me a meaningful look, her eyes wide as she nods toward the parking lot. Looks like she wants to get out of here as badly as I do.

"Sounds good. I still have a few things to do too, so I'll see you later." Jace gives Tanner a squeeze and kiss before handing him back to me.

Patricia grabs his arm. "Call if you need anything, okay?"

"Will do, thanks." His gaze flickers to mine. "I'll call you, okay?"

I nod, the words stuck in my throat.

"Have a safe drive home." One more wave at Tanner, and then he turns around and walks away.

After a moment of staring after him, Patricia touches my arm. "Come on, Millie. Let's get out of here."

"Okay." I trail after her in a daze, going through the motions when we get to her small SUV, buckling in Tanner before going to the passenger side and getting in my seat.

The first few minutes of our drive are quiet, and I wonder if Patricia is giving me time to absorb what happened. Unfortunately, we hit traffic pretty quickly, which seems to be the end of quiet time.

At least, we're lucky and Tanner passed out and can't throw a fit because of the stagnant traffic. That child hates sitting in an unmoving car, absolutely hates it. I think I still have a bump at the back of my head to prove it from when he threw one of his toys at me. All because the light at an intersection was broken and we had to wait for several minutes to cross it. No chill.

"He'll come around, I promise. Jace is like his dad. They are terribly sore losers, especially when it's something they usually excel at. Their pride takes their sweet time to get over it, but then it'll all be good again." She grabs a Starburst from the middle console and hands me a pink one, knowing they're my favorite.

"Thank you." I take the candy and quickly unwrap it, eager to let the familiar strawberry taste soothe my confused feelings.

Maybe I just imagined the distance between Jace and me? He just lost a race that was very important to him, a race I'm sure he thinks he shouldn't have lost. I mean, everyone would be a bit down after something like that. Right?

"If we have to, we'll just keep going like we have this week when he was gone, okay? You watch Tanner the normal time, and then I'll take over for the night." Patricia plays with another Starburst wrapper while slowly guiding us through the evening traffic.

My head snaps over to hers when I finally understand her implication. "You don't think he's coming home tonight?"

She shrugs and blows her lips, a motion that Tanner normally finds hilarious. "He might, but there's a chance he's going to hide and lick his wounds for a few days. Normally he'd do it at home, but since he doesn't live alone anymore, that's not possible."

I don't know what to say, and my thoughts immediately bounce all over the place. Wanting to be mad at Jace for possibly abandoning his son because of a bruised ego. Feeling sympathetic because he lost something that was important to him.

And also upset at the thought that he'd stay away and not see me after we've barely seen each other all week.

We're at my house quicker than I thought, and despite how much I adore Patricia and her company, I can't help the need to flee. After a quick goodbye, and one more look at a still-sleeping Tanner, I rush into the house, heading straight for the comfort of my bedroom.

Suddenly, I have this incessant urge to be alone and analyze this week. This whole month.

If tonight showed me anything, it's that I'm in deep with Jace.

Because there's no denying the fact that he doesn't want me around when he's hurting, which feels like a stab straight to my heart. Whereas, I turned to him immediately after things happened with my mom.

If this thing between us meant something to him, wouldn't he let me in and help him get through this too?

I want to be there for him, I want to help him in whatever way I can.

But none of this matters if he shuts me out.

And I'm not sure what that means for us.

TWENTY-SIX

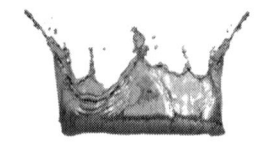

JACE

Em: I'm here if you need me.

Em: I'm getting worried. Are you okay?

Em: I miss you.

Countless calls and voice messages from Em and a few from my mom I still haven't listened to. Then nothing for a couple of days. I looked at these messages a million times in the first few days, but I'm not ready to talk to any of them yet. My mom has the hotel room number if she really has to reach me.

I don't want to hear the pity in their voices, knowing how much I disappointed them. I'd rather wallow some more. Watching the race another hundred times because my mind is unable to let go of it.

Even though I already dissected it with Coach. And with Hunter. I *know* what mistake I made, and I still can't get past it.

The door opens and Noah strolls in with takeout bags in one hand and a drink holder with two large foam cups from the smoothie place in the other.

He stops a few feet in front of the bed and looks at me. "I'll feed you if you get ready. It's time, man. No one likes to lose, but it's not the end of the world either."

Noah has always been the quietest out of the four of us, but a great friend. His support is often silent, showing in his actions rather than his words. And now he's here, bringing me food, *and* giving me advice.

Have I been that bad?

I rub my tired face and take one more look at my phone before I put it aside. I stop and sit ramrod straight when my brain finally processes the words on the screen.

Em: Remember Tanner's preschool meeting. I forwarded all the details to your email last week.

His preschool meeting? When is his preschool meeting?

My heart skips a beat as I search through my foggy brain, remembering how Em and I talked about it a few weeks ago. I'm about to switch to my emails when I see the next message.

Em: We're getting ready to leave now. See you soon.

My heartbeat quickly increases as I look at the time stamp before my eyes flicker to the clock. Fuck. She sent it an hour ago.

"*No.*"

The realization of what's happening hits me. I'm about to miss my son's meeting with his preschool teacher.

Under other circumstances, this might not be a big deal, but this is one of Tanner's *firsts* since he's been with me, and I wanted to be there for all his firsts after already having missed so many.

And now this.

I've been so wrapped up since my lost race that hiding in my hotel room from the rest of the world seemed like the best thing to do.

"Shit."

"What is it?" Noah puts down the food and drinks on the nightstand and pulls over one of the chairs.

"I fucked up." My eyes burn, and I rub my hands roughly over my face. I don't even have any anger left in me. I've drained myself of all energy this week.

Noah keeps staring at me, so I inhale deeply and try to sort my thoughts. "Today's Tanner's first meeting with his preschool teacher. I didn't see Em's reminder texts until now."

His eyebrows raise.

I shake my head. "I've been avoiding her messages."

He doesn't look surprised. "I figured."

Crap. Am I that predictable?

"Normally I do what I want to do."

Noah leans forward, placing his elbows on his knees. "But it's not just about you anymore. There's someone at home waiting for you, *counting* on you."

My body locks down, immobilizing every piece of my being.

I'm such an asshole.

And now I missed Tanner's meeting with his teacher.

Damn it.

"Dude." Noah slaps me on the shoulder. "Go. I'll check you out."

I jump out of bed and get ready in record speed, tripping over my feet as I grab my bag and stop in front of Noah, who's now settled into the plush chair by the window to eat his food.

"Thanks, Noah. I owe you."

"Don't mention it." He holds out one of the drinks and the bag. "I'll talk to you later."

The drive is a blur, and when I reach my street, Em pulls into the driveway right in front of me. I'm afraid I might rip the door off its hinges when I get out as fast as I can, but I don't care.

Em's halfway leaning into the car to unbuckle Tanner. I can't see more than his hand, but this sudden need to hold my son crashes into me like a powerful wave, making my steps falter for a moment.

How could I have been so stupid to just hole up like the rest of the world doesn't exist? Like the *people* in my life don't exist? My mom might be used to this from previous situations —not that she's ever deserved this treatment either—but I have a child now, for fuck's sake.

And then there's Em.

Guilt paralyzes my insides as l watch her heave Tanner out of the car and put him on the ground.

When he spots me, his whole face lights up. "Dad-dy."

Oh fuck, he actually said it.

He runs toward me as fast as he can, his feet tapping

across the cement. His mouth is stretched into a big smile that makes my gut clench.

I don't deserve this guy.

I catch him effortlessly and hold him close to my chest. "Hey, buddy."

He pulls back and grins at me. Then he leans in once more, squishing his face in my neck as his little fingers dig into my shoulders.

My grip tightens, and I hold on for dear life.

Stupid, stupid, stupid.

The backs of my eyes burn, and I take several swallows as he leans back and squeezes my cheeks.

"Did you have a great time at school?" My voice is raspy, my sole focus on Tanner's cute face. With his chubby cheeks and his wavy brown hair. His blue eyes the same as mine.

And then she comes into view.

Em.

Gosh, she's fucking beautiful. She's wearing her Millie-attire—big-ass yellow tutu, yellow bow—and for once, it doesn't throw me off. Because I *know* she wore it for Tanner and his preschool visit. Probably so he felt more at ease, because that's the kind of person she is.

Thinking of others first.

The opposite of me.

Her hair catches my attention, the sun highlighting her red strands, almost making it look aflame.

Gorgeous as always.

What's missing though is the easy smile I'm used to seeing.

I really fucked up.

"Hey." I want to reach out and touch her, but something in her gaze makes me hesitate.

"Hi." Her eyes roam my whole face like she's taking inventory, and I do the same.

Her mesmerizing eyes, her cute nose, those dang freckles, and those delicious lips.

How's that possible that I didn't realize how much I missed her?

I feel like an absolute moron, frustration over my actions sinking into my bones like a dead weight, impossible to shake off.

"Let's get him inside and to bed. He almost fell asleep in the car, and you know how wired he gets when he's overtired." Em gets her bag and Tanner's water bottle out of the car, and we head inside.

The door shuts behind us, and I don't give her a chance to say anything. "I'll put him down."

She's in the middle of taking off her shoes and stops to look at me. "Okay."

I kick off my shoes and walk to Tanner's room with him after a quick stop at the bathroom. I go through the motions of getting him ready, putting him in his pull-up before getting him in his sleepsack.

He knows the drill and pushes his arms through the armholes before I zip it up.

"Daddy." He smiles at me, and I want to sink to my knees and beg him for his forgiveness, even though he doesn't know what I did.

Somehow, that makes it even worse, and I have the inexplicable need to rub my chest.

I pick him up and hold him close. *Needing* that

connection with him. "I'm so sorry I wasn't there today, buddy. I promise, I'll do everything I can to never let anything like that happen again."

He snuggles closer into my neck, his fingers creating small pressure points on my back.

I close my eyes and sway.

When I learned about Tanner's existence two months ago, I never would have thought I could enjoy this. And this week I surely acted like it didn't mean anything, which I regret. Deeply.

That was the old Jace, pre-Tanner Jace, and I left that man behind at the hotel earlier. For good.

Tanner's hand moves on my back, and I take that as my cue to sing. Right now, he's obsessed with *Twinkle, Twinkle Little Star*. Today's version is more of a whisper-singing, but Tanner doesn't seem to mind. I follow that up with a hummed version of *Brahms Lullaby*, and right on cue after the last note, Tanner leans back in my arms, clearly ready to go to sleep.

Such a smart boy.

Even though I don't want to let go, I kiss him goodnight and put him in his crib, where he immediately flips onto his stomach. He pushes his booty up in the air before I even make it to the door.

I almost bump into Em when I try to sneak out and mouth, "Sorry."

I take in the long dress she's changed into. It gently hugs her curves, and everything I feel for this woman comes back with a vengeance.

After closing Tanner's door quietly, I wordlessly grab her hand and pull her into the living room.

My thoughts are jumbled while I'm still trying to figure out this mess. All I want to do is sit down and hold her, but I know that's not enough. The least I can do is try to explain myself. Apologize. Tell her what was going on.

I've got to do something.

My muscles feel weak, my mouth dry as she gets comfortable next to me, leaving a few inches between us.

I hate it, but can I really blame her?

But I focus on the fact that she hasn't pulled her hand from mine. That's a good sign, right? "I know I have to explain some things to you, but first, tell me how things went with Tanner today. Please. If you don't mind."

The tension leaves her face and her mouth relaxes. "He did really well. The teacher was friendly and made him feel at ease. I wasn't sure how nervous he was going to be, which is why I changed into my Millie costume, which was probably silly but . . ." She shrugs.

Just like I thought. "Thank you."

"Of course. She was impressed with his signing, which will make communicating with her and the other teachers a lot easier. The classroom is wonderful, and Tanner loved it. He ran from one toy to the next with a huge smile on his face. I think he's going to have a blast."

The sense of loss curses through me. I absolutely loathe that I missed this experience with him.

I close my eyes for a moment and exhale loudly. "I suck at this parenting thing. I'm barely ever home and screw things up constantly. I don't want this for him. I want to be the best damn parent he could possibly have."

Em is quiet, like she knows I need to get this off my chest.

This feeling inside me is horrible, this gnawing sensation

of failure scratching at my organs, leaving me raw and exposed. But as I don't have any words to describe this turmoil, it's leaving me empty throughout.

Em's need to comfort seems to kick in and she squeezes my hand. Sickeningly enough, I'm happy about it, needing and wanting it right now. "I hate to say it, but I think that's what parenting is all about. It's definitely not easy. At times you think you'll never do it right, but you keep trying to do right by them."

Now I'm the quiet one, staring at our hands.

"And you love him, Jace. I see that every time you're with him, and that alone is worth more than parenting the correct way every minute of every day. If you expect perfection when it comes to parenting, you're trying to achieve something impossible and only set yourself up for failure."

Her thumb brushes over my hand. "You were both thrown into this situation without warning, and from where I'm standing, you've been doing a good job. Just keep loving him, Jace."

Her voice breaks during those last words and I look into her watery eyes.

Shit. I didn't even think about what nerve this must hit, and my heart breaks into a million pieces for her.

Unable to hold back, I slip my hand out of hers and cradle her face. "Baby, I'm so sorry. I didn't want to make you sad."

She shakes her head and pulls back. "I know."

"I screwed up. Not just with Tanner but also with you. I wasn't thinking straight. It was selfish of me to disappear for days. I'm sorry." My voice cracks, and the same wave of regret

I experienced with Tanner rushes through me. Just like earlier, I want to fall to my knees and beg for forgiveness.

I swallow a few times. I knew this wasn't going to be easy, but it's the right thing to do. Both Tanner and Em deserve my apologies, and so much more.

"I called you." Her voice is barely a whisper. "I messaged you."

I close my eyes and shake my head. "I know. And I should have answered. I'm so sorry, baby. Neither you nor Tanner deserved that treatment. I swear, I won't ever ignore you again. I can't even explain why I went into hiding. Saying I'm a sore loser sounds so lame."

"No one likes to lose."

Typical Em. I make a mistake, and she's trying to make it easier for me.

My brows draw together. "Probably, but I handled it poorly. I was so upset because I should have won that race."

The tension in my voice is undeniable, but I don't try and hide it from Em. I want to be honest with her.

She tilts her head to the side, her features soft. "What happened?"

I laugh but there's no humor in my voice. I don't think I'll get over it anytime soon. "Stupid beginner's mistake, which makes the whole thing even worse."

She stares at me, probably no clue what I'm talking about, but how could she?

I sigh, replaying the scene in my head. "I lifted my head a few feet before the wall. That rookie mistake cost me my win." I have no idea why I did it either, which is what has pissed me off the most. I. Know. Not. To. Do. That.

A second, or even millisecond, can make or break your win. And I know that.

This time, I lost.

"That must be so much pressure." She squeezes my hands.

"It is, but that's no excuse for the way I acted. I should have come back and explained what was going on instead of hiding away and feeling sorry for myself. I should have talked to you."

"It's okay. Thanks for explaining what happened."

I don't deserve her, but I want her so badly. "Will you forgive me?"

She nods. "Just talk to me next time, okay?"

Her shoulders go up the tiniest bit, and I have to touch her.

Without warning, I grab her and pull her in my arms. "I promise I will. I've missed you so much."

"I've missed you too." Her voice is muffled against my shirt.

My heart speeds up. Exhilarated. Relieved. Happy.

When Em moves around to get more comfortable and puts her arms around my waist, digging her fingers into my back before grasping fistfuls of my shirt, I know I'm in trouble.

I meant it when I said I missed her, and my body seems to be playing catchup now that she's in my arms.

Holding her, feeling her warmth on my fingertips, her delicious scent invading my senses.

I pull back, wanting to see her.

Needing to fix this between us in every possible way.

Her eyes are big and filled with emotions as she stares at me. So beautiful.

I wait, wanting her to take the first step.

Her gaze flickers back and forth between my eyes and my mouth.

When she licks her lips, I groan, unable to control myself as my fingers dig into her waist.

And then she kisses me.

Pulling at my hair, pressing her breasts against me, *grinding* on my already-hard dick. Her flesh is soft underneath my hands, her warmth seeps into my lap, her taste undeniably sweet on my tongue.

She's absolutely intoxicating, and I've never felt like this about anyone else before.

"Hold on, baby." Standing up with her, I walk us into the bedroom.

Wanting to feel her.

Needing to feel her.

I'm finally *home*.

TWENTY-SEVEN

EMILIA

Jace shuts the door behind us, leaving the baby monitor on the dresser. I didn't even realize he took it.

I'm glad he doesn't break our connection when he walks us toward the bed. After sitting on the edge, he starts kissing his way down my neck, and I'm ready to melt on the spot. His mouth is warm, and my pulse throbs against his lips as I let out a breathy moan.

So sensitive.

I've missed his touch so much. Maybe I should feel ashamed, but I was ready to jump him when he came out of Tanner's room. I know his murmured words were for his son and not for me, but I heard them anyway.

And not just that. I *felt* them. Deep in my heart. The pain and regret was so tangible that I felt like crying.

Yes, his behavior was a bit clouded this week, but at the same time, I see him learning from it. I also really appreciated his honesty, and that he allowed himself to be vulnerable with me. A lot of men think they can't, or rather shouldn't, but it was important to allow us to move past this.

When his pelvis pushes against mine, lust overtakes my thoughts, and I push back against his hard length.

Impatience is burning a hot path through my body, and I need to be with him. I need to re-establish our connection in every possible way.

"Take off your clothes, Jace."

After staring at me for a moment, he grins and flips us over. "Yes, ma'am."

It takes him less than a minute before he stands in front of me in all his naked glory. Gorgeous, gorgeous man. All tight skin over lean muscles. That proud erection between his legs.

I grow wet at the sight of it, and Jace must have caught my impatience. Before I know what's happening, he's pulled me off the bed and my dress goes flying. My underwear is next and then we stand naked in front of each other, our breathing labored even though we aren't touching.

Then he grabs me by the waist and throws me back on the bed.

My breasts bounce with the movement, but I barely notice it because I'm still shocked he just did that. No one's ever done anything like that before, and it's oddly exhilarating. So primal and hot.

Jace crawls over me, grabbing my boobs and squeezing them before devouring them with his mouth.

His movements get sloppy and his pupils darken. He looks as desperate as I feel. My body is out of control, and I'm trembling underneath Jace's touch. Pulling his hair. Scratching his back.

My silent begging reaches its limit when my hips shoot

upward and I start rubbing, grinding, pushing. Whatever contact is possible, I make it.

Jace finally takes pity on me and kisses me. He devours my mouth like he might never get to kiss me again, and it's beautiful.

His emotions are laced into this kiss, seeping into my essence, to the exact part of my soul that was starving for it.

I pull back, my lip popping free from his as a whimper escapes my lips. "Jace, please."

He blinks several times as if to clear his head. "What do you want, baby? I need you to say it."

"I want you."

"You already got me, baby. I'm so into you, I can't even think straight sometimes."

"I need you inside of me." My voice is shaking like the rest of my body.

Thankfully, I don't need to tell him twice, and he's got a condom on in record time.

The heat that started between my legs continues to spread throughout my whole body, the flames licking at my insides and threatening to consume me.

I've never been this ready for someone. Heck, I don't think I've ever been this wet in my life.

Nothing and no one has turned me on as much as this.

When I think he might just push inside, he pauses and stares at me. Then he captures my mouth, his lips moving with mine like they were meant for each other. He sucks on my lower lip, and my hips buck up on their own accord, my body reacting to everything he does.

"Now, Jace." I don't care how often I have to beg.

And boy, am I deep in this. So much deeper than I ever thought I would be.

My thoughts evaporate when he grips his hard length and rubs it along my entrance. Back and forth over my swollen flesh until I'm ready to lose my mind.

Pushing up, I brush against him. Any inhibition or embarrassment about my wants and needs have definitely flown out the window.

With Jace, I feel like I can be me. I don't have to uphold any strange idealistic idea of how I should behave. He's not trying to make me someone I'm not.

The way he makes me feel right now—out of control and desired—makes the back of my eyes burn. It's powerful and feels... freeing.

"Eyes on me, beautiful." Jace's voice is sharp and tight, like he's ready to lose his control soon.

The fluttery sensations in my chest and stomach intensify when he pushes my knees toward my chest. Positioning himself once more, he pushes his tip inside, immediately closing his eyes and exhaling harshly.

My insides stretch and adjust as he slowly comes into my body. Eventually, he stops when he's in to the hilt. It's intense, and I need a moment to get used to the new sensation, not remembering ever feeling this full.

Jace lifts one hand, his gaze focused on our joined spot, rubbing my swollen bundle of nerves with a precision that brings tears to my eyes. I reach for him, almost blindly, wanting to feel more of him. Wanting him to move. Wanting him to kiss me. To touch me. All of it.

I want *everything* he has to offer.

His hand goes up to my breast before going back to my

hips, his touch possessive and intense as he slowly starts to pull out and push back in. In and out, the rhythm so blindingly seductive, I'm lost in it.

When he finally leans down and covers my body with his, I wrap my legs around him and push into his butt with all my might, unable to get enough. Chasing an orgasm I know will be even more intense than the last one I had with him.

"Oh gosh," I gasp as he changes angles, hitting a spot that magnifies everything.

"I could watch you all day long." Jace kisses me so hard, I know I'll feel him on my lips hours from now.

But I give back just as much, utterly lost in the sensations, never wanting this to end. His movements get faster, the friction so powerful, I feel the sparks all the way down to my toes.

The air is filled with skin slapping against skin and our harsh breathing. My boobs bounce between us as Jace leans back and pinches my nipples.

I can't hold on any longer, letting go, flying over the edge so hard, I stop breathing for a moment. My body is flooded with the most intense pleasure I've ever experienced. It's blinding, making me see stars as the buzz continues to travel through my body.

The shudders of pleasure continue until Jace stills, growing even larger inside me as he opens his mouth and lets out an almost animalistic growl. "Oh, fuck."

I stare at him. Holy crap, that was sexy.

The air rushes out of my lungs in one big *whoosh* when he collapses on top of me.

"Shit, sorry." He pushes up on his elbows and stares into my eyes, his strong arms enclosing me like a cage. "Just give me one more moment to stay right here, allowing me to memorize the way you look right now."

Despite everything we just did, heat travels up my neck, and I chuckle. "Stop it."

He grabs a hold of my waist and rolls off me, pulling me to the side with him.

We face each other, only inches apart, and Jace grabs my hands, pulling them up to his lips to give each fingertip a kiss. "You are absolutely perfect, from top to bottom, and I doubt I'll ever get enough of you. Ever."

My cheeks are blazing now.

This moment is absolutely perfect, and I want to shield it from everything, unwilling to let anything in this bubble, afraid to ruin this moment because I can't remember the last time I felt this happy, this satisfied.

"I feel the same way." I'm hyper aware of all the places we touch. Our hands, our knees, one shoulder, our feet.

Jace leans in.

Our noses.

He comes closer.

Our mouths.

It feels like our hearts are touching too, and for some reason, it makes me want to cry.

This feels so good.

Almost too good, and that scares me.

I savor the kiss, not ready to let go of this happiness.

Jace pulls back, suddenly squirming as he lets go of my hands. "Crap. Sorry, babe. The condom."

"Oh." I totally forgot about that.

He takes care of it and gives me one hell of a show when

he walks to the bathroom naked before coming back to bed and pulling the bedding over us.

This time, he grabs my hands and puts them on his chest, allowing me to feel his steady heartbeat. It's accelerated, and I wonder if it's because of the sex or if there's a different reason.

He lifts his fingers and brushes his thumb over the bridge of my nose and down over one of my cheeks. "My beautiful ladybug."

I laugh at the term, remembering my embarrassing stunt in his living room last month. It feels like years ago instead of weeks.

"I love your freckles." He eliminates the space between our faces, kissing the path along my nose and cheeks he just traced with his finger.

It's oddly intimate, and my nerve endings tingle.

"And your smile." He peppers my lips with small kisses until I smile so big he's kissing more teeth than lips. "You have no idea how happy you make me."

"Yeah?"

He chuckles since it's obvious I'm fishing for compliments and holds his thumb and pointer less than an inch apart. "A little."

My chest rises on a deep inhale. "I'm glad. You also make me a little happy."

Jace's eyebrows rise in a challenge, and I don't see the tickle attack coming until his hands are on both sides of my ribcage, knowing exactly where I'm ticklish.

Within moments, I'm gasping for air.

Jace seems to enjoy himself immensely, a huge grin on his face. "Only a little, huh?"

I feel an impending side stitch forming and raise my hands in the air. "I surrender."

Jace pauses but doesn't take his hands off my body. His hot skin makes mine feel like it's on fire.

Are all men like breathing and talking furnaces?

"You surrender?" Jace puts his face right in front of mine, locking eyes with me.

There's something in his gaze that wasn't there before. I can't pinpoint what it is, but it's intense. I've never been . . . watched like this. Seen.

"Does that mean you like me more than just a little bit?"

I gulp at the question. It's unexpected, and a bit . . . scary.

Is he asking me because he wants to say something to me but wants me to go first? Or is he simply curious to hear about my feelings but has no intention of telling me his?

Neither changes anything about the way I feel about him of course, but one option certainly makes me more vulnerable than the other. And no one likes to have their feelings trampled on when they aren't reciprocated.

I decide to play the game some more to see if I can get a better feel of his intentions. "Maybe?"

His expression is serious, determined, and I'm about to die of nervous curiosity. "I sure hope you do because I really like you. I like *us*. I like where this is going. Em, I'm—"

His phone goes off somewhere in the room.

"My mom." Jace leans in and plants a kiss on my lips. "Just the person you want to talk to after having sex."

I shake my head and laugh. "Oh my gosh. Don't say something that."

"Better to say it to you than to her."

"Naughty."

He winks at me, and I watch him as he moves around the room to pick up our discarded clothes, throwing mine to me before getting dressed. It's a sight to behold, and while I enjoy the hell out of it, my mind is still stuck on the last moment of our conversation.

What was Jace about to tell me?

It can't be what I think it might have been, right?

Or is it possible he feels the same way I do?

TWENTY-EIGHT

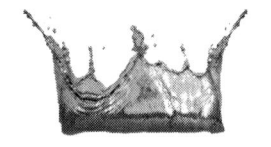

JACE

My almost slip feels like years ago, even though it was only last week. Talk about bad timing though. Not my mom's. I'm actually grateful she interrupted me from spilling the beans to Em. In retrospect, I realized it might have not been the best timing to confess my love to her after I'd just ignored her for days.

Not to mention after having sex with her for the first time. The last thing I need is to be accused of my love confession having any connection with that, because sex with Em . . . It was absolutely amazing. Better than my wildest dreams.

The way we fit together, the way she made me feel . . . like she was meant for me. I can't stop thinking about her.

She makes me believe that I might be able to have everything I want after all. And who wouldn't want the whole package? A job I love, an awesome boy, and a gorgeous and incredible woman by my side. Could I really have it all?

Apart from the fact that I love spending time with her, I also can't get enough of her. I won't deny that getting her naked as often as possible is my new favorite thing, which isn't nearly often enough when your hormones still think you're a teenager. But there isn't a lot of time with my schedule and an energetic toddler at home.

My mom just left on a trip with some of her friends, but as soon as she's back next week, I'm going to beg her to take Tanner for the weekend, so I can fuck Em on every possible surface in my house from morning to night.

Maybe that will be a good time to arrange something special to tell her how I feel. She deserves for it to be more than just a blurted-out post-coital admission.

Someone slaps on my shoulder and I flinch, my heart jumping until I see it's Ryan. "Shit, man."

He chuckles, slapping my shoulder once more before letting go. "Dude, I've been calling you across the parking lot since you stepped foot outside the building. Looks like you were daydreaming with your head in the clouds."

I try to glare at him but can't keep the smile from spreading, and he shakes his head. Because he isn't wrong. I barely notice my surroundings these days. "What's up?"

"Just wanted to make sure you wouldn't forget about the party next week. Harper's been busting my ass to make sure everyone's coming."

Harper and Ryan had an unconventional start to their relationship, but they are quite the couple. Despite their age difference, amongst other things, they worked things out and are happy. It's hard to miss whenever I see them together.

"She still hanging in there?" I check my watch, something I've already done a million times since my training session ended and Coach held me back to talk some more strategy for the next few months as we prep for the Olympics next year.

Ryan nods. "She is. Driving me crazy with her need to organize a birthday party for me that I don't even want when she's eight months pregnant, but it makes her happy. And that's all I need."

I'm starting to understand how that works. The need to make the other person happy, no matter what. I'd do a lot to see Em happy.

Apparently, I was lost in my thoughts again because Ryan pokes my shoulder. Hard.

"You're bringing Millie to the party, right? Harper can't wait to meet her."

That snaps me out of my thoughts for good. "Oh yeah?"

"Yup." Ryan gets his car keys out of his pockets. "Hunter's been telling us all about her, and I think Millie might have another fangirl in Harper. She's been watching her videos and whatnot, talking about how awesome she is."

I groan. "Hunt's got a big mouth."

"He does, but he means well."

"I know." I pause. "But yes, I was going to ask her if she wants to come with us."

"Good. About time we finally meet her. Harper said you've been selfish with Tanner and Millie, and that it's really time for her to find a girlfriend out here."

We both laugh at that. I have no doubt Harper would say something like that.

The love-sick expression on his face is unmistakable though, and I wonder if I'll look like this one day too when I'm talking about Em. Or maybe I already do? Especially when she's pregnant like Harper. An image of Em with a child growing inside her belly—*our* child—fills my chest with a lightness that's oddly energizing.

Ryan laughs. "Shit, Noah was right. It's impossible to have a conversation with you these days. Go home. I'll see you tomorrow."

We part ways, and I head home more eager than before.

"Honey, I'm home." It's super cheesy, but I can't help myself. My conversation with Ryan has only cemented my feelings for Em, and I feel like yelling it from the rooftops.

Em's quiet footsteps sound on the floor when I toe off my shoes. I turn around with a smile on my face, ready to pull her in my arms and kiss the hell out of her, maybe more depending on how long Tanner's nap will last.

But my smile drops the second I see her.

Her purse is strapped across her upper body, her laptop bag on the floor next to her as she struggles to put on her shoes. Even though I'm still a few feet away, I see her hands shaking.

"Em, what's going on?" I rush toward her but stop in my tracks as she lifts her head and glares at me.

"I can't believe you did this to me. After everything that went down last week and all the promises you made." She's breathing hard, still yanking on her shoe. "I told you how important today's appointment is."

My mind races, my eyes going to my watch. "What are you talking about? There's still over an hour before you have to leave."

"I had to leave half an hour ago. I called you a million times." She pinches her lips together. "You said you'd be here. You promised, Jace."

Shit, not again. I pull out my phone and see that she's right. Missed calls, messages, and voicemail notifications.

"Crap. I'm sorry, Em." I brush my hand through my hair, feeling like an ass. "But I don't understand. It says three ten on the calendar. I checked it ten times to make sure I got the correct time."

She finally got her shoe on and storms into the kitchen. I follow her, shaking my head as if that would help me make sense of this bizarre situation.

This whole conversation has already left a sour taste in my mouth, and I flinch when Em reaches the calendar and stabs it with her finger.

"There. One thirty." She stabs it a few more times as I get closer. "They're never going to hire me now."

I squint to see the numbers on the calendar. "Em, it says three ten."

"No, it doesn't." She shakes her head, still pointing at the numbers. "This is the only thing I've ever asked of you, and now it's all over. You've ruined *everything*."

Her nostrils flare, and her mouth is pulled into a tight line. She stomps her foot on the floor and hits her fist on her thigh. "Damn it, I'm so angry with you. I've asked for one thing. *One* thing. This was my only chance."

Tears build in her eyes but she locks her jaw, from the looks of it, willing them to go away before they spill over. Trying to stay strong because she thinks she needs to be.

All the while, I'm confused, still not understanding what's going on.

She starts walking back and forth behind the counter.

Then something she said registers.

"What do you mean that this was your only chance? And

hiring you?" Cold dread washes over me as my mind tries to make sense of this when there's only one possible answer. But I don't want to accept that. "What was so important that you missed?"

That stops her in her tracks. Instead of continuing to glare at me, her gaze strays to the floor.

I take a step closer, my throat suddenly tight. "Em? What's going on? What appointment was it?"

She mumbles something I can't hear.

"What was that?" I'm trying to stay calm, but I suddenly have a sickening feeling in my stomach, and it makes my blood boil. *I hate when people hide things from me.*

Lifting her head, she looks at me, holding her wobbly chin high. "My audition for *Kinder Street.*"

Under different circumstances, I would have applauded her for holding her head high, for standing up for herself. But right now, the thought of her leaving us, of leaving *me*, pushes me over the edge, and a wave of anger rushes through me so violently, I have to take a step back.

What the actual fuck?

She was going to audition for *Kinder Street*? Today?

"Why is this the first time I'm hearing about this? Were you planning on leaving this whole time? Was this just a game to you?" I'm trying my hardest to keep my voice level, but I don't think I'm very successful.

I feel like I just got kicked in the balls.

Em averts her gaze and tugs at the collar of her shirt. "What? No, of course not. I was going to tell you when I got the job."

"The show is on the other side of the fucking country, Em. I know what this means."

That shuts her up, and I'm glad. I really need a minute.

Deep breath in. Deep breath out.

Normally, I like to pride myself on my self-control. Whenever I have to deal with anger or other negative emotions, I'm able to wrap them up nicely and let them all out in the pool or at the gym. Physical outlets are my go-to form of therapy.

I can't even remember the last time I was ready to blow up like this.

Losing the race last week was brutal, yes, but that was frustration and disappointment geared toward me.

This time, it's Em.

All Em. If she gets the job, when will she look after Tanner? Or would she work on the weekends? No, that doesn't make sense. The only option would be during the day . . . instead of being here with Tanner. And of course, it would mean she'd be leaving me as well.

"Were you going to tell me in the same breath that you quit your job here and left us?" The calmness in my voice is a tad eerie even to my own ears, and I think she notices it too as she gapes at me with her mouth slightly open.

"No, no, no. That's not how it is at all." She pauses for a moment, and then she squints at me, her brow lowering. "Also, *you* were the one who told me to chase my dreams."

"Oh, now it's my fault too that you were planning on leaving us? Because it's not already bad enough that you blame me for missing your audition?"

Why the fuck would she leave us—leave me—when it's been so good?

Or am I the only one feeling that?

"But it *is* your fault." She raises her voice and throws her hands up in the air.

"Maybe next time you should write the numbers in the correct fucking order."

The words are out of my mouth, and I regret them the second I say them. *Shit.*

Em flinches, her eyes glazing over as she swallows loudly and nods. When she closes her eyes for a long moment and presses her lips together, I want to punch myself in the face for that asshole comment.

I take a step toward her and her eyes snap open. She immediately holds her hands up to warn me off, stepping around me and making a beeline for the front door.

"Em, wait. I'm sorry. I shouldn't have said that. That was out of line."

She spins around, her cold gaze hitting me like an ice storm. "It was. Especially after everything I told you about my parents and how they made fun of me. I trusted you and gave you my heart, but I should have known better. The only way you can feel better about yourself is by making others feel less."

I trusted you and gave you my heart.

What is she talking about?

"I . . . I have to go."

I'm too stunned to reply, too frozen in spot to go after her as the door shuts behind her.

Ironically, she shuts it quietly.

The opposite of what I'm feeling right now.

Everything inside me is loud and angry.

The only way you can feel better about yourself is by making others feel less.

I don't do that. I don't fucking do that.

And she's planning on leaving us. Leaving Tanner. Leaving... me.

I go in search of the baby monitor to check on Tanner and take it downstairs with me to the gym to deal with this the only way I know.

Physical exhaustion.

I really hope he'll sleep for a very long time, because this will take a while to work through if it's even possible at all.

Because Em is leaving.

Damn it.

TWENTY-NINE

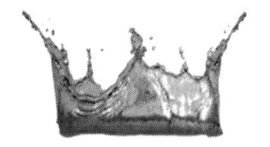

EMILIA

Nicole took one look at me this morning and told me to take a shower. Apparently, we're going somewhere. I didn't take a shower but left the house with her. I mean, what else are hats for?

My best friend has been with me through tears, ice cream attacks, and blank staring-into-nothing episodes all week. I call this phase PJ1—post-Jace week one.

It's been interesting, to say the least. My emotions have been all over the place, and I can never be sure if I might burst into spontaneous bawling or not.

Two days ago, I got teary-eyed at the supermarket when I saw the granola bar Jace likes—banana and peanut butter-chocolate chips.

Long story short, I've been a mess.

I texted Jace the day after our fight and told him I was sick and couldn't work, and I've been avoiding his calls and messages. I'm actually not even sure if I have any sick days, so maybe he fired me in one of the voicemails he left me.

I'm not sure when I'll have the guts to listen to his voice or read his messages.

Thinking about him is already painful enough.

Add missing out on my dream job on top of that, and my heart's been broken. My spirit crushed.

Nicole is quiet as we hike up the trail in Tilden Regional Park. It's still as gorgeous as I remember. The path up the hill is rocky but well worth the view when you're at the top.

I was really hoping that she was right and getting outside would help. It hasn't so far, but at least I'm getting some exercise, and I'm safe from food-induced meltdowns.

We've been up here for a while now, sitting on a bench, staring into the distance—thanks to a rare clear sky. My thoughts are tripping all over themselves, but it's not like I've been able to contain them anyway. They've been eating at me day and night.

My dream job... gone.

My dream guy... unclear. But for now... gone.

It's too much

"All right. That's all the time you get to wallow." Nicole turns her body to face me, propping her arm on the back of the bench.

"Mmm." My perfect reply lately. I've discovered it's pretty versatile.

"Millie, look at me." Her gaze is soft, one corner of her mouth slightly lifted. "You've been absolutely miserable. I know what he did wasn't okay, but don't you think you should at least try to talk to him? Not to mention, you technically still have a job."

A sad sigh moves past my lips. "I know."

I'm a coward with a capital C. My hurt pride mixed with

a healthy dose of guilt is a real killer.

Because not only do I miss Jace, but I miss Tanner with my whole being too.

Telling Jace I'm sick and can't work wasn't a total lie because Nicole is right, I've been absolutely miserable. A broken heart should get you some sick leave. It takes a lot longer, and is far more painful than any other injury or sickness I've ever had in my life.

And instead of getting better, it feels like it's only getting worse every day.

The longing to be with Tanner, the yearning for the man I've fallen crazy in love with over the last few months. It's so much, too much. My chest feels like it's been robbed of something vital, and is consequently withering away without it. Escaping to a dark place where hope is a foreign word. Leaving me with no control.

No matter how many times I try to smile or say I'm doing okay, it never reaches my center. My body is disconnected, the link to my heart severed, and I can't shake the feeling that I've lost a part of my essence.

I could have forgiven him for being late, even though I was incredibly mad and disappointed about that. But everything that came after?

His anger, the words he spoke to me, and the look on his face as he said them. The furious glare he shot me, his eyes stormy and cold as he dropped his hands to his sides to form clenched fists.

Then the sudden stillness when the realization of his words hit him. The color fleeing from his face as he reached out to me.

But the damage had been done.

For twenty years, I'd heard my parents berate me, mock me, dismiss me. Their words hurt, but they've never come from any place but self-centeredness and loathing. With Jace? I felt he'd accepted me for who I am, dyslexia and all.

Maybe next time you should write the numbers in the correct fucking order.

But I'd been wrong. Very wrong.

He was supposed to be *my* person. His opinion matters.

My own guilt over not telling him about my audition is constantly in the back of my mind too, but I'm ignoring that. Jace's faith in me was what helped me try. What I don't understand is why he got so angry and so suddenly.

If he'd let me explain, I would have told him that I wanted to see if I could work out something with the producers. Maybe I could work from one of their West Coast studios instead of the East Coast? Or sell them my program?

To be honest, I wasn't sure what I was going to do. This has been my dream for so long, I didn't really think much past that thought and what consequences might lie on the other side.

Now, the man who had been my advocate, became my enemy. The man who had disappeared for days after his lost race, had no time to listen to me.

Clearly, ignorance is my biggest friend right now, especially when Jace might have been right about a few things, after all.

Hindsight truly is a bitch.

"What if we can't work things out? That scares me." The words are so quiet, the wind almost carries them away.

Nicole reaches out and squeezes my arm. "There's only one way to find out. You need to know what you want, and I think we both know what that is. I understand why you didn't tell him about the audition at the beginning, but he sees things differently. You butted heads, it happens."

"Just like that, huh?" I close my eyes and chuckle.

"It can be."

My reply dies in my throat when my phone buzzes in my pocket. I get it out, staring at the area code.

Nicole peeks at the screen. "New York?"

I shrug and push the green button. "Hello?"

"Miss Davis?" An unfamiliar male voice greets me.

"Yes."

"Hi. My name is Richard Moore."

Richard Moore? Why does that name sound familiar?

"Hi, Mr. Moore."

"Please call me Richard."

"Okay, Richard. How can I help you?"

"I understand this might not be the norm, but I'm calling to talk to you about an opportunity." He pauses for a moment. "I'm with Moore Media."

My wide eyes find Nicole's as I squeeze the living daylights out of her hand, because holy shit.

That's why his name rang a bell.

I stand up so quickly that I get dizzy as a result.

My hand flies to my mouth before holding on to the back of the bench for support.

Moore Media has worked with some of the most successful shows in the children's entertainment industry and is a big sponsor of *Kinder Street*. I've heard of the elderly man being very involved in everything, so it makes sense he'd be at the audition.

"Miss Davis? Are you still there?"

I nod, even though I know he can't see me. "Yes, yes. I am. Sorry."

He chuckles. "Okay, perfect. I'm sorry things didn't work out with the audition, but I heard about your last-minute family emergency situation."

Ah yes, that little white lie.

Well, technically Tanner is like my baby, and I couldn't leave him alone, so it's rather a lie of omission in my books, but I try and not think about that too much.

Nothing I'm proud of but my hands were tied, and I panicked. "I'm so sorry. I feel terrible about that."

"I think most of us have had situations like that before." He sounds reassuring, so I want to believe he means it and isn't just saying it to make me feel better. Not that it really matters in the end.

I wait for him to say more, wondering what reason he could possibly have to call me. My fingers dig into the wood of the bench, and I can only hope I'm not catching a splinter. That would be my luck.

Nicole gives me room to roam, but her eyes are on me.

Richard clears his throat. "As you may know, I flew to California for the auditions. I was looking forward to meeting you."

"You were?" Reality slowly sinks in, and I'm becoming more and more aware of how stupid I must sound with my short replies.

Thankfully, Richard seems undeterred by my lack of communication skills. "I was. I read your application and was really interested in hearing more about your program. It sounds rather impressive and unlike anything I've heard of before."

My heart flutters, and I take a calming breath before answering him. "Thank you so much. I can't tell you how much that means to me."

"From what I understand, the program is finished?"

"It was a small production, but yes, it's finished." Pride blooms inside my rib cage, spreading throughout my whole body like a comforting blanket. This program is my brainchild, and no one could ever take that away from me.

With everything happening this last week with Jace, and the missed audition, I haven't taken the time to think about what I'm going to do with it.

Theoretically, the possibilities are endless, but also come with a price tag that's way too big for my savings account. Especially after I paid Brandon for all the work on the videos.

"I read the description of your program and watched the intro video you sent. I have to say, teaching music not only with instruments but also signs is absolutely brilliant, and I'd love to talk to you about it some more and see what you've come up with. My schedule is rather busy right now, and I don't have the time to fly to California any time soon. How do you feel about coming to New York instead?"

Again, silence stretches between us as I try to get my emotions under control.

My breathing speeds up and, when I look at Nicole, she tilts her head and mouths, "You okay?"

I nod and close my eyes.

I must be the most unprofessional person Richard has ever talked to, but I'm absolutely floored by his words, and don't know how to handle both his interest in the program and the compliments.

"If you need time to think about it, no worr—"

"No, no." Let's add rudeness to my list. Ugh. "Sorry, I meant I'd love to meet up with you. That would be absolutely amazing. Thank you."

This man deserves a medal for being patient with me, and I promise myself to get a grip, because I do not want to screw this up. This is a once-in-a-lifetime opportunity, a second chance, and I'd never forgive myself if I failed.

"Great, great. I'm glad to hear that." It sounds like he's typing on a keyboard. "My assistant Andrea knows my schedule better than I do. I'm forwarding her your contact information, so she'll be in touch with you shortly to arrange everything. I'm looking forward to meeting you in person."

"I can't wait. Thank you so much for everything."

"Thank you, my dear. I have a feeling this will be the start of something great. I'll see you soon. Take care."

I stare at the phone after we hang up until Nicole grabs my hands. "Please tell me this was what I think it was because yes, yes, yes."

I tell her what Richard said, the whole conversation still surreal when we finally make it back to the car after a long hike down the hill.

The high of the call is still there, but the sadness is slowly creeping back in too. The first thing I wanted to do after ending the call was to pick it right back up and call Jace to tell him.

And I can't.

Or rather, I won't.

I let my head fall against the headrest and close my eyes for a long moment.

"You've got this, Millie." Nicole is there, as always, giving me the time I need to figure out what the heck is going on with my life.

"Thank you. For everything." I smile at her and reach for the keys just as my phone buzzes on the middle console.

Patricia's name flashes on the screen with an incoming text message. My heart skips a beat, unsure if I'm stable enough to see what she wants. She knows what happened, mostly at least, and has been keeping me updated with cute pictures of Tanner since she's watching him for Jace. Thank goodness for summer break.

We've also been able to do a few video chats. Seeing Tanner's cute face makes me equally happy and sad.

I hate not being able to see him in person, but I know I can't handle seeing Jace right now. Not yet.

Still, every time his mom texts or calls, I'm afraid it has something to do with Jace. Or worse, that it's actually him using her phone to get me to answer. I'm clearly paranoid.

"You want me to read it first to see if it's safe?" Nicole grabs the phone and holds it between us.

"No, it's okay. But thank you." I might as well get it over with. I grab the phone and swipe the screen to read the message.

Patricia: Hey, sweetie. Just wanted to make sure you're still coming to Tanner's birthday party next week.

Crap. I totally forgot about it. Not that it'll be Tanner's birthday but that Patricia mentioned organizing a party for him.

My thumbs hover over the screen as I try not to panic.

Does that mean Jace will be there? *Stupid question. Of course, he'll be there.*

The better question is, will I be ready to see him?

"Of course you're going." Nicole's leaning over the middle console, giving me a reassuring thumbs up. "Maybe you can talk to him then? It'll be less intimidating when other people are around. And it'll be all about Tanner anyway, so you can focus on him."

I think on that for a moment. "You might be right."

Emilia: Hey! When is it again?

Patricia: Sunday.

It's Friday today, so still over a week until then. With a possible trip to New York before then too. That will give me time to mentally prepare myself, so I'll be able to face Jace. It's not like I'm going there to see him anyway. That day will be all about Tanner and Tanner only.

I smile at the thought of seeing Tanner again, of taking him in my arms and squeezing the daylights out of him to make him giggle.

Emilia: I wouldn't miss it for the world. Let me know when you have time this week for a video chat. I'd love to see that little monkey before I forget what he looks like.

A lump forms in my throat and I have a difficult time

swallowing. At this rate, I'm never going to make it home today.

Patricia: He misses you so much and would love to see you. I can call you in the morning when I'm at Jace's.

His name looks like a blinking neon sign on the screen, and I know I won't be okay seeing him next week. But somehow, I have to deal with it. For Tanner.

Emilia: Sounds perfect. I've got to go. We'll talk in the morning.

I need to stop before she asks how I'm doing. I don't think I have it in me today to talk about that with her.

Nicole smiles wildly and hits the dashboard with her palm. "Since that's settled now, let's go home. You need a hot shower and a cozy date with some sappy TV, a box of tissues, and our main men, Ben and Jerry."

I snort at that remark, but we both know that's exactly what I need. Because I might have gotten another chance at my dream job, but my heart still feels broken. I feel . . . despondent. Because I've lost my other job of a lifetime and something I'd begun to dream about.

Jace. Tanner.

A family of my own.

THIRTY

JACE

"Man, you look like shit." Noah claps my shoulder before taking a seat on the couch opposite me.

"I still can't believe you fucked things up so badly." Hunter glares at me, and it's not the first time he's done it since he practically threatened me with violence last week if I didn't spill the beans to him.

Ryan shuts the door of the game room and walks past the pool table to the two couches nestled in the corner. "Will you guys watch the cussing when the door is open? Harper will have your balls if she hears you."

He sits down next to me while Hunter's still pacing, shooting me icy glares in between. I ignore him and turn to Ryan. "You sure Harper is okay with Tanner? I don't want her to overdo it."

Ryan's eyes go wide as he shakes his head. "Don't you dare say something like that to her, or try and take Tanner away from her. She'll castrate you for either. She's so looking forward to having a baby that she'd babysit Satan's spawn at this point."

"Huh. That's an . . . interesting way of looking at it. You too?"

"Babysit Satan's spawn? Fuck no."

We all chuckle, and I punch him in the arm. "I was talking about you being baby hungry too."

One corner of his mouth lifts before dropping again. "Not really. I mean, I'm looking forward to meeting our little one, but that doesn't mean I want to be around everyone else's kids all the time. They're stressful."

"So true." It just slips out, but then I shrug because heck, it is true. Kids are beyond stressful, but at the same time, they also fill a void that no one or nothing else can.

Tanner is living proof of that.

"So, what happened?" Ryan leans back on the couch, one of his long arms extending along the back of it.

"Women suck, that's what happened." Noah's words are quiet but loud enough for us to hear in the otherwise quiet room.

Hunter throws his head back and groans. "Noah, one day I'll get you drunk so you finally tell us who pissed in your cheerios."

Noah glares at him, too much of a quiet and calm guy to do or say more.

Ryan points at the couch Noah sits on. "Hunt, sit your ass down. You're driving me nuts walking back and forth."

Hunter curses under his breath but sits down. He's the youngest of us and listens to Ryan the most, who coincidentally, is the oldest.

After letting out an irritated breath, Ryan looks back at me and tilts his head. Waiting.

I shrug. "We had a time mix-up and she missed an

appointment that was important to her. We got into a fight, and when she told me what the appointment was for, I lost it and said some shit I didn't mean."

"What was the appointment for?"

"Another job."

Three loud hisses echo through the room.

Ryan rubs a hand over his face. "Shit, man."

"I know."

"A different nanny job?"

I stretch my arms overhead before linking my hands behind my head, leaning back on the couch to stare at the ceiling. "No. It was for a TV kids' show. It's always been her dream to work there and they invited her to an audition."

The moment replays in my head, the hard stares and nasty words that were spoken, and it takes me a minute to realize that it's quiet around me. Too quiet.

Why is no one saying anything?

Lifting my head, I first look at Ryan and then at Hunter and Noah. They give me almost identical looks. Raised eyebrows and an exasperated notion in their eyes. "What is it? Why are you staring at me like that?"

Noah is the first to break the silence. "You're an idiot."

"Why would you say that?"

"Because you are." This time it's Ryan.

I don't need to look at Hunter since he thinks I'm an idiot when it comes to Em anyway. For some reason, he's on her side no matter what. Traitor.

I blow out a noisy breath, feeling the thrum of my own pulse in my veins. "What the fuck did I do? She's the one who did all of it behind my back, ready to jump ship the first chance she got."

I clench my fists, almost wishing for a fight to let out some of this negative energy, but none of my friends look surprised or bothered by my outburst. They probably know I'm full of shit.

"Have you talked to her since?" Ryan is certainly the calmest of the group. Maybe it's because he's in his mid-thirties. He also completely ignores my rambling.

"No. Over a week of absolute radio silence. She should have told me. It's not a hard thing to do." I'm trying to hold on to my anger, but even though the storm inside my stomach is still agitated and ready to roar, it's also threatened to be overpowered by something much stronger.

Regret and agony.

"I totally understand that, believe me. But you know what happened with Harper and me. I'm not saying your situation is the same of course, but if I'd given her a chance to explain, if I'd actually taken the time to give her a few minutes and listened, we probably could have saved ourselves a lot of heartache and time."

Ryan's serious gaze bores into mine, and I think he's trying to make sure I actually listen. "Don't repeat my mistakes and have your head stuck up your ass because of a false sense of pride. Just saying."

Damn.

I keep staring at him until the sound of the door opening pulls my attention away.

Harper pokes her head into the room and gives us a tired yet happy smile. She's carrying Tanner who has his head buried in her neck. How she carries him with that huge belly is a mystery to me, but she doesn't seem to mind. "I think someone's ready to go home."

I push off the couch and walk over to Harper, gently taking Tanner from her. He's still awake, mostly at least, but definitely ready to go to sleep.

We say goodbye to everyone and Ryan walks us to the door.

"Think about what I said, okay? Don't let your ego stand in the way of your happiness. You'd regret that for the rest of your life." He claps my shoulder once. "Now go get your boy home safely. I'll see you later. Thanks for coming over."

"Happy birthday, man."

After buckling in Tanner, I get in my seat and take my phone out of my pocket to put it on the charger. It slips out of my hand and lands next to my foot. The tumble must have activated the screen a few times because when I pick it up, I stare at a picture of Em, Tanner, and me.

My mom took it on the day Em and I went after her and Tanner to the park. Things had just started with Em and me, and it was a fun day.

We both look so happy, and it pains me to not have that anymore. Because I want it.

I miss it.

I miss her.

I miss *us*.

Plugging in the phone, I turn down the music and begin our drive home.

As I suspected, Tanner's out seconds after we hit the road, the rumbling of the motor and the movement of the car working better than any sleeping machine ever could.

There's not a lot of traffic and I welcome it, my thoughts occupied with this evening's conversation. Ryan's words repeat in my head over and over.

Don't let your ego stand in the way of your happiness.

Is that really what I'm doing? I mean, yes, I can be honest with myself and admit that my ego has taken a beating. Having Em think about leaving me, leaving *us*, for another job, is a hard pill to swallow.

Another conversation pops into my head, one I had with Em right after her mother stomped all over her feelings. I'd wanted so badly to make her feel better. To make her believe in herself.

If it's your dream to be a part of that kids' show, then do it. Fucking chase that dream like the devil's right on your heels because you deserve it. You deserve the world.

Fuck. And here I am, doing exactly what her mom—her whole family—has done to her, her whole life. No wonder she looked so wounded.

I'm such an asshole.

Bright headlights shine straight in my face and pull me out of my thoughts. The car in the oncoming traffic is swerving farther into my lane with each passing second.

My heart takes a lurch as every muscle in my body goes on high alert.

Fuck.

The damn car is coming straight for me.

I honk the horn and pull the steering wheel to the right. Sharply. Too sharply.

It takes me several seconds to correct the car, to gain control, and I come to a stop on the side of the road.

Holy shit.

My life just sped by, and this whole incident probably took less than thirty seconds.

The rearview mirror shows the other car is happily back

in its lane, the driver probably not even aware of the heart attack they just gave me.

A quick look to the back confirms that Tanner's still knocked out cold, his quiet snores oddly comforting.

I push the warning hazard button and drop my head against the steering wheel. After drawing in several shallow breaths, I still feel like screaming. I need to get rid of this pressure, his intense this tightness in my chest. I can't stop shaking.

Leaning back, I try to empty my mind of all thoughts and focus on my breathing. Something I've perfected over the years for my training. I like to think of it as a secret weapon, because it allows me to focus on my races without any distractions.

It doesn't work as well as it normally does, but at least it allows me to calm my breathing to an almost normal pattern. My hands have mostly stopped shaking too, and I grab my phone without real conscious thought.

I want to call Em.

I have to call her. *Need* to.

She and Tanner were all I could think about during those panic-filled seconds when I thought I might crash straight into the oncoming car.

These two have been the main occupants of my brain for weeks now. Months really, if I'm honest.

Don't repeat my mistakes and have your head stuck up your ass because of a false sense of pride.

I know Ryan was right. I see it with a clarity that wasn't there before.

I pick up my phone with trembling hands and pull up her

contact, pushing the call button after taking a few more steadying breaths.

It goes directly to voicemail. Shit.

After a few more tries, I give up and throw my phone on the passenger seat. It bounces off and lands on the floor. Figures. I glare at it for a moment but pick it up anyway. Em might call me back.

Maybe it's better to do this in person anyway. Apologies aren't nearly as good on the phone. Tanner's birthday party is in two days, and I hope like hell that Mom's right and Em is going to show.

If not, I'm going to find her. No matter how long it takes.

Because I was wrong. Terribly, horribly wrong. How could I hurt her so carelessly? How could I throw words at her that I knew would cut deep? Selfish asshole. That's what I am.

All I can hope is that Em forgives me. She forgave me for hiding away for days, now I need her to forgive me for breaking her heart.

Because going forward, I know something with absolute certainty. She is my future. She is *our* future.

THIRTY-ONE

EMILIA

"So, tell me about New York." Patricia looks up from where she's putting bows around mason jars.

Somehow she coaxed me into helping her with the preparations of Tanner's birthday party tomorrow. I'm in charge of filling up treat bags.

At Jace's house of all places.

Apparently, I'm that easy. As if the impending torture tomorrow—seeing Jace—isn't bad enough, being here has made me feel . . . homesick.

Where everything started.

Where everything evolved.

Where I fell in love with Jace.

Where he broke my heart.

And I didn't even get to soothe it by seeing Tanner, because he's gone with Jace.

It's been two weeks. My heart suffers from withdrawal symptoms.

"So, how did it go?" Patricia picks up the decoration jars she finished and places them gently in a box on the table.

I clear my throat, pushing away all thoughts of Jace and my shattered dreams.

Instead, I focus on the woman who has become very dear to me over the last few months. "It went well, I think. I hope."

"Did Mr. Moore say when he'll know more?" She's done with the mason jars and begins to tear open several bags of mostly green balloons—perfect for the dinosaur-themed party. She dumps them on the table in front of her before she starts blowing them up with a balloon pump.

"He said it will be a few days, maybe a week or two, before he'll know more. He needs to look into a few things first, talk to some people, whatever that means." The meeting was two days ago, but the anticipation—the torturous wait—is already killing me.

"What does your gut tell you? Do you have a good feeling about it?"

After quickly becoming one of my biggest cheerleaders, I appreciate that she's just as curious as I am. I truly don't know how I would have survived these last few weeks without her.

How can this woman have so much faith in me when my own mother despises me? I sigh. And then I replay the meeting in my head like I've done so often over the last forty-eight hours.

An easy smile forms on my face when I remember Richard's enthusiasm. "He definitely liked the program. He was also very blunt about the improvements it would need in order to succeed in any commercial form, but I already knew that. I'm not sure what's going to happen since it's not just up to him but also his business partners, but I trust his expertise. He's been involved in some of the best programs out there."

"That's great to hear. You know I'm rooting for you."

"Thanks, Patricia." A sudden rush of gratitude rushes through my system. "For everything."

She forms a knot at the bottom of a balloon before placing it in a large trash bag. Then she walks over to me, placing both of her hands on my upper arms. "Everything's going to be okay. *Everything*. I just know it."

I smile at her. "I hope so."

Then the doorbell rings and Patricia drops her hands. Her eyes widen for a moment before she chuckles nervously. "Um, that's for me. I have to get that. You go finish those bags. They look perfect."

I nod, wondering who or what's at the door that has her acting so weird.

She grabs something from the kitchen that I can't see before speed-walking to the door.

Hushed voices come from the entrance, but they are too quiet to make out anything that's said.

"What the hell, Mom? Where are you going?" The male voice is loud and clear, right before the front door closes with a loud bang.

I freeze.

This can't be happening. No freaking way. Patricia said he *wouldn't* be here. Technically, I guess she wasn't lying since he wasn't here when I got here. That woman.

Footsteps echo down the hallway, and for a moment, I consider hiding somewhere. But then I remember my car. Patricia was unloading boxes in the driveway when I got here, so I parked across the road. Jace may have seen it. Oh Patricia.

And now, I'm not ready to face Jace yet. Not today.

I'm still standing there like an idiot—a dinosaur treat bag in one hand and chocolate-covered pretzels in the other—when he rounds the corner.

His eyes are focused on the phone in his hand, and I don't think I've ever been this quiet in my entire life. I don't dare blink as I watch him push the screen a few times and lift the phone to his ear. "Come on, Em. Pick up your phone please."

That voice.

I've forgotten how much I love it. It's deep and sexy. And it makes me feel all these emotions that I didn't want to feel anymore. I've tried so hard to not think about him since I last saw him.

"Dammit." He throws his phone on the kitchen counter and brushes a hand through his hair.

I've missed weaving my own hands through his thick brown hair.

When he lifts his head on a sigh, his blue eyes land right on me.

His mouth falls open as he blinks rapidly. His shoulders fall. His chest caves.

"Em?" His voice cracks with emotion, and I swallow hard.

My mouth is so dry, I can barely open it enough to wet my lips.

Since I don't know what else to do, I lift my hand—dinosaur treat bag and all—and give an awkward wave. "Hey."

He shakes his head like he can't believe I'm here, gesturing toward his phone. "I just . . . and you are . . . I can't believe you're here. I just tried calling you again."

His gaze doesn't leave mine, like he's afraid I might disappear if he looks away.

Oddly enough, I feel the same. Even though I was nervous to see him tomorrow, I also can't deny that there was the smallest speck of joy and anticipation knowing I'd be able to lay eyes on him again soon.

"What are you doing here?" He takes a step closer but stops again. "Why haven't you answered my calls? I got worried when it started going straight to voicemail a few days ago."

"I . . ." It feels like something's stuck in my throat, and I have to swallow several times until I think I might manage to get out a sentence. "I lost my phone in New York a few days ago."

Jace frowns. "New York?"

I forgot he doesn't know I flew to the East Coast. "Yes. I had a business meeting."

"Oh."

My breath snags on something inside my chest, and it pulls me out of this awkward moment. I set the bag and treat on the table and straighten my dress with long, nervous strokes. "I should probably go."

Jace stares at me as I pick up my purse from the chair next to me. I only make it a few steps when he composes himself and walks toward me with an outstretched hand. "Please don't go."

His frantic gaze searches mine, quietly pleading.

"Where's your mom?"

He waves one hand toward the hallway. "Don't ask me. I think she's gone crazy. First, she tells me to ring the bell when I get here, and then when she opens the door, she practically snatches Tanner out of my arms and runs off with him, yelling over her shoulder to please finish the decorations and that she'll be back tomorrow with the birthday boy."

That sounds so much like Patricia I actually want to laugh. I refrain though, biting on the inside of my cheek instead.

"Can we talk? Please?" He gestures toward the couch, and after trying to clear the fog from my brain, I sigh and nod. I walk over to it and sit on the edge.

"What do you want, Jace?" I try and push the sadness away that's clinging on the edges of my consciousness, but it's hard to see him. I feel deflated, this situation sucking the leftover energy I had left right out of me.

I know I had to talk to him eventually, that it was unavoidable. But I don't know if I'm . . . No. It's not about being ready, it's my fear of being rejected. Forever. Not only because of my family's ridicule of losing another man.

What if Jace has wanted to talk to me to tell me to leave and not return? I'm not sure how I'd survive that. And that's my greatest fear. I love him, but it may not be enough to keep him.

Jace sits down a few feet away from me, probably noticing that I chose the easiest spot to escape. For good reason.

He leans forward, placing his elbows on his knees, and threading his fingers together under his chin. "How have you been?"

I'm not sure how to handle this. Trying to act normal is beyond weird. "Good. You?"

Definitely the most awkward small talk ever.

"Sure, sure."

"What?"

He grimaces. "Sorry. I just can't believe you're here. I feel like I haven't seen you in years."

"I know what you mean."

He scoots a little closer, and I wonder if he's even aware of his movement. I have to consciously fight against the urge to lean into him, because that's what my body wants. What my heart truly wants. But it's also still bruised. Jace hurt my feelings.

We all make mistakes, especially in relationships, but his wasn't a small one. He hit the freaking jackpot of hurt feelings, the one thing that would dig so deep, it's hard to get over.

Ironically, had this happened a few weeks or months ago, it might have been easier for me to get over it. But since I've known Jace, I've developed this new level of pride and confidence when it comes to how I should be treated.

How I *deserve* to be treated. It took me a while to recognize it, and to get a good grasp on it, but it's there. Burning strong and proud in my veins.

"I didn't go to my parents' dinner last week." I'm not sure why I tell him, but for some reason, I want him to know.

That gets his attention and he straightens. "Why?"

I shrug and stare at my hands. "I was just fed up. I think the whole scenario when I saw my mom with her friend mixed with our . . . altercation just pushed me over the edge. I was so tired of being anyone's punching bag, so I told her as much. I won't visit until they can act like civilized people and treat me with the respect and humanity I deserve."

My conversations with Nicole have helped a lot, forcing me to take a really good look at myself and my life too.

Despite the pain, these past few weeks have proven to be a soul-searching experience. *A necessary one.*

When several seconds have passed, and Jace still hasn't said a word, I can't resist the urge to look at him. There's a gleam in his eyes that wasn't there before and a satisfied smile curves his beautiful lips.

He reaches out with one of his hands but pulls it back before touching me. "Aside from the fact that I wish I could erase our *altercation*, I'm so proud of you. I know that wasn't easy for you."

"Thank you. It was a long time coming, and I wish I would have stood up for myself earlier, saving myself plenty of heartache over the years, but it is what it is. I'm trying to focus on the future instead of torturing myself with what-ifs from the past." I finish my speech on a loud exhale, feeling lighter than before.

Did I want to share this with him? Was that one of the things that has been weighing on me?

"My coach would be really proud of you right now. I know I am. He always says there's never anything good coming from looking at past failures. All it does is imprison you, hold you back, and give you a late start into the future." He chuckles softly. "That man says the most random things sometimes."

"But it makes sense."

"It does."

The sense of camaraderie I've previously felt with Jace is still very present, and gosh, it feels so dang good. I've missed him. Not just Jace, my lover and the man I've fallen madly in love with, but also Jace, my friend and confidant.

He's intelligent and funny, protective and strong. I still

haven't forgotten what happened, but I also can't deny the comfort from being in his presence.

He clears his throat, the rich noise making the hair rise at the nape of my neck, sending delicious shivers down my back. "Now about us."

I look him straight in the eye, the beautiful blue of his irises captivating me. "What about us?"

"Oh, Em. There's so much about us. So very much, baby."

THIRTY-TWO

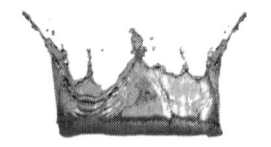

JACE

Don't screw this up.

Don't screw this up.

Despite my outward bravado, I'm scared shitless about doing or saying something stupid and screwing this up with Em.

And that can not happen. It's not an option.

Not now. Not ever.

She bites her lip and averts my gaze. Shit. I've zoned out again and just stared at her like a moron.

All I want to do is fall on my knees and beg for her forgiveness. To take her into my arms and inhale her sweet scent. To go back to the way things were before our fallout.

When she turns her head in my direction, her beautiful eyes focus on me, and my breath stalls in my chest. Something happens every time she looks at me. We connect on a level I can't fully grasp, let alone begin to explain. It's raw and deep. It makes me feel vulnerable yet strong at the same time.

She lifts her chin but her features stay soft. My gaze

flickers to her mouth. That soft bow of her upper lip perfectly curved and just waiting to be sucked on.

"I'm sorry." The words rush out of my mouth, the urge to make this right, to fix things, taking on its own life. "I'm so terribly sorry. I'm a total ass for my stupid comment, and I'll never forgive myself for putting that look in your eyes. Never."

Em's throat works as she swallows. Once. Twice. "What you said was mean and uncalled for, even if I wrote the numbers wrong."

"I know. Nothing makes my behavior okay. Two wrongs never make a right, and I overstepped. You caught me off guard and I got mad, but I should have dealt with it better instead of hurting you, and for that I am truly sorry."

"I know you are."

The look on her face is killing me. I've seen it twice, the first caused by her family, and the second by me. I never want to see it again. "I'd move the earth if it meant I could take it back."

"I know you would."

"Tell me what it takes for you to forgive me." I lose the battle with my fidgety fingers and grab the hand that's closest to me, savoring the brush of her fingertips on my palm as a gasp leaves her mouth.

Hope stirs in my chest when she doesn't break the contact. "I've missed you so much, and I'm not beyond begging. You have become my person so quickly that I will do whatever it takes to make this right again with you. As long as it takes to have—"

Her hand shoots up and covers my mouth with her fingers. "Will you actually let me get a word in too?"

My lips move against her fingertips but no words come out. Her gaze flickers to my mouth and I watch her face transform. A warm blush pinks her cheeks, her magnetic eyes turning into liquid pools of desire.

When her fingers brush across my lips, I close my eyes to relish in the sensation. The contact couldn't be more innocent, but my blood is boiling, the hunger for her so strong, I might go up in flames.

I grab her wrist and pull her hand away from my mouth before I give in and start sucking on her fingers.

It takes her a moment to catch up with the motion and her hooded eyes lift to mine. Her chest heaves in quick succession, her breathing growing faster and more audible as we stare at each other.

I push through the lust-covered bubble I'm in and ignore the fever that's spreading throughout my body. "Baby."

Her hands tremble in mine, and oddly enough, it gives me the courage I need to keep going.

When I'm sure I have her full attention, I squeeze her fingers. "I love you."

Em closes her eyes. When she opens them, they are shiny, and she nods almost compulsively. Taking our tangled hands, she lifts them up and presses our connected palms to her heart.

The gesture is too much, and I can't wait any longer. Extracting my hands from hers, I capture her face, gently caressing her cheeks with my thumbs before leaning in. There's less than an inch between our lips, and I'm desperate to close the distance.

"I need you to tell me, baby." Our breaths mingle, her

sweet scent filling my nostrils. "I need to hear the words. To know that I can make this right. That you'll forgive me."

It takes me a moment to feel her hand on my chest. But instead of pulling me closer, she pushes me away, and my heart sinks.

She wets her lips, and I want to fall to the floor in relief when the corners of her mouth lift in a soft smile. Because she wouldn't do this if she had bad news, right?

When she lifts one of her hands to brush over my cheek, I lean in to her touch.

"We both should have handled the situation differently. I'm sorry for not telling you about my audition. I was scared and didn't want to set myself up for failure in case things didn't work out. I also didn't want to upset you, or worse, disappoint you." Her voice is soft, breaking at the last words.

"You could never disappoint me by going after your dreams. I told you to chase them, just to throw it back in your face. That wasn't fair, and I'll never forgive myself for ruining your chance. But I'm so proud of you for going after them." Turning my head, I press a soft kiss to her palm.

"Maybe it wasn't meant to be. It might have opened another door, but I'm not sure yet."

"Does that have something to do with your trip to New York?"

"It does." She pauses, her gaze dropping to my lips again. It seems like I'm not the only one having trouble focusing on our conversation.

"Will you tell me about it?"

"I will . . . Later." Her pink tongue snakes out of her mouth once more to wet her lips, torturing me in the process.

"There are more important things we have to take care of first."

"Oh yeah?" *Please let it be what I think it might be.* "Like what?"

She leans in, pressing her warm lips to mine before pulling back to look at me. "Like this."

The relief is so strong, my body tingles and I hold on to Em for dear life.

Another soft kiss to my mouth, this one lasting longer and ending with a slight tug on my bottom lip, sending my nerve endings into an absolute frenzy.

"And this."

She travels along my cheek and over to my ear, and I'm reminded of the time I did something similar to her. The first time I got to taste her. The memory alone makes me groan, my dick so hard, it's almost painful.

I can feel her smile on my skin. This little minx knows exactly what she's doing. Somehow, that thought turns me on even more.

Her lips nibble on my earlobe, her teeth grazing it gently.

"I love you." Her whispered words go straight into the deepest vault of my memory to keep it safe.

And into my soul.

And my heart.

"What was that?"

We both know I heard her, but I need to hear those three words again.

"I love you." Her gaze doesn't waver from mine. It's strong and steady, like her voice. "So very much. You and Tanner are my world."

That does it. I grab her by the waist and stand up with her.

She giggles as she tightens her hold around me. "What are you doing?"

My hands move lower, grabbing her ass, squeezing the soft flesh. "What does it look like I'm doing? I'm planning on making up for all the lost time."

I pull her ass closer and she bites her lower lip.

Fuck, I won't make it long.

"Your mom and Tanner won't be back until tomorrow?"

I turn us around to open my bedroom door with my elbow. "That's what she said."

"Oooooh."

Another pull. Another moan.

I reach the bed and put her on the floor, immediately working on her clothes. I don't even know what she's wearing, nor do I care. I pull, unbutton, unzip, and pull some more until she's finally, finally naked. I'm pretty sure I heard something rip but that's the least of my concerns right now.

Em covers her mouth with her hand and giggles.

That pulls me out of my sex haze. "What?"

"That was the most caveman thing anyone's ever done to me."

I growl in response and bend to capture her mouth with mine. I devour her, suck her lips, and taste her tongue until she moans so loudly, I think I'm going to lose my fucking mind. "Bed. Now."

"Not until you're naked too."

She makes quick work of my clothes while I watch her like a hawk, unable to take my eyes off her. Afraid this is all just a dream.

That she's here.

That she's forgiven me.

That she *loves* me.

Apparently, she's also trying to give me a heart attack by dropping to her knees and taking my throbbing cock in her mouth, not even giving me a chance to say a word, let alone catch my breath.

As much as I love her mouth on me, the need to be inside her, to become one with her, is stronger.

Pushing my hands in her hair, I grab her head and stop her. "Baby . . . on the bed. *Now*."

She blinks once before letting go of me, licking her lips before getting situated on the bed with her legs spread wide open for me.

Inviting me.

Welcoming me.

The condom tests my patience to the limit, and when I finally climb over Em's body, I have to stop for a quick taste.

"Is all of this for me, baby?" She whimpers under my touch, bucking up into my mouth as I hit her sensitive bundle of nerves.

Another moan, this one so throaty and sexy, I almost come right then.

"I didn't hear you." I spread her wetness around, paying extra attention to her swollen nub.

"Yeeeeees." She lifts her head and glares at me, making me chuckle.

Apparently, that has pushed Em to her limit, because before I know what's going on, she's up on her knees, pushing me down on the mattress.

When she climbs on top of me to straddle my hips, we both groan.

She sinks down on me, and desire pulses through me in a sudden flush of warmth, spreading from the groin outward.

This woman is doing it for me on so many levels.

"Jace?"

I look into her eyes. She looks wistful . . . sad. "What is it, Em?"

"I'm giving you my heart. Please . . ."

Oh my beautiful girl. The trust she's placing in my hands. I don't deserve her.

"Em, I will take care of your heart. I will never be so careless again, I promise. I love you, so very much."

"I love you too. So much."

And then a realization hits me like a ton of bricks.

Knowing she loves me, that we're in this together, for good, changes everything. I don't think I've ever been so in tune with anyone before. Sexually. Emotionally.

I don't want this with anyone else.

Ever.

Neither Em nor I are perfect, but we're perfect for each other. She'll be there to help me manage my flaws, while also driving me nuts with hers. But what matters most is that at the end of the day, I go to sleep with the person that completes me in the best, most imperfect way possible.

THIRTY-THREE

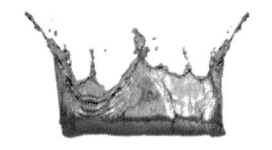

EMILIA

Panic fills my chest when I wake up the next morning. Was this a dream?

Talking to Jace. The sex. The declaration of love?

My goodness. My heart squeezes at the thought, at everything that's gone down in the last twenty-four hours.

I keep my eyes closed, squeezing them for good measure so I won't peek.

This emotional high feels so good, I need another moment to dwell in it.

A soft chuckle makes me reach out before I slowly lift one eyelid.

The heaviness in my chest gives way to lightness when I look straight into Jace's beautiful face.

His brown hair is a mess—the perfect sexy bed hair—and his blue eyes crinkle at the corners. I love this face. I love everything about this man.

The corners of my mouth lift, mirroring his expression.

"Good morning, gorgeous."

"Hey." My voice is thick with sleep as we stare at each

other. Something we've done a lot since yesterday. Catching glimpses of the other one at every possible chance, wanting to make sure they're still there. Needing to ensure this is really happening.

Because if it's up to me, *this* is it.

Despite the fact that Jace isn't perfect, he's my perfect match. Just as he's accepted me with my faults—I'm not delusional and know I'm far from perfect—I have done the same.

Yes, he hurt me.

But I know I hurt him too.

And like he said yesterday, two wrongs don't make a right. Neither one of our actions were excused because they were okay, but rather accepted as both of us having flaws.

My love for Jace is patient and kind, just like I hope his is for me.

In some respects, I'm actually happy this fight happened. It allowed me to see not only how Jace reacts under pressure, but also, how he handles tough situations and when he makes a mistake. Because in my eyes, that's what shows real character.

Whereas my parents have done me wrong my whole life, I can't remember seeing regret in their eyes, not once, or any of them ever attempting an apology for their behavior.

Jace's immediate pain and regret was so strong and palpable, it was almost like a third person in the room with us.

But my own pain was stronger and won, his actions ripping my heart wide open. That allowed the sorrow from all those times when my family had done me wrong to escape, inadvertently projecting it on him as well.

I didn't realize I'd locked it all away until that very day. Until it all boiled over, and I finally had to face the fact that I'd been nothing but a doormat to my family.

Jace's hand reaches out to brush away a strand of hair that fell out of my ponytail. "You okay? You look sad."

I lean in to his touch.

"Just thinking about everything that happened." I clear my voice, not wanting the emotion to show in my voice. "And my family."

Jace's smile drops. "Oh, baby. Don't. Knowing that I acted like them for even a few seconds kills me. I will make it up to you for the rest of my life, you have my word on that."

Another brush of his finger on my face, the touch comforting.

Jace closes his eyes and when he opens them again, they're watery. "I'm so sorry, baby. So incredibly sorry."

Seeing him taken over by his emotions triggers my own, and I blink rapidly. "I know you are. I really do."

I lean in and press my mouth to his.

When I pull back, we both sniffle, and I have to laugh. "Goodness, we're a mess."

Jace gives me a small smile. "I like our mess, even when it's not always perfect. That means it's real, that *we're* real. And I very much love that and will fight for it as long as you let me."

I grab his hand and squeeze it. "I like the sound of that."

"Yeah?"

"Yeah."

Tanner bounces in my arms, clapping his hands in excitement. He got home half an hour ago with Patricia and hasn't left my side since.

Which suits me just fine because there's nothing like it. Holding him in my arms, feeling him, smelling him. Incomparable.

Patricia hasn't stopped smiling since she saw that her plan of getting Jace and me in the same room to talk things out worked better than she'd hoped.

Jace and I somehow managed to get out of bed this morning to get everything ready for Tanner's dinosaur-themed birthday party. Hanging up what felt like two hundred balloons, setting the table with mostly green and brown table decorations, as well as putting together the food Patricia prepped.

Fun things like prehistoric dirt a.k.a. chocolate pudding, and other delicious treats, including separate tiers for herbivores and carnivores.

It's precious and Tanner loves it, ogling everything with big eyes.

It's still not enough to distract me from the situation at hand though.

My hands are clammy as I try to wipe them on my jeans as best as I can with Tanner hanging on me. Even though I'm also grateful he is so clingy since there couldn't be a more perfect shield for facing Jace's friends for the first time than this little monkey.

Jace comes up behind me, placing a quick kiss on my cheek. "Are you ready to meet them? They will attack soon if we don't make the first move." He chuckles in my ear, and it helps. Maybe.

"Okay." I'm nervous, because I know how important it is that your partner's friends like you.

Because that's what Jace is, my partner. The thought makes me smile as we make our way across the room to the group of people.

And holy moly.

Or rather, holy hotness.

Jace is by far the best-looking one, of course, but I'd be blind to deny how handsome the other guys are.

All tall, wide shoulders, and long, muscular limbs.

Before I have a chance to embarrass myself by trying to memorize their every detail, Jace smiles at me and puts his arm around Tanner and me.

"Guys, I'd like you to meet my Em. Or Millie as some of you know her by."

The thought of them knowing me from my show never crossed my mind, but the possibility warms my cheeks as I wave awkwardly. "Hey. It's so nice to finally meet you."

Tanner leans forward with an outstretched hand to get high fives from everyone before happily chatting away.

"Babe, this is Hunter, Noah, and Ryan." He points at each of the guys as he says their names. Then his finger stops at a woman, a gorgeous, very pregnant blonde. "And this bouncy ball is Ryan's better half, Harper."

"I'm so excited to finally meet you. Tanner and I have watched your show, and you're amazing. I've been waiting for some more female dynamic in this group forever." She takes a deep breath, her hand fluttering to her chest. "Phew, I'm already out of breath again."

Immediately feeling at ease with her, I chuckle. "Thank you. How much longer do you have?"

"A month, give or take." She rubs her belly. "Depending on when this prince or princess decides it's time."

"Aww, you want it to be a surprise? How adorable. Congratulations, you two." I glance up at Ryan before looking back to Harper.

"Thank you." Perfectly synchronized.

Harper takes a step closer. "You wouldn't happen to know anything about water births, would you?"

She lowers her voice, but I'm sure everyone heard her.

The confirmation comes when Jace chuckles next to me. Tanner giggles too, mimicking Jace's behavior before becoming fascinated with my hair, pulling on different strands and brushing his fingers through it.

Ryan groans. "Babe, we're not setting up a pool in our house. We've talked about this. I don't like the idea, it's too risky. Now leave poor Millie alone with that."

Harper pouts. "But it's supposed to be so much more comfortable for the baby to come out of my va—"

Hunter interrupts Harper and holds up his hands. "That's my cue to leave."

Noah nods. "Me too."

They both nod at me and smile—Hunter more so than Noah—before sauntering toward the food.

Ryan and Harper are immersed in a whispered conversation about different birth techniques and Harper not talking about her vagina in public. I turn my head toward Jace, who's already staring at me with a bright-eyed look on his face.

"What?"

His gaze flickers to Harper before he leans in closer. "I can't wait for you to be pregnant."

The comment is unexpected and I pull back. Oddly, after letting it settle for a moment, it's not unwelcome.

"Oh yeah?"

"Uh-huh. I also think we should get back to practicing as soon as possible." Then he shifts his focus to Tanner, who's apparently started to chew on my hair without anyone noticing.

Great.

Jace holds out his hands to Tanner who jumps into his dad's arms after reluctantly letting go of my hair. Jace tickles him, the bell-like noise of Tanner's giggles echoing throughout the expansive room. "I think Tanner wouldn't mind having a brother or sister sometime down the road. Right, buddy?"

Of course, Tanner smiles, and I laugh when Jace presses their faces together, matching cheesy smiles and all.

These guys have become my two main men so quickly that my brain is still playing catch-up sometimes. My heart, on the other side, never had a chance. It's secured the two most special places for Jace and Tanner, happy as a clam.

Holding up only my thumb, index finger and pinkie finger, I face the palm away from me and gently move it left and right. "I love you."

"I love *you*." Jace closes the distance between us and gives me a quick kiss.

Tanner waves his fingers around, trying to copy my hand movement before throwing his arms around our necks, pulling our heads together. "I-o-u."

No one says a word before Jace and I pull back at the same time, staring at each other and Tanner with tears in our eyes.

Jace blinks a few times before clearing his throat. "Did he just say what I think he said?"

I nod frantically. "I think he did."

Jace ruffles Tanner's hair while I smother his cheek with little kisses.

This is life.

This is happiness.

Ups and downs and all these moments in between.

My perfect imperfect life.

EPILOGUE

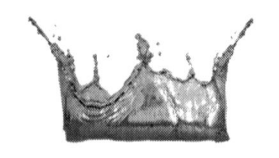

JACE

ONE YEAR LATER

"Are you ready for tomorrow?" Em's breath tickles my neck as she cuddles against my side on the couch.

She's only wearing shorts and a tank top even though the air conditioning is on full blast in our hotel room in Tokyo.

I'm the last one to complain though, absentmindedly rubbing my hands up and down her smooth skin, trying to focus on her question and not on my needy dick. "Yup."

Her hand comes up to my chest as she chuckles, my favorite accessory sparkling on her left ring finger. I was planning on waiting to propose until the Olympic craziness was over in a few weeks, but I couldn't wait any longer and asked her last month.

It was similar to today. We were cuddled up on the couch the night before the Olympic trials in Nebraska. The only difference is that this time, it's the real deal. The finale of sorts. The reason I've been busting my ass off the last year.

It's been crazy and intense getting ready for this event, but I have a feeling that it was all worth it.

I've been feeling pretty good in the water, especially since things have settled down in my life and Em moved in with Tanner and me last year. With her roommate Nicole moving out anyway, I was able to make a good argument and get her to agree.

Coming home to my two favorite people every day is the best thing.

And what a difference a year can make.

I've never had a crazier time in my life, or a happier one.

Things with Em's parents haven't changed much in the last year. Em told them straight out that if they wouldn't start treating her—and us—with respect, she wouldn't go see them anymore.

My strong, beautiful ladybug.

Of course, Em wouldn't be Em, if she wouldn't still drop by for birthday or Christmas wishes, but that's where it ended. Especially considering that her sister is still married to that dick of a husband. We definitely don't need that drama in our life.

I turn my head when her fingers brush over my cheek, gazing into her mesmerizing eyes.

"You zoned out. Do you want to go to sleep? You know I wouldn't mind."

We just put Tanner to sleep in the adjacent bedroom, so it's still fairly early. But tomorrow is the first day of the Olympics, which means I have an extra-long and nerve-wracking day ahead of me.

Yet, I'm ready to smash this. Ready to succeed and make this the highlight of my professional career.

"I'm not really tired yet, but I have a few ideas of what we could do in bed instead." I waggle my eyebrows at her and she laughs.

A tiny flutter tingles inside my chest like it does every time she's happy. It's a simple thing but essentially tied to my own happiness. The bond between us goes both ways, good and bad, and I cherish every step we take together on this path.

No matter what the goal is, no matter how hard it is, I'm certain we'll get there. My confidence in us is strong and unwavering.

My need for her grows when her hand travels down my torso. What a tease. I'm about to pull her on my lap when her phone vibrates on the table.

She kisses my cheek before scooting to the edge of the couch to reach for it. She swipes the screen and slaps her hand over her mouth, but not before a loud gasp echoes through the room.

I immediately sit up and touch her back. "Everything okay?"

Her head bobs up and down as she keeps scrolling on her phone screen.

When she turns her head to look at me, her eyes are filled with tears, and I'm by her side before she has a chance to blink, leaning closer, wanting to comfort her.

"What's going on, baby?"

She blows out a shaky breath, and I can tell by the way her lips quiver that she's trying to hold back her emotions. "Richard messaged."

Sweet relief floods me, because I know in my gut this isn't bad news.

Missing the audition last year turned out to be the best thing for her career. Richard has quickly become one of Em's biggest supporters, and together they were able to find enough investors interested in her children's music program to create a professional production.

Not only is the program now available to purchase, but it has also found many online supporters—both young and old—around the whole world.

I nudge her elbow. "Well . . . what does he say?"

"He—" She chuckles and shakes her head. "He did it, babe. He secured a deal with . . . with PBS Kids." Her voice is quaking and laced with joy as she loses the fight with her tears. "They want to turn my program in to a TV show."

My mouth drops open as I gape at her. "No way. Holy shit."

She nods, laughs, and cries. All at the same time. "I know."

I push my hand through my hair. This is her dream, something so big she thought it would be unachievable. "This is amazing. You deserve this so much, baby. I'm so fucking proud of you."

"I still can't believe it." She blinks rapidly and just stares at me. "I'm so happy. First the engagement, then the positive test, and now this. I can't believe it."

"I'm so happy for—" My smile drops as my brain catches up with her words. I tilt my head, my brows furrow. "Wait. What did you just say?"

Her tears flow quicker down her cheeks as she chuckles and hiccups. "We're having a baby."

What the . . .

It takes me a long moment before I begin to wrap my

head around this piece of news. A laugh breaks from my chest. This is fucking awesome. "Are you serious right now?"

She presses her lips together and nods, now crying in earnest as sobs begin to shake her body. I pull her on my lap and Em throws her arms around my neck.

"We're going to have a baby. I can't believe it. I love you so fucking much."

Taking her to the bedroom, I plan on showing her just how much.

This is it.

The last race of my professional swim career.

And there's no better way to end it than with my friends in a men's medley relay. Hunter, Ryan, and Noah are next to me as we get ready to head to the pool.

Ryan bumps into me. "You ready, man?"

I nod.

Hunter grabs me by the back of my neck and pulls me in until our foreheads touch. "Let's do this, dude. Go crush it, you hear me?"

I nod again, my throat too tight to talk.

We walk out in silence, and I keep my focus on the water, swimming the race in my head like I've done a million times before.

And then it's showtime.

The crowd roars as Hunter dives back from the wall with his strong backstroke. He's ahead of the other swimmers before he even finishes his first lap. I grin when he taps the wall after his second lap with several feet between him and his runner-up, breaking the world record like the beast he is.

Ryan is next. His strength has always been breaststroke. Despite his age, he's still the world record holder, and I know he has this in the bag too. His form is perfection, his head in line with his body.

It's my turn next with butterfly, and I give it my all, leaving my dreams and all my hard work in the water. My heart has been in this for so long, wanting to be the best, that losing isn't an option.

My vigorous training, my previous wins, have been preparing me for this Olympics. To being better. To being the best. I'm tired, but the hunger for success keeps me going, making me one with the water.

Muscle memory takes over, and I glide powerfully through the water.

My mind is almost numb, except for that voice in my head.

I'm so proud of you, son. Look how far you've come. You did it. You really are the best as I always knew you were.

My dad's voice echoes in my head as my one hundred meters go by in the blink of an eye.

I thought hearing my dad's voice would leave me with a hint of sadness, but instead, pride fills my chest.

This is for you, Dad. This is for you.

It's easier to focus on my racing heart and breathing rather than my emotions as I watch Noah do his magic with his unbeatable freestyle laps. His form is flawless, his strength impeccable as he pulls away from the others with every stroke.

My chest feels tight as I watch him finish his second lap and reaching the wall, bringing our win home.

When everyone's done, he lifts himself out of the pool, and the four of us form a huddle.

We're a team, a unit, and the momentous significance of this moment isn't lost on any of us. We all know this will never happen again for us.

This moment will be etched in my brain forever.

To me, we'll always be the kings of the water.

When we part, they slap my shoulder before grabbing their things from the chairs. I keep my eyes downcast as I listen to the announcer reminding the crowd that this was my last race. That I'm retiring. I swallow.

Cheers and applause erupt in the aquatic center as I lift my head and gaze up in to the stands.

Lifting my arms, I turn around and wave, bowing my head to give thanks, even though it doesn't feel like it's enough. My eyes prickle as I scan the crowd for someone very specific, or rather, specific someones.

Calmness settles over my heart when my eyes land on Em and Tanner. They are all I see, all that matters.

My eyes flicker up to the big screen where everyone witnesses the dance these two perform in my honor—congratulatory cardboards and all.

Em looks as stirred as I feel and doesn't hold back from sharing her crazy with our boy. I hope this will never change. It's exactly the kind of crazy that was missing in my strict life, and I can't wait to see what the future has in store for us.

I'm now the most adorned Olympic medalist in history—and officially retired—and it's nothing compared to what life has given me this last year.

One smart little boy who has the biggest heart I've ever witnessed. He makes me proud daily, and I'm looking forward to watching him grow up.

Then there's Em. The most beautiful woman that by some miracle loves me back and is now growing our baby.

One amazing mom. Loyal friends. Wonderful fans.

If that doesn't make me the luckiest man on earth, I don't know what does, and I'm planning on enjoying every last minute of it.

AUTHOR NOTE

Thank you so much for reading my words!

If you enjoyed *Fresh Meet*, it would mean the world to me if you could leave a review. Word of mouth and reviews go a long way, and I'd appreciate it so very much.

For more books and bonus scenes, please visit my website www.jasminmiller.com

ACKNOWLEDGMENTS

This book. These characters. Gah. Jace, Em, and Tanner have made my heart so incredibly happy. Telling their story was a bit memoir-ish in some places (kids scenes) and constantly tugged on my heartstrings. And they made me smile a lot. I like smiling. :)

The biggest thanks goes to my husband. I couldn't have done it without him. He had my back, as usual, making sure I was able to keep my deadlines. His support has reached new levels, as has my appreciation for him. His constant encouragement keeps me going. Then there are our little monsters. As usual, providing me with plenty of inspiration for my books. Maybe we can tone down the accidents a bit though please, okay? Thanks. Regardless, my heart is yours. Always and forever.

Suze and Alicia. I have so much love for you two. You're the icing on my cake, the cheese to my crackers. Thank you for helping me work out the kinks in this story and for being there for me when I need you. Which is a lot. I'd be lost without your help and guidance and constant encouragement.

Kristen and Stephie. Thanks so much for the extra eyes on my story. I appreciate your time and support so incredibly much. Your feedback always helps, and I'm beyond grateful to have you.

Marion, this baby wouldn't be what it is without you. Thanks for the honesty and love you showed this story. And for believing in me. You helped make this story shine the way it was supposed to. Thank you from the bottom of my heart!

Judy, as always, I'm beyond grateful for your fantastic proofreading skills. It soothes me to know you have my back.

Najla, thank you so much for dealing with my fussy self! I adore you and your work! The cover is absolutely stunning.

My lovely ARC and promo teams. I have so much to thank you for. The wonderful reviews you write. The kind messages you send me. The beautiful pictures and posts you create. Spreading the love about my stories. I appreciate you guys so very much, and you're incredibly special to me. Your support means everything.

Awesome Peeps, you're my favorite place online and for good reason. I'm so lucky to have so many of you fantastic peeps in my group, and you never fail to put a smile on my face, and that means the absolute world to me.

My readers. You guys. Goodness. You make my heart so incredibly happy. Thank you for picking up my books, for reading my words, for giving me and my stories a chance. I won't ever be able to tell you just how much that truly means to me. You make me believe in myself. You keep me going.

🖤🖤🖤

ABOUT THE AUTHOR

Jasmin Miller is a professional lover of books and cake (preferably together) as well as a fangirl extraordinaire. She loves to read and write about anything romantic and never misses a chance to swoon over characters. Originally from Germany, she now lives in the western US with her husband and three little humans that keep her busy day and night.

If you liked *Fresh Meet* and would like to know more about her and her books, please sign up for her newsletter on her website. She'd love to connect with you.

www.jasminmiller.com
jasminmillerbooks@gmail.com
Facebook.com/jasminmillerwrites
Instagram.com/jasminmiller
Twitter.com/JasminMiller_
Facebook.com/groups/jasminmillerpeeps

Printed in Great Britain
by Amazon